The CEO Came DOA

Book Five
In
The Alvarez Family
Murder Mystery Series

Heather Haven

The CEO Came DOA © 2016 by Heather Haven

The Wives of Bath Press
5512 Cribari Bend
San Jose, Ca 95135

http:// www.thewivesofbath.com

Cover Art by Heather Haven and Jeff Monaghan
With special thank to FaceBook friends
Edited by Baird Nuckolls
Layout and book production by
Heather Haven and Baird Nuckolls

Print ISBN: ISBN: 978-0-9896712-6-2
eBook ISBN: ISBN-13:978-0-9896712-4-8

The Alvarez Family Murder Mystery Series

"You won't be able to put it down!"
Sheldon Siegel, New York Times Best Selling Author

"Heather Haven is one of the funniest mystery authors around and The CEO Came DOA is her best book yet. Fast-paced with non-stop laughs. It doesn't get any better than that. A must-read 5 star series!"
National Best Selling Author, Cindy Sample

"You'll go from edge-of-your seat suspense to rolling-on-the-floor laughter. Hang on to your derriere. If you have not read Ms. Haven's books, please do so. I highly recommend."
Rochelle Webber, author

~

Murder is a Family Business – Book One
Single Titles Reviewer's Choice Award Best Book 2011

A Wedding to Die For – Book Two
Global and EPIC Best eBook Mystery of the Year Finalist 2012

Death Runs in the Family – Book Three
Global Gold Best Mystery Fiction 2013

DEAD....If Only – Book Four
Global Silver Best Mystery Fiction 2015

Acknowledgements

I would like to thank BrainyQuote.com for all the wonderful words said by Silicon Valley greats used at the start of each chapter. All the name brands within the book are of quality and worth. If they were no good, the Alvarez Family wouldn't bother with them. Life is too short.

I would like to acknowledge Charly Taylor for her help with my Spanish phrases and the people who helped make this book a reality by bringing me up short, and telling me what's what. Beta Readers. What would an author do without them? Thank you Mary Wollesen, friend, quilter, and reader extraordinaire; the Cellophane Queen, a talented cyber writing pal with a ready wit and eagle eye; Margie Bunting, who is a natural born line editor; Carter Schwonke, writing group buddy and superb writer with many fine published short stories to her credit; Cindy Sample, friend and fellow mystery author who writes the funniest chase scenes I've ever read; Grace DeLuca, cousin, friend, and writer of mysteries and allegories, proving that maybe just a little talent runs in the family; and lastly Baird Nuckolls, friend, editor, business partner, and gifted writer in her own right.

I am surrounded by the best. Thank you for being in my life.

Dedication

This book is dedicated to my mother, Mary Lee, who I miss terribly; to my husband, Norman Meister; and to families everywhere. My Alvarez Clan has a little bit more drama than real families out in the world but the thrust of what holds every family together is, I hope, running rampant throughout this book. No matter what the dynamics, the fact of the matter is when you share love, respect, and work together for a better future you are family.

The CEO Came DOA

Heather Haven

It had not yet been named Silicon Valley, but you had the defense industry, you had Hewlett-Packard. But you also had the counter-culture, the Bay Area. That entire brew came together in Steve Jobs.
Erik Qualman

Chapter One

Life was good. I was happy. Let me count the ways. Any day now my sister-in-law's water would break, and my first niece or nephew would get on with things. I was dubbed Investigator of the Year by the Professional Private Investigators Association of California. No one was more shocked than my mother. I lost five pounds. No one was more shocked than me. And I was getting married in less than a week to a man who thought I was just about as great as I knew he was.

Meanwhile, I was doing my favorite kind of job, which is not chasing bad guys over rooftops, often my sad lot in life, but ferreting them out while sitting on my duff in the air-conditioned office of a small startup company. Looking for a saboteur, I was either sifting through documents via my laptop during the day or searching offices late into the night.

Called Read-Out - a dull but appropriate name – the startup was a bio-tech company claiming to have developed a ground-breaking computer chip. The scuttlebutt was that when said chip was placed under the skin of a human or other mammal, it detected a multitude of conditions and major diseases related to that particular species. In addition, the chip could predict potential problems for the next five-year period with eighty-nine percent accuracy. For a small fee, there would be monthly transfers of information to a medical data center or your doctor.

This last bit perked up my ears, because breast cancer has run through many of the women in our family. I lost both grandmothers to the disease. The Read-Out chip promised a whole new level of early detection. Consequently, there was a personal interest in my seeing Read-Out thrive. If only half of what they touted was true, I was committed to finding the saboteur of their upcoming IPO.

For those not familiar with the Mother's Milk of Silicon Valley, an IPO or Initial Public Offering is the first sale of stock by a company to the public, mega millions in the making for investors and vested staff, none of which was me. Even though these ventures are Silicon Valley's bread and butter, a lot of public offerings are pretty ho-hum.

This time, however, there was a slightly different slant on the proceedings. A trusted someone within Read-Out was trying to destroy it even before it gave birth to itself. Hard-won inside information was being systematically leaked to like businesses, compromising its very reason for existence. Millions of dollars had already been poured into this startup, so the powers-that-be were in a panic to find the culprit.

Enter Discretionary Inquiries, the family business, started by my now deceased Mexican immigrant father, Roberto Alvarez. Together with my mother, Palo Alto blueblood Lila Hamilton Alvarez, he started an investigative service like no other. We specialize in the apprehension of miscreants who steal intellectual property, software, hardware, patented inventions or otherwise, from companies who have the legal right to call them their own.

Speaking of calling, D. I. is what everybody calls Discretionary Inquiries. That is everyone except L. H. Alvarez, mother mine and head chieftess of the family business. D. I.'s leader is a woman who balks at abbreviations, chewing gum,

10

or crossing milady's legs anywhere but at the ankles. Her motto is, dress as if you are doing a photo shoot for the cover of Vogue or Esquire 24/7. And as I am but a lowly investigator, I do what she says…most of the time.

But despite her mandates, this time I got to do my ferreting in jeans and a sweater; not the standard getup required by She Who Must Be Obeyed. I would have looked even more out of place in a designer suit and heels than I already did, me being female and considered an Old Bag Geek at thirty-four years old.

Ninety-eight percent of the one hundred and forty employees at Read-Out were male, and aged somewhere between puberty and sprouting chin hairs. To try and fit in, I gathered my long, dark hair at the nape of my neck in a thick ponytail, donned horn-rimmed glasses, and gave the spinster aunt look a try. It didn't work.

Recently one of the older techies – had to be twenty-two if a day – hit on me and told me he'd never seen violet-colored eyes as beautiful as mine, all the while staring at my chest. He then proceeded to ask me over to his apartment to play the newest version of Swords and Gremlins. I stopped wearing eye makeup immediately and took to very loose-fitting shirts. Just call me granny.

Other than that, life was good, as I said. Maybe a little too good. That's probably why I shouldn't have been surprised to see a dead man hanging from the center beam of the boardroom, wearing nothing but his jockey shorts. And it wasn't just any man, but the co-founder and CEO of Read-Out, D. H. Collier.

One of the recent celebrities on *Dancing with the Stars*, Mr. Collier had been eliminated in week two, told to go home, and work on his rhythm. I stared up at him. He couldn't do that now.

Collier's lifeless body strung up by a hemp rope was a shock to me. Not only because I found him dangling before I'd had my morning coffee, but I'd been told he was in

11

Switzerland. I made sure he and I were the only two people in the room before I pulled out my phone and hit three numbers.

"This is 9-1-1. State the nature of your emergency." The dispatcher's voice was matter-of-fact but high-pitched. I recognized it immediately.

"This is Lee Alvarez, Amy. I'm in the boardroom of Read-Out, at 51461 West Caribbean Drive, Sunnyvale. Third floor. I've just found the body of D. H. Collier. He's dead. Hung himself."

"Are you sure he's dead?"

"Oh, yeah. I'm sure. Several hours at least."

"Are you in any danger?"

I looked around me again. "No, but thanks for asking."

"Okay, Lee. Don't touch anything. You know the drill. Someone will be there in five minutes."

I did know the drill. As a PI, I had the criminal justice system and public safety protocols down pat. In addition, Amy and I took our Emergency Medical Service certificate together, she for Santa Clara County and me for D. I. Amy passed with flying colors; I scraped by. I'm not good with blood.

I disconnected and looked up at the specter-like view. Not to be graphic, but my insight into the man being dead for several hours was due to the accumulation of fluids in his hands and feet. They tend to settle when a body is at severe rest. Like dead.

My insight into it being D. H. Collier was due to living on this planet. But in case one had just arrived from Mars, a six by nine-foot headshot of the billionaire, flaring nostrils and all, clung to a wall of the lobby next to the elevators.

Unfortunately, the humongous photo had an IMAX effect on me, which was not good. Too much, too big, and a headache coming on. I found it a helluva way to start each morning. I don't know how the permanent employees did it.

But nonetheless, here was one of the wealthiest and best-known men in the world, certainly one of Silicon Valley's superstars. Fifteen years ago, at age forty-two, he'd even had a brief May-December marriage to a seventeen-year old who went on to become the legendary rock star, known as 'The Scintillating Sharise'. Other than for dumping him, Sharise was best known for her long blonde tresses, abbreviated costumes, and red bowler hats. She could sing pretty good, too, but that always took a back seat to her outlandish lifestyle.

Their divorce shortly after the birth of their daughter created headlines in the San Francisco Chronicle and other newspapers across the globe. You still couldn't open a magazine or watch ET without seeing Collier's image at least once a week carousing with some long-legged beauty decades younger than him.

The other co-founder of Read-Out was Craig Eastham, Chief Technical Officer or CTO, and as different from Collier as you can get. Eastham was responsible for overseeing all technical aspects of the company. He was a quiet guy, and avoided the spotlight as fervently as Collier sought it out.

In fact, the only time I saw Craig Eastham was a few days earlier when he'd scurried to his office like a shy bird. Head hunkered down and shoulders slumped, he'd muttered a greeting so quiet, I wasn't sure I'd been spoken to at all. And of course, he was married to the same woman for decades, a big bore for the media. They lived on a ranch in Woodside with their children, dogs, and llamas.

I hit one of my frequently called numbers, Frank Thompson, Palo Alto Police Chief and family friend. He answered on the third ring.

"What's wrong?" His voice, although gravelly from sleep, sounded alert.

"Frank, it's Lee. Listen, I --"

"I know who it is; I can see who it is. What's wrong?"

"I've found a dead body, Frank."

"Again?"

13

"What do you mean, again? I only found one...okay...two...no, three others and they --"

"Never mind that. Who is it? Where are you?"

"D. H. Collier. Read-Out. I'm here in Sunnyvale, but I'm calling you because he lived in Palo Alto." I looked down at the stepladder lying on its side beneath the man's hanging feet. "On the surface of it, it looks like he committed suicide, Frank."

"Good God."

"I just wanted to give you a heads up. Being who it is, this is going to be huge."

"Did you call 911?"

"On their way."

"Are you okay?"

"About as okay as I'm going to be after finding a dead body before six o'clock in the morning."

"Sit tight. I'll be right there. I'll give Hank Broas a call and formally ask permission to crash his party." The Sunnyvale Chief of Police, Henrique Broas, was an old golfing buddy of Frank's. He went on.

"And don't let anybody else in the room. I don't want anyone messing around with the evidence. And that includes you," he said. Unnecessarily, I might add.

I hung up and switched on the camera part of the phone. For later reference, I took quick snaps of the body, stepladder, and clothing. Then giving the body a wide berth, I took close-up images of the clothes next to his shoes and socks, all placed neatly on the conference table.

My phone said five forty-seven am. I may have been the first person in on this fine Monday morning, but I knew others would be trouping in soon. Such was the life of a start-up, a devotion of twelve to fifteen-hour days, seven days a week. I placed another call on my speed dial, this time to mother mine.

"What's *wrong*, Liana?" Apparently any phone calls from me before six am elicited this reaction.

14

"The founder and CEO of Read-Out, D. H. Collier, is dead, Lila." I always address mom as Lila when we're in work mode. She always calls me Liana. Period.

"David Harold Collier? Good *Lord!*" Leave it to Lila to not only know his full, given name, but to use it. She drew in a deep breath. "How?"

"He seems to have taken his own life. Hanged himself in the boardroom. At least, it looks that way on the surface of it. It's a pretty bizarre set up."

"*Explain* yourself. Other than it being a *suicide*, what makes the event *bizarre*?"

My mother has the annoying habit of stressing certain words in a sentence to make sure you get her meaning. Genetics being what they are, I pray every night this habit does not transfer itself to me. So far, so good. *However*, I explained myself.

"Clothes neatly folded on the conference table, shoes sitting beside them, socks folded and placed inside. He's only wearing his jockey shorts. Baby blue, not white. And of course, the necktie. Your average sturdy hemp."

"Don't be flippant, Liana. It *doesn't* become you."

"Sorry. It's my way of coping. This is very, very strange."

I heard the rustling of fabric, as she moved around in bed. "I'll get dressed and be *right* there. Give me *twenty* minutes. Is Gurn still in Washington?"

"Yes, he comes back tonight. But don't bother coming here, Lila. Seriously. I'm just alerting you."

"Did you call the police?"

"Of course. And I also called Frank. He's on his way." Chief Frank Thompson, aside from being a close family friend, was also my godfather. He could hassle me like nobody else, but I was like his second daughter, the one he fretted over.

"Good. Are you all *right*, dear?" Lila switched to mommy mode. I switched to daughter mode. Switching abounded.

"I'm a little shaken but fine, Mom. Thank you. I don't know how long I'll be stuck here. I'm sure I have to answer a lot of questions from the police. After that I want to talk to whoever will take over."

"Isn't that *whomever*, dear?"

I ignored her question. "It might be Rameen Patel. He's the CFO, but I don't know that for sure."

"You don't know that he's the Chief Financial Officer or that he's Rameen Patel?"

"I don't know if he's the one slated to take over. Maybe it's Eastham or one of the other board members."

"Then that's what you need to *say*, Liana," she said primly. "Otherwise, it is *confusing*." In times of duress, L. H. Alvarez tends to lock in the proper and efficient way of doing a thing, never missing the opportunity to beat you over the head with it. Between the stressing and the duressing, I was getting a double-whammy.

"The police will be here any minute, Mom. I should go. I'll call you later with any updates."

"Yes, please do, dear. And *try* to stay calm."

"I'm calm. Why wouldn't I be calm? I'm calm."

"You don't *sound* calm."

"But I am," I said through gritted teeth. "Bye, Mom."

I went back to the door and stood sentinel at the only way in or out of the conference room.

Silicon Valley is a mindset, not a location.
Reid Hoffman

Chapter Two

"So what happened?" Detective José Garcia looked at me, his writing pad and pen poised to ensnare my every word. Like his chief of police and a lot of people in this area, he was of Portuguese descent. In most Latin countries, the name José Garcia is akin to being named John Smith. You know there are people out there with the handle, but you rarely meet one. When you do, it's hard not to say, 'hey, do you know you've got one of the most common names in the world?'

But I couldn't say that to this guy, not even as an icebreaker. José Garcia was around my age, one tough cop, and didn't care much for PIs. Sometimes I liked to give him reason. I scowled before answering his question.

"Weren't you paying attention? I must have told you five times," I said.

"Tell me again."

"You know, I already gave my statement and signed off on it."

"Tell. Me. Again." Garcia leaned in and managed to hiss the three words, even though there wasn't one 's' in any of them. He also had bad breath, but I told him again.

"Read-Out hired D. I. to investigate recent attempts to sabotage their IPO. It's scheduled for next month." I looked at my watch. "It's nearly seven o'clock. When can I get some coffee?"

"Who hired you specifically?" He jumped in with the question as if he might trap me into giving a wrong answer.

"Our contract was with Rameen Patel. He's the CFO. He hired us on behalf of himself and the board members. The contract is on file, if you want to see it."

"Oh, I'll want to see it." His voice held a challenge tinged with contempt.

"Fine." I shrugged. "Have your people call my people and we'll send you a copy."

"I'll want the original."

"The original it is."

It really was too early in the morning to have a schoolyard brawl with someone, so I was compliant, even agreeable. It threw him, I could tell. In a less combative tone he went on.

"What were you doing here at five-thirty in the morning?"

"For the past week I've been here under the pretext of being Rameen Patel's new personal assistant, so let's not blow my cover unless absolutely necessary. Every day the guard lets me in before anyone else arrives. I have access to the mainframe, personnel passwords, and product codes for all the computers. First thing in the morning is when I go through employees' computers; when no one is here. Right now I'm dealing with emails for the past nine-months. There are thousands of them."

Garcia shook his head. "What a job."

He let out a laugh. So did I.

"You're not kidding. Boring takes on a new meaning."

His demeanor changed instantly. No more cordial, nice guy. Not that he ever was.

"Well, don't think you're going to spice things up by involving yourself in this suicide. I've heard about you. I'm the detective here."

"Garcia, it's all yours," I said, deciding not to take umbrage to the 'I'm the detective' crack. "Collier happened to be hanging around in a room I walked into." I thought for a

18

moment. "I could have phrased that better. Let me just say, I've never been introduced to the man. Besides, I'm getting married soon. I've got so much going on, I'm happy not to be involved in this."

He warmed up somewhat. "That's right. You're marrying that CPA guy with the strange first name. Gash or something, right?"

"Gurn," said an authoritative voice over my shoulder.

We both turned to see Chief Frank Thompson coming up from behind, dark skin glowing, a crease in the pants of his uniform you could slice a loaf of bread on. He was handsome in a Denzel-Washington's-Other-Brother-Only-I'm-Tougher sort of way. He deigned to cast us both a half smile before he spoke again. Frank has this authority thing down, even though he officially has none in Sunnyvale.

"His name is Gurn Hanson. Good morning, Garcia. Be sure to thank Chief Broas for allowing me to watch from the sidelines. There's going to be hell to pay back in Palo Alto."

He stuck out his hand to shake Detective Garcia's. Garcia took his hand eagerly with an instant smile.

"Our pleasure, Chief Thompson." Garcia's demeanor switched from aggressive to pleasant. There's something to be said for the effect of a well-ironed uniform. Garcia slathered it on a little more. "We always cooperate with other townships when we can."

Frank nodded. "As do we. You about done here?"

"Yes sir, just wrapping things up, Chief. I'll go see what forensics has." With an almost subservient gesture, he turned and left.

"He's one for the books, Frank."

Frank watched him stride across the room with a thoughtful gaze. "Take it easy on him, Lee. José just lost his wife in a car accident. He only wants to do a good job."

"I didn't know that." I was surprised, feeling a surge of remorse for being combative with Garcia, if only in my mind.

"I mean about his wife. I assumed he wanted to do a good job."

Frank moved away toward a corner of the room. I followed. He wheeled on me, black eyes sparkling with intelligence. Then he glanced back at the room filled with men and women who specialized in death.

"I've worked with most of these people. They're a good group. Whatever happened, they'll know in a matter of days if not hours. Did I hear you say you were working undercover?"

His change in subject didn't surprise me. I merely nodded. He went on.

"I thought you were getting married. At least that's what the invite says. Doesn't that take a lot of planning, especially for one as grand as your wedding is going to be?"

I groaned before answering. "Mom's running the show, Frank. She's doing everything. My job is to show up Christmas Eve dressed in white."

"I thought as much when I heard some of the details."

"She feels I cheated her out of a big wedding when I eloped the first time way back when. Then Richard and Vicki went to Vegas and got married one weekend when she wasn't looking. This time she wants to have the wedding of her dreams."

"What about the wedding of *your* dreams?"

My godfather looked at me with a half-cocked smile. When it came to my mother, I was known to bark, roll over, and play dead.

"I'm fine with it. Truly."

I'd stuttered on the word 'truly'. I made an attempt to keep my voice bright and chirpy. I came across like a parakeet on steroids.

"I've got a really pretty dress, white velvet; down to the floor. And a veil that's about sixty-yards long. The bridesmaids' gowns are lovely and Christmas-y. Dark green or crimson velvet, they got to pick. Not like the usual carnival sideshow I've often had to wear, myself."

"So Faith tells me."

Faith was his only child, two years my senior, and a practicing pediatrician at Stanford Hospital. She'd been invited, along with much of the female population in Palo Alto under age fifty, to be one of my bridesmaids. I now had ten of them, plus my matron of honor. At the rate Mom was going, there wouldn't be room for me at the altar when it was my turn to march down the aisle.

Frank looked at me and I looked at Frank. His tone was even but the words firm.

"You might want to slow Lila down or your wedding just might show up in Ripley's Believe It Or Not."

I didn't answer, but let out a gurgle. I often roll over and play dead with Frank, too. He and Mom have had a long and uneasy alliance. Before Dad's death three years previous, Frank had been my father's best friend. He was also godfather to my kid brother, Richard, as well as me. But Frank and Mom were like oil and water, adding an occasional lit match for good measure.

Without saying so, Frank and I mutually decided to change the subject. He cleared his throat before speaking.

"Any suspicions as to why one of the richest men in the world, who seemingly had everything, would kill himself, Lee? You've been working here. What is the word around the water cooler?"

"Water cooler gossip has said very little about him, Frank." I thought for a moment. "And when you can get somebody to say anything, he's referred to as either a god or a demigod. It's almost as if saying anything negative is blasphemy."

"Interesting. I didn't even know he was in town. Last I heard, he was in Switzerland."

Before I could answer, there was a commotion in the center of the room and we both turned to watch the coroners' people lowering the body onto a gurney. After a moment, Frank pushed again.

21

"So what do you think, Lee? You got a guess as to why he would do this?"

I shrugged in a noncommittal way. "Maybe he got bad news from his doctor. Cancer; something like that."

"Maybe. They called his doctor for the files a few minutes ago. We'll know soon." He scanned my face. "What?"

"There is something --"

"I thought so."

"But it may have nothing to do with this. I don't want to talk about it here. Let's go get some coffee."

Frank shifted his weight and looked around him, as well. "Okay, why don't we — "

He was cut off by a high-pitched screech.

"Daddy! Dad-eeeeeeeee!' The voice sounded like it belonged to a distraught teenage girl. It had an effect on everyone within earshot. They froze in place, heads swiveling toward the lamentable cries at the door.

A rail thin but tall girl, clad in a dull, grey dress and wearing platform sandals over thigh-high socks, tried to force her way inside. Arms and legs flailing like a colt caught under a fence, she tried to push through the two officers who held their ground.

I recognized D. H. Collier's fourteen-year old daughter, Skye, from the photo on his desk. She was also the daughter of Sharise, although the performer kept a low profile on it. As far as I knew, the kid had lived with her father since birth.

"Let me through. Let me see him. Daddy!" The girl screamed as strongly as she fought. For as featherweight as she looked, Skye Collier was giving the two uniformed men a run for their money.

A woman about my age came up behind the girl and tried to pull her off the officers, speaking in a soothing, contralto voice all the while.

"Skye, honey, stop. Stop this. You can't see him now. Come on. Come with me. There's a good girl."

"Katie, they won't let me see him," Skye wailed. "It's not true, is it? Daddy can't be dead. No."

"Shhh, honey. Come on with me. Let's go home and have a lie down. We'll talk about this on the way home."

"But it isn't him! It can't be."

"It is, Skye." The nanny's voice trembled, but was firm.

Skye shook her head. "No, he's still in Switzerland. He can't be back in Palo Alto and dead. That can't be true. Say it's not true."

"You shouldn't be here," said Katie, pulling the girl close to her in an embrace. "You shouldn't have asked Marty to drive you here. His job was to pick you up from school and bring you home, not here. How the reporters got hold of --"

"But I had to see." Skye's interruption was loud and high pitched. "I had to..."

The girl broke off and looked around the room. Met with stares and silence, her fierceness dissipated. Skye leaned against the short but solid woman and sobbed uncontrollably, long brown hair covering most of her face.

Frank turned to me, speaking in a whisper. "That's her nanny, Katie Hall. She's been with her since the kid was born."

"How do you know that, Frank?"

He looked at me sheepishly. "Oh, I hear things."

"Tales of the Rich and Famous?" I threw in the wildly popular TV show.

Before I could say more, the now-compliant girl paused in the doorway and looked in our direction. Her honey-brown eyes caught mine and the intensity in them took my breath away. When she spoke, her voice sounded as old and as knowing as the Sphinx.

"He didn't do this. I don't care what they say. He would never kill himself." Skye Collier looked squarely at me. "Don't let them say daddy killed himself. Please." She burst into sobs again and was led away by her nanny.

I watched them leave then shuddered. Frank leaned his head toward the walkie-talkie resting on his right shoulder then pressed a button with his fingertip.

"Yamaguchi, you there?" There was an inaudible reply. "Collier's daughter and her nanny are leaving now. Make sure the press doesn't bother them or follow them home. Stay there until you hear from me."

There was another inaudible reply, but Frank seemed to understand it. Finished, he turned his attention back to me. I shuddered again.

"You cold?" He ran a soothing hand over my shoulders.

"Did you hear that?" My voice was hardly more than a croak. "She was talking to me."

"Chalk it up to what's happened." He scrutinized my face. "Hey, you need to sit down. Let's get you that coffee."

Frank pushed me out the door and down the main hallway. We entered the large Community Room, more or less the heart of the workers' life here.

Three of the four walls were each painted a vibrant color; bright yellow, cobalt blue or lime green. The fourth wall was a stark white in front of which stood the anything-you-want-for-free cafeteria, one of the perks for working at Read-Out.

A chrome serving bar ran the length of the cafeteria, separating it from the rest of the humongous room. Stacked trays and utensils were on either side of the bar. On the left, self-serving machines were loaded with sandwiches, fruit, snacks, and hot and cold beverages. The other end held an open, stainless steel kitchen.

A short order cook waited in the kitchen to make bacon, eggs, hotdogs, hamburgers, French fries, or one of three hot meals, complete with vegetables and dessert. No takers at the moment, the cook leaned against a cold and unused wall oven, arms folded over the starched white chest of his uniform.

Opposite the cafeteria, lattice paneling in a glossy, bright white cordoned off a section of the lime green wall. A ping-

24

pong table, two arcade games, *Guitar Hero Arcade* and *Site 4, Area 51*, plus four tables topped off by board games, such as *7 Wonders* and *Battlestar Galactica* waited inside the lattice for weary workers needing a break. The rest of the room's indoor/outdoor purple carpeting was dotted with shiny Lucite tables and chairs in hot pink and lipstick red.

There was a strategy behind the edgy colors of the Community Room. The thinking being it's good for employees to get away from their screens now and then, but they still need to stay sharp and competitive. The room didn't make me feel competitive, but overstimulated, discombobulated, and anxious to take a nap. Maybe it was an age thing.

A handful of employees sat scattered throughout the room. Some talked in hushed tones, some stared out at nothing. I knew the stare. I've been known to stare out with the best of them, startled and saddened by unexpected death, no matter how many times I'd seen it professionally.

I went to one of the three Nespresso hotel-sized machines and made myself a double cappuccino. Frank took nothing, but guided me to an empty table in a corner. After we sat down he came to the point.

"You need to go home, Lee. This has been a shock. Nothing more can be accomplished here, anyway, until we get the reports. I promise to keep you in the loop."

I took a long gulp of the life-giving brew before I answered. "Up to a point."

Even white teeth flashed a smile, filled with warmth and humor. "As you say, up to a point."

We both laughed before I spoke again. I felt myself begin to relax.

"Don't worry about me, Frank. I'm okay. I just needed a pick-me-up. There's a lot I can do. And you know how the first twenty-four hours are critical."

"That's in a kidnapping, not a suicide."

"Maybe, maybe not."

"What does that mean, 'maybe, maybe not'?"

"Nothing. I heard one of your people say they couldn't find Collier's car. How did he get here?"

"We don't know yet, but he had a fulltime chauffeur that drove him everywhere. That's the one the nanny mentioned. Marty, an old buddy D. H. Collier gave a job to years ago when he hit it big. They'll be talking to the chauffeur soon, if they haven't already."

I thought for a moment. "Of course, Collier could have taken a cab, Uber, or been dropped off by a friend."

"True enough, Lee, but it's up to Broas' men to find that out. Tell me what you didn't want to say in the conference room."

I looked around me. Even though no one was nearby, I leaned in anyway. "D. H. Collier was the one sabotaging the upcoming IPO."

Frank stared at me in disbelief. "The CEO and co-founder of the company? Good God, why?"

"That I don't know. But there's some pretty damning evidence."

Frank mused. "Maybe someone else found out. Maybe that's why he committed suicide."

"If he did."

"Don't get ahead of yourself, girl. Let's get back to him sabotaging his own company. How do you know that?"

"First off, he'd been neglecting business for almost two months. As the CEO, Collier should have been on top of things, driving Read-Out forward. Instead, he has dozens of unanswered emails on his computer from staff and execs, especially from Eastham, begging him to act on certain matters."

"And he didn't?"

"Not that I could see. This is a crucial time, what with the upcoming IPO. Collier spent the last three weeks in Switzerland, incommunicado."

"Maybe he took care of business from there. He could have used another email address or phone, not the business one."

"No. Richard checked it out a few days ago. *Nada*. And if my brother doesn't find it, it's usually not there to be found."

My brother, Richard, is the head of our IT Department, and I add with no small amount of sisterly pride, a computer genius. He's been responsible for much of our company's success in technically driven Silicon Valley.

"And there's more, Frank. Last night I found some shocking things in Collier's Chinese Puzzle Desk."

"What the hell is that?"

"It's a gorgeous piece of furniture he had built last year; carved ebony wood. The man had taste; I'll give him that. This type of desk is known for its hidden drawers, difficult to locate. But I'm good with Chinese puzzles."

"Let me get this straight, you found some hidden drawers in his desk?"

"You betcha. Four of them."

I looked at Frank. He looked at me. A moment passed before he spoke up, his tone agitated.

"Well, is this a dramatic pause or are you going to tell me what you found?"

"Sorry, mind working." I tapped the side of my forehead.

"Well, give it a rest and get on with the conversation."

"Okay, okay. Two drawers held several flash drives of highly classified documentation emailed or messaged to a handful of rival companies."

"How do you know they were classified?"

"The word 'Classified' was emblazoned at the top of most files, but all you had to do was read them. Internal memos re medical stats; six-months worth of controlled studies, including failure rates in detecting specific diseases; the how-to of their successes; highly sensitive info like that."

"Why would he do that, send rival startups information that could destroy a business he was instrumental in founding? That sounds insane." Frank's sputtering would have caused me to laugh under normal circumstances.

"And that's not all." I picked up my coffee mug. Frank spoke up.

"Is this another one?"

"Another one what?"

"Dramatic pauses."

"Oh, sorry. I was going to take a swallow of coffee."

"Well, don't until you tell me what else you found."

I put the mug down. "In another drawer I found a drive containing Bitcoins for one point three million dollars from Ultimo Meds, one of Read-Out's archrivals. I see you are just as surprised as I was."

"One point three million dollars! Bitcoins, Bitcoins." He thought for a moment. "Refresh my memory, Lee. Bitcoin is the new electronic money, right?"

"Fairly new, yes. Bitcoin is digital currency that isn't backed by any country's central bank or government."

"That doesn't sound like something I'd want."

"Think of it like a new twist on the old barter system, Frank. Bitcoins can be traded for goods or services with vendors who accept Bitcoins as payment. In the past, Bitcoins were controversial because they could have been used to anonymously transfer illicit funds or hide unreported income from the IRS. Bitcoin policy now requires transactions that involve traditional, government-backed currencies to be attached to an identity, but they still have a bad rep."

"Was D. H. Collier's identity attached to these?" I nodded. Frank went on. "And each Bitcoin is worth what in hard cash?"

"Approximately twenty-five dollars to a Bitcoin, give or take. Once again, there was one point three million dollars worth on the flash. Now most people who get handed over a million dollars in any form would have done something with it, not let it just sit there. But I guess to billionaires it's chump change."

28

"The flash was lying in a drawer?"

"All by its lonesome."

"Was it dated?"

"Six weeks ago."

Frank leaned back in his chair. "Good God."

"As an aside, in another drawer I found Collier's last will and testament, in the old-fashioned form, written on paper. Once I realized what it was, I didn't do anything with it, not even give it a quick read. Looking back, I wish I had. I'm going to drink my coffee now, because I've told you everything."

Frank digested this information. "All of this was in hidden desk drawers."

I nodded as I slurped. Frank continued his thought.

"Apparently, Collier didn't think anybody else was good at Chinese Puzzles besides him."

"It's not usually on one's résumé, but I have a knack for that sort of thing."

"You're sure he was the saboteur?"

"If it looks like a rabbit, hops like a rabbit, and has a one point three million dollar carrot in one of its drawers, I'd say yes."

"Did you remove the flash drives?"

"Only to copy to D. I.'s cloud. Then I put them back."

Frank got a pensive look on his face. "I'd like to see those files. But first, you should turn them over to the Sunnyvale investigative team in Collier's death. There may be pertinent information there."

"Whatever you say. I don't mind sharing, Frank, as long as it's reciprocal."

He stared at me then shook his head. "Oh, no you don't."

"Come on, Frank. Haven't I been forthcoming with you?"

He continued to stare at me. I smiled at him, knowingly.

"I knew it! What have you got, Frank?"

"You are such a brat."

"What have you got, Frank?"

He thought for a moment, and let out a deep sigh. "Okay. It seems there's a private entrance to Read-Out used only by D. H. Collier, with unmonitored video access."

"Wow! I wondered about that. I saw the backstairs, but couldn't get any access or information on who used it."

"Everyone knows Collier was big with the ladies, especially the young ones, despite the fact he was a bit long in the tooth."

"Maybe because of it," I offered.

"Yeah, well, some men need to keep their pants zipped."

"Temper, temper."

"Apparently, he brought his conquests here to seduce, probably because of his daughter being at home. And he didn't want his amorous deeds videotaped, so he set up a non-video-able spot for his assignations here at Read-Out, using a standard hotel keycard to get in. He used it last night around midnight shortly before he hung himself."

"The keycard number was recorded?"

"Yes. As you can see, Lee, this is a plain and simple suicide. Nothing for you or D. I. to be meddling in."

After his brief lecture, he was quiet for a moment. Then that glint showed up in his eyes, the one he gets when odd things show up in a case.

"Funny, though. I had a conversation with the Chief Financial Officer, Rameen Patel, a while ago. He didn't mention any internal conflicts. Maybe he doesn't know."

"I suspect he does, Frank. CFOs are known to have hidden agendas. They're the ones answerable to the Securities and Exchange Commission if the 'i's aren't dotted and 't's aren't crossed. He may have been trying to police some pretty strong personalities, people who often have emotions running high."

"You have the gift for understatement." Frank let out a snort. "Silicon Valley's loaded with brilliant but egotistical babies." He leaned in. "What do you know about, as you say,

30

the strong personalities here? You must have learned something in your snooping."

I looked around to make sure we weren't overheard. "Once again, nobody talked about it, but I get the impression the late, great D. H. Collier was controlling and competitive. Even people he was supposedly tight with had problems with him. Take Craig Eastham. He and Collier founded the business together, but they were as different as night and day. Eastham stayed in the shadows while Collier stole the limelight and took credit for everything."

"So they didn't like each other?"

"Major. Eastham sent Collier an email a few weeks ago where he said Collier should get over himself and stop believing his own press. Collier replied Eastham could do something physically impossible. Most of the time, they used Patel as an intermediary, who neither one of them particularly liked, but respected."

"Sounds pretty hostile."

"It wouldn't be the first time a CTO crossed swords with the CEO on the QT. God, I hate all these initials, and people who use them...said the PI."

Frank ignored my attempt at humor, but seemed to agree with me. "So the relationship between Collier and Eastham wasn't what people would like to think. Remember what happened at Apex Media a couple of years ago? The two men who started it were best friends."

"Sure, one is dead and the other is in jail for killing him. Just goes to show, Silicon Valley can corrupt a lot of ordinarily nice people."

"You're sounding far too jaded for a bride-to-be, Lee."

We both laughed.

I looked down at my coffee before I spoke again. "You know, Frank, I hoped to keep this revelation under wraps, at least until I got a chance to talk to Eastham and Patel. Maybe there's something here I don't know."

31

"Nobody will hear anything from me about your unsubstantiated conjectures."

"Thanks. For whatever you said." I closed my eyes and exhaled, leaning back in the chair.

"Lee honey, you're exhausted."

"I am. I was here until around eleven; Chinese Puzzles don't open willingly. And then when I got home, *Double Indemnity* was on with Barbara Stanwyck. I had to watch that."

"You and your 1940s movies," said Frank. "Your father should have never introduced you to them."

"Are you kidding? They made me who I am." Frank harrumphed, as I sat upright, struck by a thought. "If I'd stuck around another hour, I might have seen Collier when he came in. Maybe I could have prevented this."

"And there's another unsubstantiated conjecture. You need to go home. There's nothing more --"

"I don't know, Frank," I interrupted, leaning forward. "I can't get those baby blue jockey shorts out of my mind."

"Go home," he repeated more forcefully.

I ignored him, ruminating out loud. "Why kill yourself in the boardroom of your own company? And why take off all your clothes to do it? None of it makes sense. I'm going to try to stick around unless Read-Out fires me. Maybe I'll learn something."

Frank said nothing, but squeezed his eyes shut, and let out a deep, noisy sigh. I went on.

"You've got to admit it's a weird way to go."

"Depends on how whacko the guy was. D. H. Collier didn't march to the tune of the ordinary drummer. That's how he got to where he was."

He took a deep breath as if to say more but stood and stretched out his long frame. "Never mind. No point in telling you again to go home. Well, I'm leaving. I've worn out my welcome in Sunnyvale. And I need to fight off the press,

32

protect Collier's home and property from the curious. Did you give your statement yet?"

"And signed it. Did it electronically. One of life's modern miracles; no trip to the station to sign off on it."

"And just as legal, too." Frank looked over my shoulder. "Don't look now, but guess who's coming up behind you at eleven o'clock."

I turned to see the CFO, Rameen Patel, striding across the room toward me. One of the oldest Read-Out people at age thirty-one, Patel had an impressive history.

Born in California of East Indian parents, he attended Wharton Business School, and worked on Wall Street auditing Fortune 500 companies. Six years later he left a good paying, secure job back east to return to California for the CFO title at Read-Out, making bupkis. He was one of thousands in the Bay Area, shooting to turn bupkis into gold with a startup's IPO.

According to more water cooler gossip, Patel was the poster boy for the success of arranged marriages, too. Maybe I had nuptials on the mind, but at twenty-two he'd married eighteen-year old Marjana, neither having laid eyes on the other until the wedding day.

Nine years later they had four girls, aged eight, seven, six, and three. For whatever reason Patel didn't drive, so every evening at exactly six-thirty his wife arrived in their Mercedes SUV and waited at the front curb, children and family dog in tow. The employees were then privy to the kind of familial huggy-poo, kissy-face usually seen in Norman Rockwell paintings.

But Rameen Patel didn't look very Norman Rockwell as he approached me. In fact, he looked more like the portrait of the "Anguished Man," painted by the artist in his own blood right before he killed himself.

There's no single right place to be an entrepreneur,
but certainly there's something about Silicon Valley.
Peter Thiel

Chapter Three

Frank backed up, gave a short nod of his head to the CFO, and departed. Rameen didn't acknowledge the greeting, but came directly to the chair opposite me and sat down, leaning in.

"There's been a catastrophe."

His voice, normally a lilting tenor, shook when he spoke and took on a raspy edge. I leaned into him squarely with one arched eyebrow.

"You mean other than your CEO swinging from a rope in the boardroom?"

Either he didn't hear or chose to ignore me. He straightened his horn-rimmed glasses with a trembling hand.

"We can't talk here. We need more privacy."

Without another word, he stood, turned, and walked away. I got up and traipsed after him, still nursing my coffee. I followed him to his office, I assumed for privacy, which didn't make a whole lot of sense.

Read-Out was a modern-thinking business, i.e. no doors on offices or communal spaces. Employees were expected to be open and non-secretive at all times, even unto their workspace. The exceptions to this 'no door' policy were the restrooms and the offices of the two founders, D. H. Collier and Craig Eastham. Upon reflection, given what I'd found in

34

Collier's desk, taking away his door might not have been a bad idea.

We stepped over the threshold of Rameen's small and unassuming workplace with a grand view of the parking lot. He went behind a modern, IKEA type black desk, the top of which held a laptop computer and over half a dozen framed photos of his family. I stood at the front of his desk and waited. I didn't have long. Words exploded from him like Yellowstone's Old Faithful and almost as wet.

"Everything is missing, the chips, prototype, and tester. Without them there *is* no Read-Out. They were our only assets. We are ruined!"

His voice rose on the word 'ruined' and he looked over my shoulder to see if anyone else had heard him. I turned, too, following his example. One of the ubiquitous geeks walked past his office, deep in conversation on his phone.

Satisfied he hadn't been heard, Rameen focused on me once again. The normally soft caramel color of his face took on a mottled, ruddy look. I thought he might have a heart attack on the spot.

"What are you talking about? What's missing and from where?"

Without uttering another word, Rameen unlocked and opened the bottom drawer of his desk. He pulled out a large shoebox labeled Clarke's Walk-Abouts, set it on the desk as if it were the Holy Grail, and took the lid off. Gentle hands belying his otherwise tense state, unfolded white tissue paper. Nine by six inches of something shimmered up at me in a textured, iridescent hue. He picked up the top paper-thin layer by the edges and displayed it to me.

"Do you know what these are?"

"Looks like computer chips. Only smaller than what I've seen."

"The box could hold around two hundred thousand dollars worth of chips. What's in here now is worth over ten. I've never asked you before, because it wasn't pertinent to

35

what you were doing. How much do you know about the manufacturing process, itself?"

I hesitated. It's hard to admit when you're a dummy. "I'm sure there are holes in my knowledge. Why don't you start at the beginning, and if you get condescending, I'll let you know."

"Very well. It's done by a process called semiconductor device fabrication, used to create the integrated circuits that are present in nearly every device we use. It is a multiple-step sequence of photolithographic and chemical processing during which electronic circuits are gradually created on a wafer made of pure semiconducting material, usually silicon. Are you with me?"

"Not really, but go ahead."

"The entire manufacturing process, from start to finish, takes six to eight weeks and is performed in highly specialized facilities."

"Those are called fabs, right?" I was relieved to know something.

"Correct. What I am holding in my hands are the results - all that are left - copies of the prototype chip. These chips are smaller and more powerful than anything currently on the market."

After his burst of pride in the product, he leaned across his desk thrusting his face into mine in one quick, jerky movement. I instinctively took a step backward. His concentration was such he didn't notice my reaction but went on in a hoarse whisper.

"The prototype is missing from David's office."

"For clarification purposes, Rameen, David is what friends called D. H. Collier; it was his first name. You're not talking about someone else?"

He pulled back with a look of confusion. "Yes, of course. David felt the D. H. gave him a certain image to the outside world. For those of us who worked closely with him, we called him David."

36

"Good 'nuff. Back to the prototype."

"It's worth several million dollars. It should have been in David's wall safe and it's not." Rameen's left eye began to twitch.

"Did you check his desk?"

"I went through the drawers, but he wouldn't leave something worth millions of dollars out where anyone could take it."

"No, they'd have to be good at Chinese Puzzles."

"What?"

"Never mind. I'll look, myself, although I didn't see anything like that on the first go-round."

"As if that wasn't enough," he said, his eyes blinking rapidly, "when I was leaving David's office I got a call from security. All the computer chips fabricated from the prototype are also missing from storage, along with the tester."

"What's a tester?"

"You really don't know much about this business, do you?" Before I could answer, he went on. "Do you know what I mean when I say a prototype?"

"The first of something that works and then duplicates are made from that."

"Close enough. Once we have a prototype, copies of it are then imprinted using the process I mentioned before, photolithography. Then the chips are cut to size, etched, tested, and scaled up. That means to reproduce the product at a profit. It's done at our site in Nevada, about four-hours away. Before we can distribute or sell them, each chip needs to be quality tested. That's where the tester comes in. It's one of a kind and very expensive."

"Let's back up for a minute," I said. He nodded impatiently. "I thought chips were fabricated offshore, such as in Penang, and then sent here."

"True, but David was trying to bring the manufacturing of silicon chips back to the states, the way it was done in the eighties. It was his *cause célèbre*, but it costs a fortune. The

37

board was against it, even Craig. Trying to do things David's way is how we got in this fix."

The last sentence was said more to himself than to me, but there was no overlooking the hostile tone of the statement. I decided now was as good a time as any to do a little probing.

"Sounds like there might have been some conflict within Read-Out other than the saboteur."

He brushed me off with a gesture one might use with a bothersome fly. "There's always conflict in a small start-up. The fact that we got to this stage is a minor miracle."

But something flickered behind his dark eyes. Rameen cleared his throat then looked down at the shimmering wafer in his hands, his thoughts elsewhere. When I saw he wasn't going to say anything more, I piped up.

"Did all this stuff go missing at the same time?"

The question brought him out of his reverie. "The chips and tester vanished sometime between six am and seven. I don't know how long the prototype's been gone. I only went to the safe in David's office moments ago and couldn't find it."

"What was something owned by the company and worth so much money doing in the CEO's safe?"

"It belonged to him. That's where he kept it. He paid for its development upfront and was about to sell the prototype back to us. I was to cut a check for it when we got an influx of foreign capital, but until then it remained in his safe."

"A safe to which you seemed to know the combination."

His face hardened. "I called the company attorney this morning. She left here about forty minutes ago. There was certain information that needed to be turned over to me immediately in the event of David's death. One thing was the combination to his safe. I've never been inside his office without being invited except for this morning." I stared at him and he stared at me. "I swear."

"Let's get back to the theft of the tester and chips. How do you know the timing of the thefts with such accuracy?"

"Along with video cams, we have a security company that does rounds every hour on the hour. When the guard did the seven am rounds, the entire stock was gone, plus the tester. Over fifteen million dollars. And without the prototype, we can't manufacture more."

I usually don't whistle, but let out a soft one. "Where were they kept? In a vault somewhere?"

"No, we're renting a house a block away. They were stored in the attached garage."

"Excuse me? You rented a garage to store fifteen million dollars worth of company assets?"

"It was only temporary. It was David's idea for a special project. He wanted the chips and tester close by the office, so he rented a small house with a garage. He walked back and forth to it when he was building the Plexiglas display case for the big bash. He worked in Plexiglas a lot; it was his hobby."

"Whoa, what Plexiglas, what display case, what big bash?"

"It wasn't for general knowledge, and didn't have anything to do with the problems we've been having, so I didn't mention it to you."

"Seems there's a lot you didn't mention to me."

Rameen took some serious umbrage to my tone, his color changing from red to purple. But before he answered he took a deep breath and managed to stay as inoffensive with his reply as he could.

"David was planning to have a celebratory bash at his own home in Palo Alto next week. All highly confidential. He sent out invitations to twenty very select people from all over the world, all interested venture capitalists. The chips and tester were going to be displayed encased in Plexiglas with flashing, colored lights."

"Sounds very Vegas."

"His was a theatrical personality. He said it would not only help to win over investors for much needed capital, but turn board members committed to offshore fabrication to his way of thinking."

"So it was his decision to bring all your assets to a nearby garage in Sunnyvale? Didn't he have to run that by somebody? Like the board?"

"You didn't know David." The CFO's agitated voice filled the room. "He did what he wanted. I've been circumventing his eccentricities from the beginning. There was nothing I could do about it."

"Why is that?"

Rameen ignored my question and rose, still holding the chips. He walked to the window. Looking out, he paused, seemingly distracted by a car entering the parking lot. He turned back to me much more in control, even bringing a smile to thin lips.

"Besides, as I told you, he paid for the prototype and several other necessities with his own money, so he had more say than normal. But he told me we were safe. He'd hired elaborate security, paying for it himself. Someone outside the company loaded the truck and drove it to the garage, not the men at the factory. Nobody knew."

"Not exactly. You knew. Security knew. And the driver of the truck knew. But regardless, if your assets have been stolen and you can prove it, you can collect the insurance. Maybe not ideal, but you should be able to recoup most of your losses."

He gave me an exasperated look, like I was too dumb to live. I felt my attitude change, turning to one of hard-line appraisal. I usually try to stay neutral in my personal likes and dislikes of our clients in order to do my job right. However, a lot of secrets and hidden agendas were popping up with this group. I don't like that.

Rameen Patel glanced over my shoulder again to see if anyone was hovering near the doorway. I went on talking, anyway. You want privacy? Put on a stupid door.

"I'm thinking your insurance company will never talk to you again, but I repeat, notify them."

"We can't do that," he stuttered, lowering his voice to not much more than a whisper again. "We're having a cash flow problem. That's why the board was in favor of the bash. If word of the thefts get out, we could lose our potential investors."

"And why would that be?"

"The video cams were disabled."

"With a code?"

"Yes."

I chewed this over. "That means a person within your organization is more than likely responsible. I can see why you don't want news of this to get around."

Rameen didn't answer but set the wafer inside the box, covered it with the tissue paper, replaced the lid, and put it back into the bottom drawer. He locked the drawer with one of those little keys that often come with furniture, the ones meant to keep your dog or cat out.

"Wait a minute," I said. "Is this why Collier wasn't in Switzerland? When was all this Plexiglas stuff going on?"

"He came back five days ago and stayed in the Sunnyvale rental. No one knew he was here, not even his daughter."

"Did he come back to get ready for this big bash?"

Rameen looked ill at ease, and began to move the photos around on his desk in quick nervous gestures. I put my hand on top of his to stop the redesign. I kind of liked them the way they were. He pulled his hand from under mine and sat down heavily in his chair.

"Initially, he told me he'd make arrangements from Switzerland for the transfer of the tester and chips to the garage, so they would be waiting for him. He didn't want me to be a part of it, even though I offered." Rameen hesitated, his face taking on a puzzled look. "Then David decided to return even sooner. When he called to tell me he arrived earlier, I asked him why. He said a...situation came up."

"What situation?"

"I don't know. He wouldn't say anything more about it."

"And we crash land on Planet Weird. Am I up-to-date now?" He nodded. "Okay, so what do you want from me?"

"I want you to find them."

"Find who?" I tipped the coffee cup toward my mouth to drain the last of the liquid.

"Not who. What. The prototype, chips, and tester."

"You're kidding," I said, choking on coffee. "It's all probably miles away by now. And in any direction."

"Please, Lee. At least try. You're our only chance."

"I don't think so. I found out D. H. Collier was the one sabotaging your company." I studied him for a moment. "You don't look surprised. Something else you didn't tell me."

"I....I...." He stuttered then turned mute, momentarily unable to form words. I was firm.

"Regardless, Rameen, I've done my job. You need to turn these thefts over to the police. And good luck to you."

He found voice. "We can't go to the police. As I said, if word of this gets out, we'll be ruined. One hundred and forty employees out of a job. Two years in the making. I've even borrowed money from family to help make this go."

"I didn't think CFO's ever put their own money into a venture."

The flicker behind his baby browns returned, but all he said was, "It was called for."

Then Rameen stopped talking and looked at me the same way my white and orange cat, Tugger, does when he's had his quota of treats but wants another. I usually give in to said feline, knowing I'm the world's biggest chump. True to my pushover nature, I found myself yielding.

"Oh, all right. Give me the address of the garage. You say it's nearby?" He nodded. "I'll see what I can do. I can't promise you anything, though."

His relief was almost palpable. "Thank you. When you get there, the security guard can give you more information on the stolen items."

"The prototype chip, I'm assuming it's pretty small. What kind of container is it in?"

"When I last saw it, it was in a black, square box about the size of a ring box. The prototype chip, itself, is much smaller, encased in removable glass." He tensed up again and looked at me. "This is highly confidential."

"Got it."

He scribbled down an address on a piece of paper and thrust it in my hand. "If word of this catastrophe gets out, the results will be disastrous."

"Understood. Confidential; Catastrophe; Disastrous."

More to himself than me, he added, "This is my fault, all my fault."

The landline phone on his desk jangled its greeting or warning about an incoming call. Rameen looked at it like a man facing a firing squad.

"It's starting. I've got to stave off the press and see that David's death doesn't destroy the company. Find the prototype, chips, and tester, Lee. Please."

"I'll give it my best shot."

At the core of Silicon Valley is a passion for 'yes.'
Steven Levy

Chapter Four

Before I left the building, I took a few minutes to check out Collier's Chinese puzzle desk hoping I might find the prototype. Everything was as I'd left it the night before. I was tempted to take Collier's will out and photocopy it or at least give it a cursory read. But better to come back later when I had more time. First things first.

I hurriedly gave the room another thorough going over for the black ring box. I hadn't seen anything resembling it the night before and didn't see it now.

But I did find a small folded map labeled East Bay Neighborhoods under his mouse pad. Did Collier bring it with him when he arrived around midnight? It hadn't been there the night before, I was sure of it.

I spread the small map before me. Crisp and clean, it looked as if it had never been opened, much less used. Big question: why would one of the world's foremost computer geeks have a paper map in his office when there was the internet? I refolded and tucked it in my pocket.

Instead of taking the elevator, I clomped down the stairs and stepped outside the three-story stucco building into a sun baking off the early morning fifty-degree temperature. I hit my brother's number on the frequently dialed list.

"Hey, Lee." Richard's voice sounded tired. As if to prove it, I heard him yawn.

"Sleeping in now, are we, brother mine? I've been up since four-thirty."

"Sorry about that. Vicki and I had Braxton Hicks visitations last night. We were up half the night."

"Who's Braxton Hicks?"

"Not 'who', what. They're contractions. We thought we were going into labor but we didn't, thank God."

I've noticed a trend these days of fathers-to-be to refer to the 'we' in a woman's pregnancy, as if taking on fifty-percent of the event. And I expect it's not just here in the Bay Area. It was Richard's plan, having attended Lamaze classes with Vicki, to be in the delivery room cheek to jowl with his wife counting breath reps and shouting out words of encouragement. Naturally, the actual delivery of the child is still up to the mother, but we'll let that one go.

This whole idea of the father 'participating' in the actual childbirth was something Mom found appalling. When Richard told her he was going to be in the delivery room during the birth of their child the entire time, and recording the experience for YouTube no less, she fell into the nearest chair fanning herself.

Then the happy couple extended the invitation to the family, as well. Our uncle, Tío, jumped at the opportunity. He views the birth of new life as the greatest miracle in the world.

Mom, on the other hand, retorted that in her opinion there were times a woman required privacy. This was one of them. Lila Hamilton Alvarez is from the school of thought where the phrase 'natural childbirth' means you're not wearing makeup. Group involvement was beyond her.

I have to admit attending wasn't at the top of my list of things to do, either. But Richard asked me, so coward that I am, I said yes. My plan was to keep my eyes closed most of the time and wear earplugs. And have lots of Valium on hand.

My brother yawned again.

"Richard, I need you to pull yourself together. We've got a big problem here at Read-Out."

"Shoot."

Just on that one word, I heard him come to an alert state and give me his full attention. A lone bus stop beckoned to me from the end of the street. As I gave Richard a blow by blow of the day's events, I hiked over to a bench beside an official sign announcing the Valley Transit Authority bus schedule and route. I sat on the cool, yellow slats and waited for my brother to react to what had happened. He didn't fail me.

"Holy crap! You've had a full morning, Lee. I'll take Braxton Hicks any time."

"And I'm not done yet. I've promised to try to retrieve the stolen booty before they get too far away. I'm on my way to garage where they were kept now."

"You're kidding."

"The watch word there is 'try'. They've had less than a two-hour head start and that's where you come in."

"So what do you need from me?"

"The research you did on D. H. Collier when we first took the case. The theft of the prototype and tester on the heels of his death is too much of a coincidence. I think he's a part of this, even though he's dead." I thought of the small map I'd just found. "Did he own anything in the East Bay?"

"Offhand I remember a four-plex theatre in San Francisco and a mini-mall near Monterey. He owned much of Union Square, believe it or not, and a lot of Yountville and St. Helena in the wine country."

"Very impressive, but let's stick to the East Bay."

"Okay, give me a minute. Let me fire up my laptop and I'll call you back." He disconnected.

A breeze fluttered through trees backlit by the rising sun and a bird or two chirped in contentment. I fought the urge to lean back and close my eyes for a quick nap. Rather, I got up and walked the block or two to the address Rameen Patel gave me, passing several small startups that peppered this region of Sunnyvale.

A few minutes later the phone rang. It was Richard. I almost dropped the phone in my eagerness to talk to him.

"What have you got?"

"He has - or had - a small house in Fremont. Not worth much, maybe two, three hundred thousand. It was his parents' home before they died. Is that what you mean?"

"Sounds promising, Richard. From what I've gleaned, fifteen million dollars worth of these computer chips would probably fit in the back of a not so big truck. But I don't know about the tester. How big are those things?"

"The type they'd probably use is about five feet long and two, three feet wide. Heavy, though. If a shoebox can hold over two hundred thousand dollars worth of chips, you might be right about the truck. Let's make certain; I'll do the math."

"Never mind the math. I'm visualizing it in my head."

He ignored me, humming as he thought. "Let me see, if the average size of a shoebox is…." Here his voice faded, but came back strong a second later. "That would have to be roughly two-hundred and sixty-three boxes. The lot could probably be held in a little over six-hundred cubic feet, or a seventy-five square foot area."

"You're giving me a headache, Richard."

He continued to ignore me, and banged on his keyboard. "If you packed the boxes tightly enough and put the tester along side, almost any U-Haul trailer should do it."

"Noted. What's the address of this house?"

"I'll send the directions to your phone. Easier that way."

"Thanks. Before I forget, I uploaded files from two flash drives I found in Collier's office last night."

"To the cloud?"

"Yeah. Proof that Collier was the one sabotaging the company."

"Nasty."

"Frank wants us to forward on the files to the Sunnyvale Police, Chief Broas. Copy Frank, too."

47

"They might not have much legal validity, obtained without a search warrant."

"I was hired by the company to find the culprit. As a licensed private investigator, I am bound to pass on any wrongdoings to the proper authorities."

"I love it when you go all legal on me, sis."

"Oh, shut up. I've got to go now; I'm almost at the garage where the chips were stolen from. Or should I say, from where the chips were stolen?"

"You've been hanging around Our Lady too long." He referenced what he called our mother on the sly other than She Who Must Be Obeyed.

"Noted. Give my love to Vicki."

I could feel him smile into the phone. "I'll tell her when she wakes up. What's it like outside? Still raining?"

"Rain clouds gone. Sunshine aplenty. It looks like it'll be the mid-sixties today. Not bad for December nineteenth."

"Noted." Richard's voice carried an impish quality. We both laughed before hanging up.

I stood in front of a small, unassuming, one-story 1960s starter home with an attached garage, badly in need of a fresh coat of paint. If it were in any other place in the world, it would cost around fifty thousand dollars. Here in the Bay Area, it was probably valued at half a mil. That's paradise for you.

The garage door was open, revealing several tall, two-inch thick Plexiglas sheets leaning against a wall. Next to them was a table saw. It looked like someone was in the middle of a project. Other than that, there were a few stacks of old newspapers, built-in cabinets, and dust bunnies. Nothing else.

On either side of the roof two motion-activated video cameras were angled toward the driveway and entrance to the garage. A tall pine tree several feet away held a third camera.

A car was in the drive, wearing the Allied Security logo proudly. A uniformed woman in her thirties sat in the driver's seat doing a Sudoku puzzle. Strolling down the cracked driveway, I glanced at my watch. Almost straight up eight o'clock.

I knocked on the car window, startling the guard. I smiled and waved. Blonde, with a sunburned complexion, she gave me a hard stare, but rolled down the window.

"You must be the PI Mr. Patel told me to expect."

"Yes. My name in Lee Alvarez. I'm here to look around and ask a few questions." I flashed my license. She looked at it, looked at me, and flung the car door open. I backed out of the way just in time.

"I'll show you around, Ms. Alvarez, but there's nothing much to see. It's all gone."

"What's your name?" I continued to smile, but it was fading.

"Wendy Lewis. You can call me Miss Lewis. You're from Discretionary Inquiries."

"Right."

"I applied for a job there. Didn't get it."

"Oh, ah." Not an intelligent reply, but the best I could do at that hour of the morning. And it did explain her almost combative attitude. "So what happened, Miss Lewis? Why didn't the video cams work?"

The woman shrugged. "Taken over by remote control. We figured out it was a ten-minute video loop fed into the cameras that the main office was seeing and not actually what was going on."

"Sounds pretty sophisticated."

"It was."

"Tell me about your schedule."

"I started work at four forty-five, like I always do. My first round was at five am. Everything looked normal to me and to the office. I got out of the car, walked the perimeter, and checked on the locks. Same thing at six. Then when I came back at seven, I found it like this, garage door open, everything gone. The office didn't know a thing; the loop was still going."

49

"Anything else besides the chips and tester taken?"

"If that's what they were. I only saw boxes and some weird looking cabinet." She thought for a minute.

"Wait a minute. There was a stack of Mr. Collier's old Superman comic books in an open cardboard box. They're gone, too."

"Thanks. I'm going to look around for a moment by myself. Is the house open, as well as the garage?"

"Yes."

I nodded. "Thanks. You can stay here."

Wendy Lewis nodded, got back into the car, and returned to her Sudoku.

A quick tour inside the house revealed high end rental furniture, each labeled on the underside. Elaborate electronic equipment was scattered around, but no laptop. The kitchen was devoid of cooking utensils and the fridge held a small variety of cheeses, crackers, and white wines. I couldn't find any personal effects in any of the rooms, other than one small suitcase filled with Collier's clothes and toiletries.

I turned to the garage and scrutinized the lock system, which was top of the line. The garage door was open, pulled up by a handle at the bottom then slid into a frame at the top. It lay flat against the ceiling of the garage, and appeared to be made of steel or something else just as impenetrable.

I checked the sides and floor of the garage opening. Welded framing at least two inches thick lined three sides. When the solid door was down, it set flush against this framing. Left and right, the sides wore three heavy-duty locks. They were the latest in fingerprint and keypad locks, large and of galvanized steel. Unless you knew the combination, each of the six locks needed at least fifteen minutes' worth of blowtorching to get into. I should know. I once had to do it.

I walked inside and crossed the fifteen feet or so to the one window on the side of the garage, which it no longer was. The glass window had been replaced by thick steel. The whole thing was locked in much the same way as the door. This wasn't damaged, either. All locks were pristine.

I returned to Ms. Lewis and her Sudoku, and tapped on the car window once again. With a sigh, she rolled down the window.

"What?"

"How big was the shipment that was stolen, roughly?"

She thought for a moment. "I only saw it the once, when it was being loaded in last week on pallets. Maybe five by fifteen feet. Something like that. And the cabinet thing was about five by three feet. Weighed a lot though, even with him using the forklift."

"Him? Do you know who he was?"

"Couldn't tell; some guy in a grey sweat suit with a hoodie. It was hard to see his face. He asked me to keep my distance, so I did."

"Okay, thanks for your help."

So the load in was around six, seven hundred cubic feet, just like Richard and I thought. I mused as I moved back down the driveway, suddenly stopped by the woman's voice.

"You know, I spent four years in the Marines. I'll bet I could take you."

I turned around to face the security guard getting out of her car again. She slammed the door shut and glared at me. I strode back and looked down at her. I'm five foot eight; she was probably around five-five. Wisps of her fine blonde hair blew in her face from the soft breeze of the morning. She spread her feet apart and took on an aggressive stance. I approached her with a slight smile.

"Now, Miss Lewis, you don't want to do that. First of all, I have a black belt in Karate. And second, if you want a job at D. I., picking a fight with one of the owners of the business is not the way to get it."

She seemed to deflate before me, doubt and insecurity showing on her face. Licking her lips, she couldn't seem to find any words. I went on.

"Do you have a private investigators license?"

She shook her head.

"How about a degree in computer science, you got that?"

She shook her head again.

"That's probably why you got turned down. Our employees consist solely of investigators and IT people. That's all we hire, besides two clericals for filing papers."

"You don't do security?" Her voice was small, sounding about eight-years old.

I shook my head. "We job it out. I'm not sure where you got the information we did, but it's not true. "

"My boyfriend said you did. That's why I applied."

"Well, shame on him, because we don't. Suggestion: next time, check out the qualifying criteria for yourself before you get a mad on."

She digested this in silence. I turned to leave and was near the curb when her voice shot out at me again.

"What if I got a PI license, Ms. Alvarez? What if I knew karate?"

A smile on my lips, I said over my shoulders, "Well, that and being in the Marines should take you to the front of the line." I looked at my watch again, continued back to the parking lot of Read-Out, and to my car.

Something new will always be the source of growth in Silicon Valley.
Steve Jurvetson

Chapter Five

It was pushing nine AM and I was pushing the last of the rush hour traffic on the Dumbarton Bridge on most likely a wild goose chase. But I had a feeling, and as I didn't have much else, I went with it. Maybe with a little luck, I could pick up the trail of the chips and tester. Hope springs eternal.

Supposedly, I was driving in the opposite direction of where the bulk of the traffic was heading. But when there are so many cars tootling around the Bay Area all the time, it's often hard to tell when rush hour begins and ends or where it's heading.

The Dumbarton Bridge is the southernmost of the highway bridges crossing the San Francisco Bay. It's also the shortest at 1.63 miles. I was crossing it in style in a turquoise 1957 Chevy, a car given to me by my father shortly before he died.

While it has all the latest gewgaws and is the gift that kept on giving, it also costs a fortune to maintain. If the distributor isn't going, the hoses need to be replaced or all the trim seals on the windows. He's an old man trying to keep up in a modern world, but I love him.

At the moment, I had the top down and the radio blasting an NPR interview with Mick Jagger. If I hadn't found a dead man dangling from a rope a few hours before, I would have called it a lovely day.

Once over the bridge, I followed Thornton Avenue through Newark until I reached Fremont, an incorporated city made up of five smaller towns. Richard's directions brought me to a modest, white Fremont house, probably from the early 70's. A narrow driveway went past the right side of the house and ended at a one-car garage in the back. The house didn't look lived in, but overall the property was in pretty good shape.

I drove to the end of the block and parked. Walking the tree-lined, residential street back to the address, I found it charming, but a fairly ordinary start to a billionaire's life.

Carrying a Bible, my hope was that any neighbors with too much time on their hands and staring out a window for want of nothing better to do, might peg me for a Jehovah's Witness canvassing the street. It's worked before.

I went to the front door, but instead of ringing the bell, I scooted to the side of the house and tried to look in the windows. Heavy curtains covered each one of them. However, when I got to the French doors, I had better luck. Instead of curtains, off-white blinds hid the inside from outside viewing.

But one slat was broken near the middle revealing a small gap. I squatted down to look inside, and saw two familiar young nerdy-looking guys sitting on folding chairs in an otherwise empty room. One had short, dark curly hair, the other blonde, long and stringy. Impossibly thin, they wore the standard geek uniform of ripped jeans and faded T-shirts.

I'd seen them at Read-Out from time to time, doing exactly what I wasn't sure. What I had noted was they were always together, coming and going on similar motorcycles. I took a quick picture of them with my phone then studied the scene.

The longhaired guy was reading a Superman comic book; a carton filled with them sitting next to him on the floor. The other kid was strumming a guitar and badly, I might add.

Richard plays a beautiful guitar, so I'm sensitive to these things.

Radiating from the crack in between the French doors was the heavy scent of pot. Just to prove the point, the comic book guy took a toke from a skinny, rolled-up cigarette and passed it on to his buddy.

I straightened up and assessed the situation. Being a detective and all, I'd say this must be the place. Superman might agree.

Assessing the situation further, I liked the fact the two were probably high on pot. Not an aggressive-making drug, that meant they might be slow on the uptake, maybe not even know what was happening until after it took place. I sucked in a deep breath and regretted it instantly. All I needed was a contact high.

At the rear of the house, tall trees surrounded the backyard providing a certain amount of privacy. Two Honda motorcycles, one red and one blue, stood on their kickstands near the garbage pails.

I passed them and looked inside the lone window on the side of the free-standing garage. Frosted over, I could still see a blobby, large yellow shape, like a rental from Penske Trucks. I went around to the front. It had an automatic garage door opener. Goody.

So as not to arouse the neighbors, I strolled back to my car for the stuff I keep in the trunk for such an emergency. I opened the passenger's car door, returned the bible to the glove compartment, and popped the trunk.

I am not neat about much, but the trunk of my car is the exception. Held within it is a plethora of supplies that would warm the heart of any Campfire Girl or con man, including extra clothing, food, and a weapon or two. I grabbed the tote bag already filled with among other things, a compass, water, and flashlight.

Into it I further crammed a tapered wedge of wood or shim, wire coat hanger, my purse, phone, and a Milky Way

Bar, even though the tote already contained two granola raisin bars. When a girl needs chocolate, she needs chocolate. Granola is not going to do it.

I slammed the trunk shut and relocked the car. It would be safe there for a time. This was a nice neighborhood. At least, until I got through with it.

Carrying the necessary tools, I went back to the white house. After checking to see if my pot-smoking friends were still doing their thing in the living room – they were - I returned to the garage.

I pushed the shim into the center at the top of the garage door, and past the rubber stripping to create a space for my wire. Straightening out the hanger but leaving the hook at one end, I inserted it into the space next to the shim. I shoved the wire inside about eighteen inches, and felt the resistance of the mechanism at the top of the opener.

The emergency pull lever was right below, so I snagged it and yanked the wire back toward me. The garage door opened, folding into the top of the garage. All in all, it took about six seconds. I have to say, it was a morning of garages, but life can be like that.

I looked around before entering the now open garage. All quiet on the western front. The yellow truck sat headfirst inside, and I examined the paltry lock on the backend that kept me from knowing what was in the hold. This was another lock made for the same dog or cat trying to get into Rameen Patel's desk. I opened that sucker in about three seconds flat with my handy-dandy picklock.

Once opened, pallets holding sealed cardboard boxes greeted me. Beside them was a small but powerful forklift. Behind the forklift was the silliest looking kitchen cabinet I've ever seen, so I took it to be the tester.

An electric platform at the end of the truck made it possible to move the heavy stuff in and out of the truck bed. I climbed up, went straight to the cartons, and ripped at one with eager fingers. Iridescent computer chips sparkled up at me. Bingo.

I gave a quick search for a black ring box, but such a small thing could have been anywhere in the truck, if here at all. Time was a-wasting and I had to get out of there.

I replaced the box of chips, jumped out, pulled the cargo door down, and locked the hold again. I charged around to the front of the truck. Both driver and passenger windows were wide open. I looked inside and saw the keys still in the ignition. Some days it pays to get up in the morning, dead bodies notwithstanding.

I climbed in, started the motor, backed the truck out of the driveway, and pulled away. Easy, peezy.

The amounts of money in Silicon Valley are staggering.
Alec Berg

Chapter Six

Retrieving my Bluetooth from the tote, I phoned Richard. There are pretty strict laws in California about talking on a phone without a Bluetooth while driving. All I needed was to be stopped in a hijacked truck containing millions of dollars worth of stolen stash taken from the property of a famous guy who killed himself in the early hours of the morning. They'd chuck me in a cell and throw away the key.

After a brief chitchat with my brother, we made arrangements for him to drive me back to Fremont to retrieve the Chevy in the early afternoon. Meanwhile, I would hide the little yellow truck in the four-car garage of the Alvarez home, where big renovations were taking place adding on Gurn's new office. My garage slash apartment was perfect. The truck would blend in with the rest of the chaos and I could take my time searching it for the prototype.

I instructed the phone to call Rameen Patel and marshaled my thoughts. It wouldn't do to be blathering like an idiot to a CFO who was on the brink of hysteria; I needed to be clear and concise, especially if I wasn't going to play this quite the way he wanted. As the number rang, I hit the Dumbarton, used my FasTrak®, and started my journey across the Bay and back to Palo Alto.

The CFO's eager voice came through on the second ring. "Lee! What news? Did you find them?"

"I have the chips and tester." I was proud. Even I couldn't believe my good fortune. "I don't know yet if the prototype is among them. We'll have to tear this truck apart to know for sure."

"We need that prototype, Lee." His voice was chastising and abrupt.

"So you've said, but two out of three ain't bad. Before I return what I've got, we need to talk about a few things."

He was silent, so I went on.

"Not only did somebody know the big secret hiding place of this stuff, but knew sophisticated codes to break in and steal them. Hold on a minute." I dug around in my tote bag for the Milky Way Bar. I was starving. I ripped the wrapping off with my bare teeth and took a big bite. Yum.

The CFO found voice. "What...what do you mean, 'before you return what you've got'? You are to bring everything back to me immediately."

Rameen Patel's parents emigrated from Bombay to the States shortly before his birth and still ran a small but thriving motel in Barstow. In fact, I think I stayed there once on a drive to Las Vegas, if I remember rightly. Pepto-Bismol pink with tons of hanging purple bougainvillea.

Even though their son was born in California, much of his thinking seemed to mimic the culture stuck fast to his parents, even in their new land. So he continued to sputter with superior male indignation while I chewed. With a mouthful of caramel I finally answered.

"Rameen, you're not thinking straight, pal. If somebody took them away from you once, they can do it again. So it's better if I protect them until we find out a few things, like who did this and why."

He was silent for a time. "Very well. I see the wisdom of that."

"Good. Now that we've cleared that up, let's move on. In your office, you said that Collier killing himself was your fault. What did you mean by that?" I could feel his hesitation.

"Come on. I need an answer. How is all of this your fault? What's going on with you?"

I could feel him bristle. "Some questions I will answer, but I am ethically bound to be silent on others."

Remembering our previous conversation in his office and how loosey-goosey the setup seemed to be, I would have laughed out loud over his statement, but had a mouthful of chocolate.

"You can skirt anything that smacks of business ethics, Rameen. Start by sharing a little back history of Read-Out. Flesh it out for me." I swallowed, took another bite of candy, and chewed while I listened to him pick and choose his words.

"David Collier and Craig Eastham were partners from the beginning. David had the ideas and medical skill set, and Craig the technical expertise. They were both geniuses with a proven track record. It was to be a straight fifty-fifty, just the two of them. No interference from investors or a board. Hiring me was necessary, as neither one of them was a numbers man, but I was ultimately answerable to him, not just because of his initial investment. If you'd ever met David, you would know he wanted to do things his way. No compromises."

"So you've said."

"But it was expensive, all the research and testing they were doing. The lab work alone cost a fortune. Almost a year ago, there was a setback. One of the labs had a fire; several people were hurt. I'm sure you read about it."

He didn't wait for an answer, but jumped right in again.

"It wound up being negligence on our part and we were sued for millions. Even David saw he would take a big hit to cover the losses. Craig was unwilling to put any more money into the company and wanted to restructure. I convinced David to let us bring in investors and a board, at a total of forty-nine percent. The two of them would still have the controlling interest with fifty-one percent. That's what I told him."

The phone went silent. I was about to ask if he was still there, figuring we had become one of those dropped calls that happen when you least expect it, but he finally went on.

"But that's not how it was. David was a brilliant man, but not as far as corporate understanding goes. As I say, he was not a numbers man. Essentially, I sold him out. I'm not proud of it, but that's what I did. I wanted to save the company."

"Does Craig Eastham know about this?"

"I couldn't have done it without his help. I won't go into all the details, but David didn't think I would betray him, for reasons I don't care to go into. And he trusted Craig. We used that trust against him." He paused then added. "We had to."

"Exactly how did you do this?"

"We talked him into signing papers without reading them thoroughly. Before David knew it, he'd turned over five percent more, which gave controlling shares to the board. They started telling him what to do, always with their eye on the bottom line. They even talked about replacing him; bringing in another CEO. Frankly, we were all in favor of it. A couple of months ago he said Craig and I killed his dream. I thought he and I were even now, but maybe not."

"What does that mean; you thought he and you were even?"

"Nothing. It's not important."

"So what was with all this Las Vegas big bash stuff? Twenty venture capitalist from across the globe, and yada yada?"

"David came up with the idea a month or two ago. We thought it meant he came around, that he saw what we were trying to accomplish, and was going to work with us."

"And that's around the time the emails and faxes to competitors with highly confidential materials started."

"Yes." I heard a sob escape from Patel. "And I'm sure that's why he hung himself. I drove him to it."

I chewed this over, as well as the rest of my candy bar, chugging over the Dumbarton going about thirty-five miles an

61

hour. Apparently, the truck had been built for yellowness, not for speed.

"So you knew the whole time Collier was the saboteur."

Patel cleared his throat and coughed before speaking.

"I wasn't sure, not really. And I didn't want to color your thinking, so I never said anything. I'd hoped I was wrong; that he *had* come around to a more businesslike approach, paying attention to profit margins. That he wanted what was best for all of us."

"Who else suspected the saboteur was Collier? Eastham?"

"We never discussed it. But it was out of our hands, anyway. The board wanted to find out who was trying to destroy us financially for the past few months, so forced us to bring you in. It may all be moot at this point, now that's he's gone. Maybe I can keep the IPO alive..."

He stopped speaking for a split second then words spilled out, quick and staccato.

"Oh, God. This is bad. This is so bad. If it gets out I tricked him into signing documents and drove him to suicide, I could lose everything. In defense of myself, if David had continued on the way he was going, the next step was to declare bankruptcy. I believed in what we were doing; the betterment of mankind. Truly I did. But I've got a family to protect. My girls, how can they face their friends, with a father in jail?" He broke down on the other end of the line.

"That's a big leap, isn't it? You didn't push the ladder out from under him, did you? Or did you?"

He didn't answer but continued to sob. Just at that moment, I saw the flash of a red motorcycle coming up beside me. I was at the halfway point of the Bridge.

"Ah...Rameen...we need to continue this conversation later. I've got to deal with something."

I disconnected just as the motorcycle pulled in front of me and slowed down, forcing me to do the same. Blonde hair flapping from beneath his helmet, he glanced over his shoulder and back at me with a malevolent smile. So much for easy peezy.

What created Silicon Valley was a culture of openness,
and there is no future to Silicon Valley without it.
Sarah Lacy

Chapter Seven

I would have tried to move into the left lane and pass him, but just then the blue motorcycle showed up to my left and stayed there. He signaled for me to pull over, exactly to where I don't know. I was already in the far right lane with nothing but a small walkway separating me from the waters of the San Francisco Bay.

I hit Frank's number on my speed dial, but the call went directly into voice mail. I left a message, anyway. "Hey, Frank. Godfathers are supposed to be at their goddaughters' beck and call 24/7. Where are you? I've got a situation here and I might need some help. Call me back." I threw the phone on the passenger's seat.

Boxed in by the two motorcycles, I was reduced to thirty miles an hour, with other vehicles on the bridge whizzing by the small caravan. The motorcycle at my side rode so close he could have reached out and touched the truck door.

In turn, I could have rolled down the window and spit on him. But the Alvarez women don't do that sort of thing, at least not most of the time. And I was a bit dry; all that chocolate.

Once we crossed the bridge the blue motorcycle swung into my lane several times, nearly sideswiping me. Not that a cycle is any match for a truck, even a small one, but I didn't feel like running over the rider. It had already been a bad day.

The motorcycle in front slowed down to a crawl. As soon as there was a patch of land at the base of the bridge, they forced me onto it. The three of us came to a stop. The two guys removed their helmets, dismounted, used the kickstand to keep the bikes upright, and started toward the truck.

Meanwhile, I opened the truck door and got out slowly. I was hopping mad, more at myself than these two, and needed to control it. I should have taken care of them back in Fremont when I had the element of surprise on my side. Stupid, stupid, stupid.

I slammed the door shut and took a stance not unlike the one Wendy Lewis had given me earlier. My demeanor threw the kid who rode the blue bike. He backed up and went to the other side of his machine and just watched. The man who'd been on the red bike withdrew a switchblade from his jeans and flicked it open, still wearing that idiotic but nasty grin on his face.

Blue Bike stared at him, an expression of astonishment at his friend's actions covering his face. I was with him.

Somebody's been seeing too many old movies at Palo Alto's Stanford Theater, I thought. This was straight out of *The Asphalt Jungle.* I heard my cell phone ring back at the truck. I thought about turning around and retrieving it, but Red Bike kept coming at me. Cars and trucks raced by apparently oblivious to the drama unfolding on the side of the road.

I pointed a finger at Red. "Don't do it. Get back on your bike and get out of here. I'm returning the merchandise to where it belongs. You need to stay out of it now before things get out of hand."

"We're taking back our truck and merchandise, bitch. And you're coming with us." Then he actually snarled. I remembered Daniel Day Lewis doing that in the *Gangs of New York.* It worked better on him. Red Bike waved the long, slender knife back and forth in the air, blade gleaming in the sun. I appreciated the gesture - so Hollywood - but Blue Bike nearly fainted.

"Jerome, nobody told us anybody would get hurt. I'm not doing this. Let's not do this."

I took a step forward. "Listen to your friend, Jerome. He's making sense."

But Jerome aka Red Bike wasn't paying attention. He was trying to stare me down. "Listen, bitch, I know who you are. I saw you stealing the truck from the bathroom window when I was taking a whiz. Does Patel's new assistant feel like getting sliced up for the job? You better do what I say." The evil smile returned, as he gyrated around brandishing the switchblade.

"Jesus Christ! I didn't sign up for this." Jerome's friend jumped on his blue motorcycle, and kicked at the starter. "I'm outta here." The motor revved to life and he took off, wheels spitting up wet leaves and dirt from the night's rain.

"Ronnie! Ronnie! Come back here!"

Jerome's shouting accomplished nothing, but it did distract him for a moment. I took a run at him, and kicked my right leg upward. Hitting the switchblade with my sole of my shoe, I knocked the knife out of his hand. It spun like a top and landed on the ground behind him. Then I centered myself and rammed good old Jerome in the stomach with my left foot for good measure. He'd pissed me off. 'Sliced up', indeed. With the wind knocked out of him, he doubled over and dropped to his knees.

"Here, let me help you up." I looked around me, went to his side, and grabbed him under his left armpit in a seemingly helpful gesture. Even if people didn't stop their cars, they might call 911 if they saw enough of this scene.

I half pulled and he half struggled to his feet, gasping for air. I dragged him to the other side of the truck, the side away from traffic and shielded from view. I leaned him against the truck door, but he slid down to the running board. Apparently, he wasn't in the kind of shape brandishing switchblades demanded.

Hovering over him, I pushed back on his forehead with my hand for a good look at his face, currently hidden by stringy, long hair. I was at a high-energy level, so the back of his head smacked against the metal door.

"Ow! That hurt." His voice carried an accusatory tone, as he reached behind him and rubbed the back of his head.

"Well, I'd say I'm sorry, but you did threaten to slice me up like bologna. So let's talk. Why don't you tell me who you're working for? It's a nice way to start the conversation."

He didn't say anything, but shook his head. I heard my phone ring again, but I was a little busy.

"Shaking your head is no answer, Jerome, and I need one. I didn't take care of you back at the house and that was a mistake. I'm going to deal with you now, even if I have to call the police to come and arrest you for grand theft. You're looking at felony charges. I could throw in threat of bodily harm with a dangerous weapon, too. Might be a long time in prison. So, I will rephrase the previous question. For whom are you working?"

The little speech of mine had the desired effect. The look in his eyes became more of a scared kid out of his elements rather than a member of a New York City street gang.

"I don't know. I don't know who it was. It was just a voice, a voice on my phone." He rubbed his stomach where my punch had landed.

"Excuse me? You did all this for a voice on the phone?"

"Somebody called day before yesterday and left a message to call him if Ronnie and I wanted to make ten thousand dollars. Sweet. I called him back and he told us where to go, what to do, everything."

"And what was that, exactly?"

"We were to take the truck from Fremont and drive it to Sunnyvale at six-thirty this morning to pick up a load left in the garage. When we got there, the garage was open, so we used the forklift from the truck to put the chips and tester into the truck. When we got back to Fremont, half the cash was left inside the house, just like he said. We were waiting for his next call with the rest of the money when you showed up. But I never met him. He was just a voice."

"So the voice was a man's?"

"I think so."

"Was it or wasn't it?"

"It was disguised. I think it was a man's voice, but I can't be..." He broke off. "I think I'm going to throw up."

"Well, do it over there in the brush. Meanwhile, hand over your phone. I want to hear this message."

"It's gone." Now he began to whine. "He told me to erase it, so I did."

He covered his mouth with his hand and stood. He pushed passed me and toward some scraggy brushes where he retched. I followed and took the opportunity to reach into his back pocket and retrieved his phone as he was bending over. I don't even think he knew I took it. I turned, went back to the truck, and leaned against the front fender.

After he was finished upchucking, he wheeled around, looked at me, and took off running, crossing to the other side of the truck and toward his bike. I took a few steps toward him, but when I saw he didn't pick up his switchblade, I stopped.

Good old Jerome threw himself on his motorcycle, not even bothering to put on his helmet, which crashed to the ground. Amid revving motor sounds and grinding gears, he took off, mud and leaves flying everywhere. I strode to where his cast off helmet lay, picked it up by its strap, and then went back to the truck.

After tossing the helmet behind the passenger seat, I once again went into my trusty tote and pulled out a baggie. I recovered the switchblade for fingerprints, got back in the truck, and heard my phone ring again. It was Frank. I answered with a grim smile.

"Situation under control, Frank, but thanks, anyway."

"I was in court. Had to turn my phone off. What's going on, Lee? You sure you're all right?"

"Absolutely. Just thought I had some engine trouble."

"Since when do you call me for engine trouble? Liar, liar, pants on fire."

I laughed. "Fire extinguished, and things are okay now. I swear. Talk to you later."

"You'd better."

"Oh, by the way, Frank. I found out how D. H. Collier could have gotten to Read-Out without a car. It seems he had a small pied-à-terre about two blocks away, no one knew about. He liked to stay there and walk back and forth to work. Want the address?"

"Now what do you think?"

I laughed and gave it to him. After hanging up, I mulled over the Dumbarton Bridge fiasco. It could have been a lot worse if those two kids had known what they were doing. Then I felt a 'niggle-niggle' in the pit of my stomach. I only get that when something is off. But what? I couldn't put my finger on it. Those damn baby blue jockey shorts. It all went back to them.

I placed another phone call before starting the engine. Richard answered right away, as if waiting for my call.

"Richard, are you at D. I.?"

"Got here about ten minutes ago. Why?"

"Have you seen Jake?"

"Yeah, I saw Jake when I came in," said my brother.

Jacob 'Jake' Gold originally came from across the pond as the Brits say, was one of the more mature D. I. operators at age fifty-nine, and more or less from the old school. His father wanted him to be a rabbi, but Jake was a man who liked more action. He always carried – unlike me, who usually left her gun in the safe at home or in the trunk of the car – and had no problem knocking some teeth loose when called upon – his phrase, not mine.

The reason why he'd lasted so long at D. I. with these old-fashioned and somewhat barbaric ideals was nobody, and that's nobody, wore a suit better than him. With Savile Row

69

on speed dial, Jake was a clotheshorse from an era where clothes made the man and the man knew it. Any time Lila had an axe to grind; Jake would saunter in wearing one of his dapperest suits, complete with the latest tie from Harley Street. They'd chat, he'd strut, and he would get away with whatever. I soooo envied Jake.

"He's done with the Stringer Games job, right? I mean, he's free, if I need him?"

"You need him? What's going on?"

I told Richard about my run-in with the motorcycle babes. I asked him to bring Jake up to speed then have him meet me at the Alvarez humble abode. I just might need some packing backup.

Then I turned the key, little yellow truckie roared to life, and we continued our journey to Palo Alto.

Silicon Valley has been a technology capital
like New York is a financial capital.
Bill Maris

Chapter Eight

Forty-five minutes later after driving in circles to lose anyone who might be following me, I pulled into the driveway of the Alvarez family home. Edging the truck under the porte-cochère next to the family room, I drove behind the house. Jake was waiting for me.

Several pickups and vans were parked haphazardly next to the garage and near the pool. In between the vehicles were mounds of gravel, bags of cement, and stacks of lumber. Four or five men were either carrying supplies or measuring, drilling, and banging away on something having to do with the new office being built inside one of the car stalls.

Naturally, once the workmen started ripping down walls they discovered in order of appearance: dry rot, termites, and substandard electrical wiring. What was supposed to have been a four-week job had turned into eight. And counting.

I maneuvered the yellow truck in between a rusting red pickup and a tarp covered mound of gravel. Jake showed up at the driver's door and leaned in the rolled-down window.

He was a tall man, running a little to fat, but maintaining a square jaw line and devilish blue eyes. I remember when I was a teenager thinking here was a living, breathing James Bond. He still carried a lot of that suave as he flashed me a smile.

71

"Hello, Luv. I hear you got a truckload of something everybody wants."

"So it would seem," I said, opening the door a little. Jake backed up and I got out, dragging my tote bag with me.

"Well, if I understand correctly, Luv," Jake said in his clipped accent, "you want me to sit in the cab and make sure no one gets rambunctious with the cargo."

"That's not all. There's a small, black ring box we need to find. Might be mixed in with this load."

"You want me to search the truck and its contents for it?"

"It would be appreciated, Jake. But if it's not here, don't be surprised."

"But if it is, I'll find it."

It was his self-assuredness plus delivery that pushed Jake to the head of the pack. Opening the door with a strong hand, he jumped onto the running board with a lightness belying his years.

"It all sounds right easy enough."

"Possibly," I said, wanting to give full disclosure. "I made the mistake of underestimating two kids on the way over here."

"Not to worry." Grinning, he swung himself behind the steering wheel. "The last time I underestimated someone was in 1984."

"Was that when you were stationed in Grenada?"

"No, that's when I married my first wife. She took me for everything I had."

I laughed dutifully as my cell rang. The image of the love of my life flashed on the screen. Moving away for privacy, I waved goodbye to Jake, who closed the truck door and settled himself within. Excited, I hit the answer button.

"Hi, darling! I wondered why I hadn't heard from you yet. I must have called two or three -- "

"Honey, sweetheart, listen to me."

Just those words alone were enough to stop my heart. Gurn never says 'listen to me' unless he has something to say I don't want to hear. He took a breath then hesitated.

"I'm listening." I put my finger in the other ear to block out carpentry sounds, retreating nearer the pool so I could hear him better. "I'm listening," I repeated.

"Sweetheart, I don't have a lot of time. Something's come up. I won't be back for two more days."

"What's happened?" The world closed in on me, as I hovered by the gate to the pool.

"It's not…I can't talk about it. But I'll be back in two days' time, three at most."

"We're getting married in five."

"I'll be back. I swear."

I squeezed my eyes shut. Yellow Pages listed Gurn Hanson as a Certified Public Accountant. As a Lt. Commander in the Naval Reserves and former SEAL, the Pentagon listed him in a whole other category. Whatever he did, it was so secret I couldn't even know about it until after we were married. And even then my knowledge would be limited. When I spoke, my voice was low and unemotional.

"Where are you going this time? Iraq? Afghanistan? Syria?"

"I…I…"

"Sorry, I shouldn't have asked. I know you can't say."

"I love you, Lee. More than you can imagine."

He choked on the last word and was silent. Wherever he was going, I didn't want him going like this. I tried to lighten the mood.

"Well, *I* can imagine how much I love *you*. I'm opening my arms as wide as I can. You can't see me, but that's what I'm doing, just like we used to do as kids." I spoke in a little girl's voice. "I love you this much. Thiiiiiiis much."

He laughed and so did I. I went on in my normal tone, now that we were back in sync.

73

"Stay safe, groom, and hurry home. We have a wedding to star in."

"I will, bride." There was the roar of a jet engine and voices in the distance. "I have to go, sweetheart. Kiss Baba for me."

Baba Ganesh was the young female cat he was bringing into the marriage. I was adding Tugger to the mix, better known as my son the cat, so ours was a feline-enriched union.

There was dead air. Gurn was gone. I leaned against the pool gate for several minutes until I heard Tío calling me.

"Liana. Liana! ¿Qué pasa?"

My uncle - or Tío - is the only person I don't mind calling me by my given name. I even hate it when my mother calls me Liana, although I can't do much about it. Lila Hamilton Alvarez doesn't believe in nicknames and try bucking her. But luckily to the rest of the world, I'm Lee. I turned to face the only person who gives me unconditional love. I was shooting for Gurn being the second.

I forced a smile, waved, and went around the fenced-in pool toward the back of the house I grew up in. Here was the Alvarez version of the Great American Dream.

"Good morning, Tío." I went into his arms for a quick embrace. He hugged me back and held on.

"¿Consada, sobrina?"

"I am a little tired."

Tío often spoke to his family in Spanish, even though his English was good, despite the heavy accent. As for me, I loved it when he addressed me as *sobrina* or his niece. It always made me feel loved and special. I leaned into him.

"It's already been a long day. What time is it, anyway? I've sort of lost track." I looked up into his face.

"After eleven. Maybe the eleven-thirty. Ricardo, he calls to say you are on your way. I make the *torta* for lunch. Your favorite." He studied my face. "Something is wrong. ¿Qué pasa?"

"No, no, nothing. I'm just a little tired, like I said."

74

Even though I usually keep nothing back from Tío, I didn't feel like talking about Gurn's latest mission quite yet. I needed for it to settle within me more.

"Where are the cats, Tío?"

"I see them last in the sunroom."

What with the banging, drilling, and buzz-sawing, we didn't want to leave the cats inside the garage apartment all day listening to the chaos. There's nothing worse than a feline with frayed nerves. Cats like continuity, with a lot of peace and quiet thrown in. There was none of that inside the garage apartment between the hours of eight and five. So during construction we shuttled our furry companions back and forth daily to the Alvarez McMansion or the Big House, as Richard likes to call it.

When my parents married, Mom's family gave them the three-bedroom, two-bath home as a wedding present. With each ensuing year, Dad built a new addition, including the third floor, until it became one of the larger homes in the area. For one of their anniversaries, he finished the house off with two mammoth thirty-foot high white columns built by Mexican artisans. These landmark columns stand on either side of the front door.

Arm in arm, Tío and I went through the back door and into the creamy yellow kitchen still dressed up like the thirties, with the exception of the latest appliances. The spacious, eat-in kitchen always felt warm and inviting, mostly because this was where Tío spent the bulk of his time.

As a retired executive chef from San Jose's famous *Las Mañanitas* Restaurant, Tío lived to cook. If he wasn't cooking for family, friends or needy, less fortunate people, he was making special dietary meals for animals at the shelter where he volunteered.

Since moving in a couple of years ago, he occupied the first floor of the house with the kitchen. Mom occupied the second floor with the office and study. Mom's idea of cooking was ordering in from *Baume*, with its Michelin star and 'Menu

75

Découverte' or food discovery. The in-laws met a few times a week for a shared meal at the dining room table; Tío's fare, of course.

The smells emanating from the kitchen made my mouth water. But I needed to find the cats, particularly Tugger, who could soothe my savage breast like nobody else, unless it was of the Gurn variety.

I pushed the swinging door open separating the kitchen from the rest of the house and hurried into the family room. The first thing I clapped eyes on was the beautiful if not somewhat overwhelming sixteen-foot high Christmas tree sparkling in the bay window. I inhaled the fragrance of pine. Heavenly.

The fat but well-formed blue spruce held at least two-hundred ornaments from the Hamilton Alvarez past Christmases. Mom adds new ones each year to the ever-growing collection. Each treasured ornament has a memory and a spot. Even the Play Dough pretzel I made for her in the 2nd grade resides on a limb, looking suspiciously like dried out doggy-do.

Between stringing dozens of lights and tying each ornaments on the tree so batting paws don't send them flying, this Christmas chore takes a full three days for the family to accomplish. Ho, ho, ho.

I didn't see the cats right off, so I called out. "Tugger, Baba! Where are you? Come to mommy!"

I heard Tugger's loud, Siamese-like yowl followed by Baba's soft, high-pitched meow. Both sounds came from the window ledge of the bay window on the other side of the resplendent tree. The scurrying sounds of eight paws on the light oak floor told me they were on their way.

I leaned over and extended my arms. Tugger jumped into them and I made room for Baba, hot on his trail. I snatched the longhaired grey and white cat with my free hand and held her particularly close for a moment. Then I looked into her emerald green eyes.

"Your daddy sends his love," I whispered. She closed her eyes and began to purr. I looked at my orange and white guy, his amber eyes half closed in contentment. I already felt better.

"*Mira*. There is something wrong, *sobrina*."

I hadn't heard Tío come up behind me. He looked at me with concern written all over his face.

"I'm sorry, Tío. I guess I can't keep anything from you. Right before I saw you, Gurn called and told me he's on another mission. He won't be back for two or three days. I just took it hard, that's all."

"*Como no*. Of course," he repeated in English. "But it is his job and, therefore, your job to accept what he does."

"Making peace with it is tougher than I thought, Tío."

"*Debes intendar, sobrina*."

I smiled at my uncle. "Yes, I must try. And I will. *Gracias*."

"And now it is time to eat."

With his salt and pepper hair, Tío was a tall and elegantly appointed man. One would never know by his appearance there was a reverence for food bordering on the religious.

"Give me the ten minutes to warm and serve." With that he went into the kitchen and shut the door behind him.

Hugging two purring cats, I wandered over to the down-filled, beige leather sofa in front of a crackling fire and lay down. Big mistake.

If valleys are the dimples on the face of the earth,
as Steven King once said, then Silicon Valley is
the deepest, most sparkling dimple of them all.
Betty Dravis

Chapter Nine

Feeling something heavy on my chest, I awoke with a start and stared nose-to-nose into slightly crossed amber eyes. A pink, rough tongue licked my nose in a greeting.

"Thank you, Tugger." Reaching up, I wiped kitty saliva from my nose as surreptitiously as possible. Tugger is a sensitive soul and I didn't want to offend.

I struggled to a sitting position, throwing Tugger off in the doing. Without a backward glance, he sauntered down to my feet where Baba lay curled up sleeping. He snuggled next to her. She cuddled into him. Their friendship made me smile.

Then I noticed shadows cast by the incoming sun were at a completely different angle than when I lay down. Just how much time had gone by? I looked at the clock on the stone mantle and saw a full two hours had passed.

I would like to say I leapt up, but as so often happens when one has had too long a nap, I felt as if I were moving underwater. I managed to stand and stretch before hearing laughter coming from the kitchen.

Followed by the cats, I swung the kitchen door open, and saw Richard and Tío sitting around the table chatting. They both looked at me with smiles on their faces.

"She lives!" Richard burst out then sobered. "Tío told me about Huckster, Lee." Richard often calls Gurn by his nickname from their NROTC days. "Sorry it's coming so close to the wedding, but you know everything on the groom's part has been done, down to the boutonnieres. He is so ready. And anything that comes up, as his best man I'll take care of it. Don't you worry."

Richard stood up midway in his speech, searching my face to see if I was flipped out or not. I wasn't. The cats and sleep helped stabilize my feelings. But at the moment he seemed like the older brother and I the kid sister. He wanted to do whatever he could to make me feel better. It was unbelievably sweet.

"I'll be fine, Richard. The wedding will be fine." I smiled and touched him on the shoulder with a quick hand. Pulling out a chair before a table setting, I sat down.

The cats ran to their cereal bowls, often containing one or more of their favorite treats if not an outright meal. Finding nothing, Tugger gave out with a yowl, followed by Baba's small plaintive squeak. Then they both sat in front of their respective bowls and stared at my uncle, expectantly.

"They like to pretend I starve them," said Tío, rising and turning to the stove. "But nearly every hour they practice how to walk side by side on a leash, and I give them treats each time. Soon they will be *dos gatos gordos*."

"Two fat cats?" I looked at my long, lean Tugger and the smaller, but svelte Baba. Wrinkling my nose, I said, "I can't see it. But is Mom still pushing for them to carry our wedding rings down the aisle tied in bows around their necks? I don't know, Tío. It sounds very iffy to me."

"It sounds a little P.T. Barnum to me," said Richard.

"I do not offer the opinion," Tío said with a shrug. "But promise to try to teach them for your mama. She is very good at planning the *fiesta grande*."

"If anyone can teach Tugger and Baba to deliver rings when and where they're needed, you're the man, Tío." I said.

Thinking of rings caused my mind to dart back to the missing black ring box housing a multi-million dollar prototype chip. Where was it? I almost asked Richard for an update, but having 'family talk' for just a few minutes cast a normalcy over the day I needed. I smiled at my uncle.

"I hate to say it, but Mom might be going a little overboard."

"Gee, you think?" Richard's voice carried laughter and non-comprehension. "You've got enough bridesmaids to fill Levi Stadium."

"And Mom might not be done yet," I said.

Tío snatched up a potholder and opened the oven to reveal a casserole dish topped with bubbling cheese. "When she do your Tía's and my thirty-fifth anniversary, it was planned down to the...the..." He searched for a word then turned to us. "What is the word for the little wooden thing you use to puncture the olives?"

"Toothpicks," Richard and I said in unison then looked at each other, and smiled.

"*Si*, the toothpicks topped with the hearts *piquitito*."

The image of those toothpicks flooded back to me. "That's right, the toothpicks with tiny little hearts on top of each one. I never saw anything like that before."

"Or since, I'll bet," said Richard. "Mom had them made special."

Tío smiled, too, but it wasn't at us. His face took on a far-away, long ago look. "That party, it makes your Tía so happy. She was the most beautiful woman in the room."

"I remember," I said softly.

"So do I," Richard said.

My brother and I glanced at one another. I could tell he, too, was thinking of a beloved aunt who died too suddenly and too young, just as our father had.

"Soon I lose her," Tío continued, "but that night, Lila, she do everything to make for us the memories. All we do is to relax and enjoy. My Maria, she was never so happy." He looked at me. "And you will be happy, too, when she does for you your wedding, *sobrina*."

I thought about what Tío was saying, weighing it against Frank's advice of slowing Mom down. Nope, not happening. Planning special events made my mother happy. She was really good at them, like everything else she put her mind to.

And if I was honest with myself, there was a part of me that just didn't give a tinker's damn about invitations, caterers, or toothpicks, with or without small hearts.

I'd learned that lesson when I got stuck taking over my best friend, Mira's, wedding a couple of years back. Besides, if Mom helped create the same sort of wonderful memories for Gurn and me as Tío keeps locked away, it sounded all right.

Tío set the casserole down on a trivet in the center of the table. Steam rose from his latest edible work of art; it smelled incredible.

"*Aquí lo tienes*," he said, and stepped back with pride. "I make for you the *chorizo con queso*." He looked over at Richard and winked.

"What happened to my *tortas*?" I looked from uncle to brother.

"Oh, I ate them while you were crashed out on the sofa." I never saw Richard look so content with himself. "I didn't have any lunch today and they were delicious."

"Why you stinker," I said, half-amused, half-surprised. "I love Tío's *tortas*, especially the shrimp ones."

"Hey," said my brother feigning hurt. "Consider it your sacrifice for Tío and me getting your car back from Fremont." He tossed the keys in my lap. "It's in the driveway."

"You picked up the Chevy while I was sleeping? Well, thank you, gentlemen. Any problems?"

Both men shook their heads.

"You didn't run into anybody hanging around nearby?"

They looked at one another and shook their heads again.

"Good. But tell me, brother mine, you snagged my *tortas* but what did Tío get out of your escapade?" I love to tease Richard.

"The joy of making you your second favorite meal. Is that not right, Ricardo?" Tío said the words with high drama, before Richard could answer.

I picked up a large spoon, heaped cheesy casserole onto my plate, and dug in. "Oh my gawd, Tío," I said after the first bite. "This is just the best. I love the *poblanos*. What you can do to a pepper. Yummy, yummy."

Tío turned to me. "But please to chew with your mouth closed. You attract the mosquitoes."

"It's actually 'flies', Tío, but point taken." Trying to be more ladylike in my mastication, I looked at my uncle again. "It's your fault. You are just too good a cook."

"*Gracias*, because I make it *muy rápido*. Just like the short order cook."

"Tío," I said, "you may be very fast, but I'd never call you a short order cook."

"Amen to that," added Richard, looking up at the clock on the wall. "Folks, I have to leave in a minute. Vicki's still at the doctor's getting checked out from last night and I need to pick her up soon. Before anyone asks, everything's fine; it's only routine. The baby's just a little late in coming."

"You're sure about all of this? You're not keeping something from us?" I was concerned and didn't hide it. "Isn't ten days overdue a long time?"

"*Bebés*, they never listen to anyone, even *el doctor*," Tío said.

"Exactly," said Richard. "Everybody at Stanford Hospital says this can happen, especially with the first one, but it should be soon. Hopefully, it doesn't coincide with your wedding."

"Are you kidding? I'd love to walk down the aisle holding my newborn niece or nephew." I scrutinized my brother's face. "You're sure you don't know which it will be, boy or girl?"

82

Richard shook his head in a decided manner. "Vicki doesn't want to know and that's fine with me. Getting back to business, Lee, while you've been down, a lot has happened."

"Did Jake find the black ring box?"

Richard shook his head.

"I thought not." I let out a sigh. "Too much to hope for."

"And he said he tore the truck apart looking for it. Right now Jake's driving the tester and chips up to Redding for safekeeping. Lila hatched out a plan to keep them there until you get to the bottom of how they were stolen or, at least, until they can be shipped out to customers. Rameen Patel agreed with her."

"Redding? Lila didn't tell Rameen where Jake was going, did she?" I speared a large chunk of chorizo with my fork.

Richard gave me a look of disbelief. "You jesteth, right? Only a select few know about our storage units in Redding. That's the whole purpose of the place."

"I hate to say it, but hiding them in Redding is a good idea, better than leaving them here. But that's why Lila's the head honcho and I'm just a peon."

"Along those lines, She Who Must Be Obeyed called you a few minutes ago."

"Lila called? I didn't hear my phone ring."

"You leave it here in *la cocina*, Liana," Tío said coming into the conversation and pointing to my bag on the counter near the microwave. "We both hear, but do not want to go into your purse."

Richard cleared his throat. "So when you didn't answer, she called me. She said to be sure to tell you that you are to show up at D. I. no later than three o'clock this afternoon. The late Collier's daughter called and made an appointment to see you – and only you - then."

I stopped shoveling food in my mouth, but continued to chew, making sure my mouth was closed. When I opened it, I mumbled, "Skye Collier?"

Richard nodded.

"The kid made an appointment to see me the same day her father died?"

Richard nodded again before saying, "And from what she told Lila, Skye Collier's convinced her own mother killed her father."

I stared at Richard, the heavenly chorizo turning to ashes in my mouth.

Everyone knows that Silicon Valley is chock full of
fabulous people who 'do good while doing well.'
Ron Gutman

Chapter Ten

As it was already close to two-thirty, I took a fast shower, threw on my favorite hot-pink suit, heels as high as I could wobble in – why not make Lila happy - and aimed the car for Discretionary Inquiries. In the heart of Palo Alto, D. I. is only six-minutes away, so I arrived with two minutes to spare. I ran up the stairs to the second floor and pulled open one of the ebony colored double doors of the family business. I never lose my sense of pride when reading the brass nameplate.

Discretionary Inquiries, Inc.
Data, Information, and Intelligence
Room 300

Still trying to catch my breath, I smiled at Stanley sitting behind the reception desk. Clad in a sensible grey business suit, he'd topped the outfit off by yet another one of his outrageous ties. This one was slimy green and neon purple swirls, set off by small orange dots. I tried to keep my attention above his neck. Our office manager and general factotum returned my smile with a large one of his own.

"Good afternoon, Miss Alvarez," Stanley said in a very formal manner. Then he jerked his head several times toward the waiting area, moving his eyebrows up and down.

85

Stanley and I don't usually stand on ceremony and rarely does he use my last name. His greetings tend to be more along the lines of 'Hey you, I see you finally got your duff in here.'

Without responding, I looked in the direction he'd indicated with his thin, waggling eyebrows. Skye Collier and her nanny were already seated and waiting, but hadn't noticed me yet.

D. H. Collier's daughter, head resting against the wall, eyes closed, long legs and arms thrown out awkwardly, looked about as tired and spent as humanly possible. Certainly, she seemed more exhausted than any fourteen-year old should ever be. She wore the same outfit as she did that morning only the dress was crumpled and limp, as if sharing its owner's grief.

Katherine 'Katie' Hall sat next to the girl, stroking her charge's arm with a hand that she neither paid attention to nor seemed aware of using. While Katie Hall was lost in thought, I took a moment to study the woman.

She was a little older than I previously thought, maybe thirty-seven or -eight. Her medium brown hair was cut in a short, no nonsense style, more for economy of care than attractiveness. Dark, brown eyes wore no makeup, and yet large and almond shaped, they were by far her best feature. Now they seemed to see nothing of the outside world, but rather something inside, so alive and intense, a frown came and went upon the woman's face.

She was dressed in an unflattering yellow polo shirt covered by a dark brown jacket of pseudo-suede. A chocolate brown skirt and mid-length boots completed the rest of her wardrobe. By her feet sat a large and clunky black leather satchel. The glint of a small, gold hoop in each earlobe was her only adornment. My hand flew up to my own ears, covered by large silver medallions, garish by comparison.

Plain was the word that came to mind when viewing Katie Hall. And yet she wasn't. Something about her said that here was a lady who paid attention to what really mattered, gave more than she got, and made a difference to everyone in her life. It struck me that this was exactly the person Skye Collier needed right now.

I walked over, cleared my throat, and stuck out my hand to Katie, even though according to Lila, Skye was the one who'd made the appointment. "Hi. I believe you are Katie Hall. I'm Lee Alvarez. You wanted to see me?"

She snapped to attention, a ready smile coming to her face. She turned in her chair and nudged the girl, who stirred to a sitting position. "Skye, Skye, wake up."

"What....who..." said Skye. When she saw me she jumped up, as only youth can do, and crowded in between the seated nanny and the standing me.

"You're Lee Alvarez, right? I saw you this morning when..." She stopped talking, tears filling already red and puffy eyes.

The nanny stood, too, or rather tried to stand, by moving her body around the gangly child. I backed up to prevent bumping the teenager on the forehead. It made me smile. It was as if Skye Collier sprouted up four or five inches only moments before, and didn't know how much room her body took up. Or maybe she just didn't pay attention to other people's personal space.

Katie gently took the girl by both shoulders and pushed her aside, as if reading my thoughts. "You're crowding in again, Skye. Be careful."

The girl brushed her off with a frenzied gesture. "Whatever, Katie." Then she thought better of it, and turned to me with an apology.

"I'm sorry. I keep doing that. Please, Ms. Alvarez, I need your help.

"Call me Lee."

"Lee, I knew when I saw you, you could help me. Then I found out you were a private detective, so see? I was right."

Stanley cleared his throat, an indication for us to take our conversation away from the front reception area and any potential clients. I spoke up in what I hoped was my lady-like professional voice.

"Why don't we continue this in my office? If you'll just follow me."

I turned to lead the way and saw an expression of marked approval on Stanley's face. Stanley is the apple of Lila's eye, not only because he runs D. I. with such efficiency, but because he shares the same 1960's sense of protocol and manners. He would have made a helluva butler at Downton Abby in another life, but by gawd, we had him and would do pretty much anything to keep him. Even his horrid taste in ties wasn't too high a price to pay.

I opened the door to my office, stood aside, and gestured for the two to enter into a space filled with Mexican and Latino art. I stepped in behind them and went around to the other side of my desk feeling rejuvenated not only by the collective talent within the room, but the blues, greens, yellows, reds, and other strong colors.

My personal taste runs to south-of-the-border, vibrant and pure. D. I.'s color scheme is maroon and grey, chosen by Lila Hamilton Alvarez, who calls the colors wine and slate. I say a rose by any other name is still dull, dull, dull.

She and I have been in a rumble about my office decorating choices for years. My stand is it's my space, I'm part owner, and I'll have what I want. Her stand is that as long as it's decorated like this, she'll never step foot inside my office. Olé!

"Why don't you tell me what's on your mind, Skye?" I sat down behind my desk and looked at the girl somewhat puzzled. "How do you think I can help you?"

She gulped. I could sense the tightness in her throat as she spoke. "My father didn't kill himself. He couldn't have. He was, like, too happy."

"Sometimes people aren't as happy as they project, particularly to their children." I was the voice of reason. Lila would have been proud.

"That's what I said, Lee," chimed in Katie.

"No, no," Skye shouted to both of us. "He went to Switzerland to have a treatment done to remove what he called his turkey neck. I mean, like, that's not what someone does when they're going to commit suicide, do they?" She glared at me.

"Not as a rule, but maybe…"My voice petered out, my mind going to the five secret and unaccounted for days in the Bay Area.

"There's no maybe," Skye interrupted. "He. Didn't. Do. It." She emphasized each word, her voice strong and bad-mannered.

"Now, Skye," Katie interjected, looking directly at me. She put a soft hand on the girl's knee to grab her attention. "There's no need to be rude."

Damn, I thought. *This woman reads minds.*

In answer, Skye burst into tears, soon convulsed by them. We sat, Katie and I, and let her tears run their course. Skye controlled herself within a minute or two, sniffed loudly, and rubbed fingers over a snotty nose. I pushed a box of Kleenex toward her. The girl grabbed a handful. She wiped hands and nose, balled the tissues up, and dropped them in her lap murmuring, "sorry, sorry, sorry," several times.

"You know what I think?" I swiveled around in my chair to the small fridge sitting behind me on the floor. "I think we should have a little something to smooth us out before we go on. Ladies, I've got bottles of Coke, regular and diet, lemonade, and sparkling water. I've also got some peanuts. Any takers?"

I didn't mention the gin, vermouth, and olives I keep for after hours, nor the frozen Milky Way bars. Those are mine, mine, mine.

"I'd love a sparkling water," said Katie. "Why don't you have the lemonade, Skye, and some peanuts? You need to eat something. You haven't eaten all day."

"Okay, I'll try. Lemonade sounds good." The kid looked at me and attempted a smile.

My heart went out to her again, just as it had at Read-Out. As I slid the jar of peanuts across the desk and passed out the drinks, I knew at that moment I would do anything I could to help her. I'm such a schnook that way.

"If you don't believe your father committed suicide, what do you think happened?" I grabbed my notepad and pencil, preparing to make notes.

"*She* did it. I know she did. I don't know how, but I know it was *her*." Skye's voice took on a nasty bent.

"And 'her' would be?" Even though I'd been told of the accusation against her own mother, I had to hear it for myself. I looked from Skye to Katie. Katie took a breath to speak, but Skye's answer shot out immediately.

"Sharise." Emotional venom fairly dripped from the walls on that one word.

"So you believe the rock singer, Sharise, who is your mother, killed your father?" I kept my words unemotional and almost formal. I wanted to offset what I felt was the girl's near breaking point.

"She's not my mother. Oh, she gave birth to me, but then she handed me over to Dad and I haven't seen her since. I don't think she even knows what I look like. And Sharise is not her real name. It's Mary Louise Fitzhugh. Nothing about that bitch is real."

"Language, Skye," Katie muttered, but there was no real force behind it.

"She is a bitch, Katie," said Skye. "She never wanted me, and she sold me to daddy for the money to start her career."

Katie nodded with a sadness that showed me just how attached she was to Skye. She reached over and took Skye's hand, squeezed it, and pulled it onto her lap. Skye squeezed back, her lower lip quivering.

"Katie's the only mother I've ever known." Skye's voice was quiet. Filled with a mixture of love, hate, and resignation, it had too many levels for someone so young.

"Do you think it was Sharise, Katie?" I focused on the nanny.

Katie hesitated, looking at Skye for something, I wasn't sure what. "I think if it were possible for Sharise to kill David, she might have; she hated him so. But I don't see how. Sharise is still in Germany. Her band has been on a three-month worldwide tour. Their last performance was Saturday night. The band left Sunday, but Sharise isn't flying into the Bay Area until tomorrow, Tuesday. She's filming a concert scene in a German movie that involves her lip-syncing to one of her songs. She shoots it tonight. She and her manager, Ty, are still in Frankfurt."

"That's a lot of detailed information. How do you know all that?"

"Part of the settlement agreement with David was that Sharise had to let him know where she was at all times."

"And if she didn't," Skye interrupted, "Daddy said he would write her out of his will."

Katie nodded. "I saw Sharise's schedule on the house calendar, which is always posted on the server. All of Skye's classes, meetings, extra-curricular activities and so forth are on it, even my chiropractic visits."

I turned to Skye. "Did you pay attention to where Sharise was?"

She shook her head. "Not me. I didn't care, but Daddy always had it up. I know Katie checked it from time to time, too. I'd see it on her laptop."

A flush covered Katie's cheeks. "A lot of David's moods seemed to be dictated by what Sharise did."

"Or didn't do," said Skye. "He still had a thing for her. That's why he made her live in the Bay Area. It was, like, disgusting." Her lip curled, making her look hard and far too worldly for her age. "I don't care what the schedule says. She did it."

I mused for a moment. "It's easy enough to check on Sharise's whereabouts. The woman's a star. A quick phone call to Germany might resolve it. What hotel is she staying at, anyway? It's three-fifteen here; that makes it just after midnight there."

I looked at Skye then Katie. Skye shrugged with a helpless but angry gesture, but Katie answered.

"She's at the Hilton. The Frankfurt Hilton."

"Okay," I said, logging onto my computer for the website and number. "This should take me about three-minutes, so it's gratis."

I found the number, reached for the landline phone on my desk, and dialed it. When the number answered in German, of course, I went into my routine, trying to sound young and very American.

"Hi! This is...ah... Melva, Sharise's assistant. You know the singer? She and her band have been staying with you. I'm her assistant."

There was a moment's hesitation and then the clerk switched over to English. And flawless English, I might add.

"Yes, madam, I am aware of that. How may I help you?"

"Well, the scintillating Sharise has lost the keycard to her room again. Honestly. I'm calling from a nearby restaurant where we're having a bite." I tried to sound annoyed then giggled. "This is the second time this week she's lost it; she can be such a *dummkopf*. When I return to the hotel, do you suppose you could give me another one? Sorry for the trouble."

"It is no trouble, madam. Please remember to have proper identification with you when you come to the desk. Otherwise, we cannot help you."

"Will do. Listen, you didn't happen to see her within the last hour or so, did you? Maybe she got a new one, herself."

92

"No, I do not see Miss Sharise since she left a few hours ago."

"Not since early this evening? Well, thanks and see you in a few."

I hung up, flushed with a job well done, and turned to the two sitting before me. Katie had been following my every word. Skye, on the other hand, never looked up once during my exchange, but glared at me now, leaning forward, eyes practically slits in her head.

"That doesn't mean anything. She did it."

Was this childish bullheadedness? Or was the kid on to something? I shrugged, momentarily giving into her obstinance.

"Then the next step is her passport usage. Homeland Security keeps excellent records of citizens coming in and out of the country. We could look into it and get back to you. It will take a lot longer, but it can be done. If for some reason, she came into the country earlier than expected, we might have something. If she didn't..." I broke off. "What do you want to do in that case, Skye? Drop the whole thing?"

"My father did not commit suicide," Skye said with finality.

"My advice would be to wait until the Sunnyvale Police finish their investigation. They're very good --" I stopped talking because Skye was shaking her head at my every word and with growing intensity.

"Each minute that goes by," she leaned in and whispered. "It feels more wrong. I don't know why I feel that way, but I do. I can't make it go away. It's, like, making me crazy."

I'd had a similar feeling of my own on the Dumbarton Bridge, only I called it a niggle. It wasn't going away, either. No matter what word you use, it can eat you up inside. Skye continued her dialog as to her mother's guilt.

"I know everybody thinks it can't be Sharise, but irregardless --"

"Regardless," corrected Katie in a soft tone.

"Regardless," the girl echoed without missing a beat. "Even if it isn't, I want you to find out what happened to my father. I have to know."

For whatever reason, I now hesitated on taking the job. It seemed like a packet of trouble, and I was getting married in less than a week to a man who was on a secret mission in an unknown country.

Then Skye added the one clinching word, "Please."

Schnook, schnook, schnook. I was hooked and knew it. I took a deep breath before I spoke my disclaimers. "First of all, this is not a job Discretionary Inquiries normally takes on. We usually deal with the theft of intellectual property or software and hardware piracy. That said, we are not cheap."

"I don't care what you cost. I want you," said Skye. "Money doesn't mean anything to me."

Says she who is heir to billions, I thought. Aloud I said, "All the information your father had on Sharise, does that include members of her band, as well as her?"

Both Skye and Katie nodded then glanced at one another. Skye seemed to give Katie unspoken consent then looked down at white knuckled hands. Katie studied me for a moment and leaned forward.

"David compiled a running dossier on his ex-wife and everyone who works or has ever worked for her. It's stored on the server."

This was straight out of George Orwell's *1984*. Big Brother is watching you. I didn't say that aloud, though; respect for the dead and all that.

"Send it to me as soon as you can. It might come in handy; you never know."

I reached inside the top drawer of my desk, but before handing Katie a card with all my pertinent information, I hesitated, remembering William Shakespeare's words:

"The evil that men do lives after them; the good is oft interred with their bones."

94

In my experience, people who did what they wanted without much regard for anyone else often paid for it one way or another, and sometimes with their lives. D. H. Collier was adding up to that kind of person. At fourteen, I wasn't sure Skye needed to know this side of her father, at least not so soon after his unexpected death.

I cleared my throat. "Skye, I want you to look at me."

Reluctantly, she looked up, honey brown eyes meeting mine. It was only then I gave my PI sermon with as much sugarcoating as a Splenda® girl could muster.

"When a client hires Discretionary Inquiries to look into something…or someone…upon occasion the client may not like what we find. People live complicated lives. There can be surprising aspects to those lives. Sometimes it's better to leave well enough alone. Are you sure about this?"

Confused, the girl didn't reply but stared at me. I said no more. When she finally absorbed the meaning of my words, she seemed shocked at the idea her father might have something to hide. I gave her the time she needed to mull her decision over. I was relieved to note Katie didn't try to sway her one way of the other, but sat quietly by her side. Finally, Skye nodded again with certainty.

"Very well, Skye. Here's another potential problem. You're underage, and I can't legally take on your case without permission from a parent or guardian."

"I'm her legal guardian," said Katie.

"Beg pardon?" I was floored, but tried not to show it.

"I am Skye's legal guardian," Katie repeated. "With David's death, Skye became my ward until her eighteenth birthday. This was set up five years ago. I have a copy of the will with me. I thought you might want to see it."

"Yes, I would." I gave her one of my best smiles as I stuck out my hand. "Just to keep things on the up and up."

Katie reached into the large black satchel and pulled out an envelope containing a document of several pages enfolded in heavy, blue paper.

"May I have another lemonade?" Skye's question was whisper soft and asked quite shyly.

"Sure. At the prices D. I. is going to charge you, it's the least we can do." Everyone laughed as I'd intended, and I swung my chair around to the small refrigerator behind me. When I opened the door, I said over my shoulder, "Would you like a frozen Milky Way bar?"

"Oh, yeah!"

Skye's enthusiasm was akin to my offering her the Hope Diamond. That's pretty much my take on Milky Ways, so I knew the kid and I were simpatico. I pulled a bar out, grabbed another bottle of lemonade, and swiveled back to my desk. I set the two in front of Skye, grabbed the thrice-folded document from Katie, and stood.

"I'll be back in a minute after I copy this. Meanwhile feel free to look around the office or read a magazine on the table by the window," I said, fully aware my desk drawers were locked, and not with doggie or kitty locks. You never know when curiosity will take the upper hand. "I've set my office up like a mini-museum, with lots of Mexican artwork you might enjoy looking at."

"Yes, I see you have some sculptures by Bustamante," Katie said. "He's one of my personal favorites." Score one for the lady in the yellow polo shirt.

"That's a funny name," I heard Skye say, as I closed the door to my office behind me.

I ran to Lila's office praying fervently she would be there and not with a client. Patty, her secretary – not assistant, as Patty didn't like that word – saw me running down the hall. With her bleached white teeth glowing in her mouth, she smiled and pointed to my mother's closed door, giving me a nod. I knocked and threw the door open at the same time.

I have always been very tech-focused, which you may almost say is the traditional CEO in Silicon Valley.
Michael Birch

Chapter Eleven

"From what you've said and what I've read of this codicil, if you wish to pursue the investigation into Mister Collier's death, you are free to do so."

We stood in Lila's office, as different from mine as you can get. Stark but elegant Roche Bobois furniture in soft shades of grey sat against darker grey walls. Wine-colored accents dotted the otherwise achromatic room in the form of lamps, books, and silk throw pillows. Brushed chrome statuary posed on lacquered grey columns and seemed to come straight out of MOMA.

On one wall a large silver-framed painting called "Silver's Woman" hung. It looked suspiciously like a younger Lila's face surrounded by silvery leaves, petals, and white orchids.

Lila turned to me. Dresden blue eyes pierced mine. Lila had called it right, as usual. What Katie had given me was not a copy of the will itself, but an addendum or codicil to it. All signed, witnessed, and notarized. I had suspected as much before I'd thrown in on Lila's desk, as wills are usually thicker things. But I had hoped against hope maybe it had been typed up in a five-point font or something.

My mind spun on. Rats! I still hadn't seen Collier's bloody will yet and I was going to have to remedy that. If I'd only known the man's daughter was going to hire me to look into the whys and wherefores of his death, I would have read it, no matter how tight the time frame had been. At least, I should have photographed it. Shoulda, woulda, coulda. But who gets what plays a significant part in any investigation.

Reminiscent of a Greek goddess, Lila swept away from the copier/scanner to stand behind her massive but streamlined desk. Blonde hair done up in a French twist, she exuded cool confidence in a robin's egg blue tweed suit, accented by satin cuffs, collar, and buttons. The color matched her eyes perfectly. She finished the ensemble off with the pearl earrings Dad had given her shortly before he died; she was rarely, if ever, without them. Today a pearl-encrusted broach in the shape of a swan rested on her left shoulder.

I looked down at my feet to make sure I'd worn matching shoes. I don't always get that right. Once I came into the office wearing one black and one navy, and have yet to hear the end of it.

"However, Liana, I am surprised you wish to take this on, given you have your wedding coming up in less than a week. Kindly enlighten me as to the reason for this."

As usual, I'd lost the thread of the conversation, caught up in my mental meanderings. "My reason for what?"

She inhaled a deep breath, sat down, and closed her eyes before replying. "The reason for your investigation into Mister Collier's death. Try to stay with me, Liana."

"Oh, right! Right. Well, Lila, I --" I broke off, flustered. "Listen, could I just talk to Mom for a minute, Lila? I would feel better."

Her eyebrows shot up with surprise, as she sat erect in her high back, pearl grey leather chair. "Of course, Liana. I am always your mother, *regardless* of what you call me."

"Good, good." I noted she hadn't used the word irregardless. My mother does not make mistakes like that. Actually, she never makes any mistakes from what I can see; more's the pity. She'd be easier to live with if she did.

I took a seat across from her, and leaned in with what I hoped was a look of sincerity. "Mom, you have done a terrific

job on my wedding, an amazing job, an unbelievable job, an --
"

"Yes, dear. Now *what* is you point?"

"Mom, Gurn is off to God knows where in the service of our country; my job at Read-Out is over because, as I told you, D. H. Collier was the culprit and he's dead; there is hammering and sawing and I don't know what all going on at the apartment --"

"Liana," my mother interrupted, her voice tight and threatening. "Get to the *point*, please.

"Okay. I've got four long days until my wedding with nothing to do but wait, Mom. Lila. Mom. Whoever." I paused. "I don't know why what I call you is throwing me today, but it is. I'm sorry about that, too --"

"*Liana!*"

"Okay, the point, the point; the point is the kid needs me. I feel for her. She's just lost her father. I know what that's like. She needs some closure."

"*Your* father died of a brain aneurism. He didn't *take* his own life."

"I know, Mom, but the end result is the same; your father is dead."

"I see."

"Also... also..."

"Also what, dear?" Her voice held a soothing quality similar to one a farmer might use to try to get his prize heifer back in the barn, with no idea why she spooked. Moooooo.

"This sounds terrible, but if I can prove he didn't take his life, it will help Skye somehow, I just know it."

"Even if you prove that someone *murdered* him?"

"Even then."

"You are *determined*?"

"I am."

"Very *well*. As far as I can see, the first round of people arriving for the wedding will be in three-day's time. You should try to have it wrapped up by then."

99

"Mira arrives. Right." Mira was my best friend and also my matron of honor flying in from San Miguel de Allende. I hadn't seen her for nearly six months and couldn't wait. "But just in case I don't....ah....wrap everything up, can you pick her up at the airport?"

My mother chaffed. "Each guest's arrival and departure time has been given to the *limousine* service, which we hired for that specific purpose. I *gave* you a copy of the schedule days ago, I might add. It contains the *minutest* of details."

"Did you? Sorry. I forgot."

"Everything is in place for the wedding, as it *should* be at this stage, down to the last detail. *Nothing* has escaped my attention."

"How about the toothpicks with little hearts on top?"

She gave me one of her withering looks before speaking. "I have *decided* to use the ones decorated with a bride and groom. More *appropriate*."

"Wow! Those two must be really small, being atop a toothpick and all."

"I see you are making *fun* of me."

"No, Mom, never. Well, yes, I'm teasing you a little, but I'm very grateful. So is Gurn. It will be a wonderful wedding. One I could never pull off, myself. Really, Mom. I couldn't do it. Thank you, Mom. I love you, Mom." I paused again, letting my words sink in. "Really truly, Mom. You're the best," I threw in for good measure.

"There is no need to be *maudlin*." But a slight smile played upon her lips.

I studied my mother as objectively as possible. She was so loving this. I was right not to try to take the wedding away from her. Besides, soon she would have a new grandchild and leave me the hell alone.

Whoops! Did I say that out loud? No, no, I was just thinking it. I used my inside voice. I'm good.

I relaxed a little and reflected. Yes, here sat the woman who was the Rolls Royce to my Chevy, the conservative to my

100

liberal, the haute couture to my thrift shop, but fate had still seen to throw us together. Chalk it up to one of life's ironies.

Whoops! Did I just get philosophical on me? Go away, inside voice. Time for a martini.

"*Speaking* of Gurn," she said, unaware of my thought processes, as usual.

"Were we?"

"Please pay *attention*, Liana. To *repeat*, Gurn's parents arrive the day *before* the wedding in time for the rehearsal dinner. I trust Gurn will have returned by then."

"That's what the man says, Mom." I stood. "I'd better get back to my office." I turned and headed for the door.

"Liana, be sure to have them *both* sign the standard agreement before they leave."

"Will do."

"And Liana."

I turned back, stopped by something in her voice. "Yes, ma'am?"

"I don't *often* say this, but you are a wonderful daughter. Soon you will be a wonderful wife. Do what you can for Skye Collier, but don't let your *job* interfere with what's *important* in your life."

"Okay," I stuttered, and walked back to my office wondering what that was all about. It was so mommy-ish, I decided to block it right out of my mind.

The more angels we have in Silicon Valley, the better. We are funding innovation. We are funding the next Facebook, Google, and Twitter.
Ron Conway

Chapter Twelve

I opened the door to my office to find Katie admiring the Frida Kahlo self-portrait, a painting of which I am proud to own. I may never be able to retire due to what it cost me, but such is life. Katie turned and faced me when she heard the door open. I looked around the otherwise empty office.

"Where's Skye?"

"She was falling asleep in the chair, so I called Marty to come in and escort her to the car. He's the chauffeur. She's in the backseat sleeping."

My Latina guilt came forward; it's a genetic thing. "Sorry I took so long. But I do need Skye to sign the form hiring Discretionary Inquiries. I'm afraid we'll have to wake her."

"If that's the one on your desk, we both read and signed it already."

I picked up the document and looked at it, smiling at the other woman. "Thanks. And here's your codicil back."

She took it from my extended hand. I continued with the business at hand.

"Once you give me a retainer, we should be done here, although I will have a few more questions later. I can probably get started as early as tomorrow morning." I neglected to mention my intended late-night visit back to Read-Out to take a gander at D. H. Collier's will tucked away in his Chinese puzzle desk.

Katie looked at me. "I was glad Skye went back to the car so you and I could talk alone."

"Oh?" I sat down behind my desk and gestured to a chair. She sat but leaned forward, almost coming out of her seat.

"Yes, I wanted to let you know that Skye is not your typical teenager."

"You didn't need to send her out of the room for that. It's no revelation."

Katie went on as if I hadn't spoken. "I think you will discover Skye is her father's daughter in many ways. She has his brilliance - she's already doing college-level work - but she also has his stubbornness, which comes, I suspect, from being smarter than anyone else most of the time."

"That can be a drag. My brother goes through that all the time."

"Then there's her sixth sense about certain things, which didn't come from David. It's never mentioned, but I think she inherited some of her mother's touchy-feely approach to life. Sharise's premonitions are often talked about in scandal magazines and such. Just how much is real, how much is publicity, I couldn't say. But Skye does seem to know certain things. It's uncanny."

I began to see why my mother asked me to come to the point. Sometimes you'd like to know what the subject of a conversation is before the new millennium.

"She sounds like a handful. Where are you going with this?"

Katie hesitated, seemingly searching for the right words. "The fact that Skye's so convinced her father's death isn't suicide has convinced me. I believe there should be total devotion to the job and it should be given top priority."

She thrust a check in my hand made out in the amount of one hundred thousand dollars. My eyebrows shot up to the stratosphere.

"This is a helluva retainer."

"Find out who killed her father, Lee, and it will be doubled. Ensure a conviction, and it will be a half-million dollars."

Suddenly I didn't like Katie so much. I handed her back the check.

"Our standard retainer is ten thousand dollars. And I give every job top priority. Ten thousand is what's required upfront. We can talk about possible bonuses at another time."

"I see I have offended you. I apologize. I am used to dealing with people who value money over everything else."

"I don't and I didn't think *you* did, either."

Dang. I just did a Lila thing, emphasized a word in a sentence and made a harsh judgment call, to boot.

"I'm not a person who values money over people." Katie's steady gaze met mine. "But I wanted to see if Skye's faith in you is well-founded. I see it is."

"I haven't done anything yet. Let's see if I can give Skye what she needs."

"You will."

With those cryptic words, Katie pulled another check out of her wallet, already made out for ten thousand dollars, and handed it to me. Saying no more, Skye's nanny stood, turned on her heels, and left.

I took the retainer, attached it to the signed form, shoved both into a manila folder, wrote D. H. Collier's name at the top, and set the folder in the outbox. Eventually, Stanley would come by and do whatever he does with these things. Then I sat wondering if Skye and Katie's faith in me was misplaced. Or if I was as mad as a hatter for taking on the job. Maybe a little of both.

Working in tech in San Francisco circa 2015
is like living in Florence during the Renaissance.
The Economist

Chapter Thirteen

Ten-thirty that night found me signed in at Read-Out and heading for the minuscule cubicle given me as Rameen Patel's assistant. Fortunately, Rameen hadn't taken me off the list of employees yet, if he intended to, so I was cool.

The late hour didn't bother the older, overweight guard sitting behind the desk, either. I was just another go-getter in Silicon Valley with no life other than the one sitting in front of the company computer day in and day out.

There wasn't any computer slated in my visit, but the guard had no way of knowing that. Mainly, I wanted to read that stupid will, finally and for cryin' out loud.

But first I'd retrieve the list of the fourteen workers who started with the company four years previously, hoping to become millionaires with the upcoming IPO. One company assassin stood in the way of any of them scaling up from an old Honda Civic and cramped rental apartment to a brand new Porsche convertible and fancy house with a pool. That made for fourteen very strong motives.

Being above board with security had some pluses. It meant I could throw a little light on the subject once I got upstairs instead of using a flashlight. I hit every light panel at the entrance and surveyed the empty, maze-like space usually bustling at least fourteen-hours a day. I walked the area to make sure no one else was around before going to my desk.

I found the list lickety-split, and without hesitation added Rameen Patel and Craig Eastham's names to it, which upped it to sixteen. I could have added the board members, but thought I'd wait until I went through this lot first.

I threw a few personal items into my tote bag, and went to Collier's office. The door was locked, but that didn't bother me none. I withdrew my tools and was inside in less than ten seconds. You gotta love these dog and cat locks. They save so much time.

Once inside, I didn't like what I saw. All four previously hidden drawers of the Chinese Puzzle desk were now open and empty. Indignant, I pulled out my phone, and hit speed dial. Frank answered right away, but sounded highly annoyed. Tough noogies.

"What's happened now?"

"Did you tell Sunnyvale about Collier's puzzle drawers?"

"Of course, I did." His voice registered surprise at my question. "You didn't expect me to keep information like that to myself, did you? I might be impeding an investigation."

"Did you tell them from where you got this unimpeded information?"

"Of course not." Now his voiced registered indignation. "I told them it came from one of my sources. Why would I involve you? And speaking of you, where are you?"

"I'm working on a few things," I was vague. Then more to myself I said, "I wanted to read that will, damn it, and now the Sunnyvale Police have it."

"Well, ask Talbot how soon you can see it. He'll probably be pretty forthcoming. It'll be a matter of public record soon enough."

"James Talbot, esquire? The Alvarez' family retainer? You mean Collier had the same lawyer as we do? The old guy gets around."

I was stunned. James Talbot was one of the world's oldest practicing lawyers. He handled Grandfather Hamilton's estate from way back when and the Alvarez legal affairs to this day.

106

The best part is he knew Mom when she was "in rompers," and is not one bit intimidated by her. Frank's voice interrupted my reverie.

"I think it's one of his sons, actually. Talbot's slowing down a little."

"Well, he's got to be a 107 if a day."

"83, actually. Same age as my father."

I looked at my watch. "I'll call him in the morning."

"You do that. Lee, while I have you on the phone, I have some information to share with you. Tit for tat."

"Tat away, Frank."

"Collier's death is being listed as suspicious."

I sucked in a sharp lungful of air. "What?"

"His doctor checked the stats from his chip implant, and found Scopolamine in his system. The lethal, chemically altered kind."

"You mean Collier had one of the Read-Out chips implanted in his body?"

"According to Doctor Newton all the employees do, including their families. Eastham even has his llamas chipped. All part of their controlled studies."

"And what did you say this Doctor Newton found in Collier's body?"

"Chemically altered Scopolamine."

"I thought Scopolamine was used for sea sickness."

"Diluted and in its natural form, it is. But this has been altered in a lab. It's called 'Devil's Breath'. Not much is known about it in the states, but it's got a history in Colombia."

"Devil's Breath? Sounds bad."

"And aptly named. It can take effect in any of three ways; inhaled, absorbed through the skin, or swallowed. It's used by the Colombian criminal set in smaller doses to control their victims; make them do whatever they want. They blow it in their faces, lace a drink or food, or hand them a piece of paper to read coated with the drug. In less than a minute it's in the system, causing the victim to lose all willpower."

107

"For real?"

"According to reports, they turn into zombies. They do whatever they're told; empty bank accounts, rob their own homes, even some cases of date rape."

"What happens if it's used in larger doses? Can it kill?"

"For the moment 'undetermined' is the official stand of the Sunnyvale Police Department. But from what I've read, Devil's Breath can be lethal if you use enough of it. And there's no antidote. Collier's death is being ruled as suspicious until they know whether he took it himself or someone gave it to him."

"Are they going to tell his daughter?"

"It's up to the Coroner's Office to release the info, even to his family. My gut feeling is no. So this is between us chickens."

"Cluck, cluck."

"Now hang up so I can go back to bed. And Lee..."

"Yes?"

"Do I want to know where you are?"

"Not really."

I hung up and sat for a time. So the kid was on to something. Maybe her father didn't commit suicide. Maybe someone made it look that way. Yawning, I vowed to get right on it first thing in the morning.

After relocking the door, I exited the building, and went to my car. That's when my phone rang. It was my brother.

"Lee! Lee! This is it. We're on our way to the hospital. The baby's coming!" Richard sounded both excited and frantic. I could hear Vicki in the background. She didn't sound so excited. But she did sound frantic, with a lot of moaning and groaning thrown in.

Who do you think made the first stone spears?
The Asperger guy. If you were to get rid of all the
autism genetics, there would be no more Silicon Valley.
Temple Grandin

Chapter Fourteen

"Isn't she the most beautiful baby you've ever seen in your life?" Even behind the mask and scrubs, I could see my brother's ear-to-ear grin.

I looked at Stephanie Roberta. The name Stephanie was given for two deceased family members, our much beloved cousin, Stephen, and Vicki's grandfather. The baby's middle name, Roberta, was the feminine version of our late father's name. Everybody was happy. Just a few hours old, the baby did look beautiful in that red-faced, wrinkled, Winston Churchill sort of way.

Vicki, too, looked remarkable considering it hadn't been the easiest delivery. My sister-in-law is a small, slender-hipped girl and Stephanie Roberta wanted a little more elbowroom than she was being given on her way into the world. But mother and daughter worked it out, as mothers and daughters usually do, and here she was at seven pounds, three ounces, sleeping in her new mother's arms.

"All right, everyone, listen up."

Our very own Nurse Ratched addressed the family at large. A sourpuss woman paradoxically dressed in red slacks and a holiday scrub top with candy canes all over it, she hadn't cracked a smile since Mom, Tío, and I were allowed into the private room. When she wasn't taking temperatures, fluffing pillows or writing in charts, she stood in a corner and glowered at us, but never said a word.

When she finally spoke, I wish she hadn't. She had a gravelly, 2-packs a day smoker's voice that makes one glad one never took up the habit.

"It's seven AM," she rasped. "And rest time for mommy, daddy, and baby girl."

"Stephanie Roberta," we all said in unison and looked at one another in surprise. The we went into gales of laughter.

Nurse Ratched didn't have a chuckle in her. She glared at us. "It's time for everyone else to leave the room. And I mean now."

We hugged the new little family as quickly as possible and trouped out the door, which was shut with enthusiasm by the nurse behind us.

Mom and Tío elected to stay at the hospital a little while longer, in the hopes they might be able to see the baby again. As I walked outside into the chilly morning hours of a California winter, I texted Gurn a message about our new arrival, even if it was a long shot he'd get it.

You are the proud uncle of beautiful Stephanie Roberta Alvarez, 7.3 pounds, born December 20, 4:43 AM. Love, L.

Dead on my feet and with a big day ahead of me, I drove home, set my alarm for nine-thirty, and crashed. I was asleep for about ten minutes when the work on the new office started again.

I looked at the clock. Yup, eight AM on the dot. I gathered up the cats and dragged myself over to the Big House, where it was relatively quiet. I reset the alarm for ten-thirty, feeling that being up all night and waiting for your new niece to be born outweighed any obligations I had to my job first thing in the morning. I couldn't have been more wrong.

The natives of Silicon Valley learned long ago that when you share your knowledge with someone else, one plus one usually equals three.
Vivek Wadhwa

Chapter Fifteen

I was startled awake by the sounds of Mom, Tío, and Richard coming into the family room. Even without speaking, I could tell something was wrong. Jumping up, I dislodged two protesting cats that fell to the sofa.

"What the…" I looked from one face to another. "What is it? Nothing's happened to Stephanie, has it? Or Vicki? Oh, my God!"

"No, no," Richard said, running over to hug and soothe me. "The baby's fine. Vicki, too. In fact, she threw me out saying the two of them can't sleep between all my crying, cooing, and taking pictures."

I relaxed and went into a teasing mode. "Ahhhh, were you cooing at my niece?"

A fleeting smile crossed his face then he sobered and shook his head. "Lee, Mom got a call from the office. It's bad news. Maybe we should all sit down."

He turned and looked at our mother. So did I. Her face was ashen. Tío came to her side and guided her to a chair. I couldn't move, but stood there already dreading the news of what I did not know.

"What's happened?"

"It's Jacob Gold, Liana." Mom's voice was hardly more than a whisper. She dropped down in the tan leather

111

wingback before she spoke again. Throwing her head back, she said, "He's *dead*, Liana. There's no other way to say it. Early this morning."

"Jake, dead?" I thought of the handsome, virile man I'd seen only the day before. I sat down before I fell down. "*Dios mio*, this can't be true."

"He didn't have any family outside of England, so he put Discretionary Inquiries down as the emergency contact." Mom lifted her head and looked at me. "Patty called me right after they notified her around ten."

My mind raced. "How? Was it natural causes? A heart attack or something?"

Mom shook her head. "They don't think so. He managed to get to the motel office before he collapsed."

"He died for those computer chips and tester, Lee," said Richard, his voice sounding harsher than I'd ever heard. "They're missing."

"The chips are gone? Again?"

Richard looked down at me, but before either of us could say more we heard Mom's voice, sounding far away and sad. She brushed at eyes filled with tears.

"Jacob worked with Discretionary Inquiries from the beginning. He was the first operative Roberto hired. He would do anything for your father, you know."

She looked at us with a fleeting memory's smile on her face. Then the clouds returned.

"They say he was acting strangely, staggering, incoherent. The police think he overdosed on something, but he never did drugs. Never!"

Her voice had a desperate edge to it, as if she was already defending the reputation of a good man that might become tarnished once a hint of drugs was linked to it. I thought of Shakespeare's quote again "...**the good is oft interred with their bones.**"

Mom went on, clasping and unclasping her hands in her lap and reiterated her stand. "In all the years I've known the man, he never once took an aspirin, never."

I leaned forward. "But he might have been given something, Mom, without his knowledge."

I briefly told them about my previous night's conversation with Frank and the coroner's findings on Collier's death.

"I didn't have a chance to tell you any of this before, what with the baby coming. Maybe the same person who killed David Collier killed Jake. I went on line last night while we were waiting at the hospital and looked up 'Devil's Breath'. It's a chemically altered use of the drug Scopolamine, a drug coming from the Borachero tree in Colombia."

"The sea sickness drug?" While it was only Richard who spoke, three sets of eyes were on me.

"It's also used to combat a pregnant woman's morning sickness. But that's in its original state. Once it's chemically altered, it becomes what's called the world's scariest drug, Devil's Breath. Unsavory types use it to take away a person's willpower, to make them do whatever you want. And from what I've read, the way Devil's Breath affects people at too high a dosage sounds similar to Jake's symptoms before he died."

"You're saying this could be tied in to the death of David Harold Collier?" Mom frowned and looked from Richard to me.

"It does sound awfully coincidental," Richard muttered.

"Richard," I said, "how much time can you give me today, if at all?" I looked at my brother. "I don't want to push the new father into work-related problems, but we might have no choice."

"Vicki says she doesn't want me to come back until around seven o'clock tonight. She and the baby need some rest. I'm good with that, so what do you need?"

"But how do they find Jake so *rápido* in Redding?"

Tío's voice carried throughout the large room. All heads turned in his direction. My uncle rarely enters business conversations, but when he does he asks good questions. Tío went on.

"You and he are both experienced at not having the tail."

"You're right, Tío. I know I wasn't followed, and I don't think anybody followed Jake, either. He was too good." I considered the alternative. "There must be a bug planted on the truck."

"A bug could explain it," said Richard. He opened his laptop. "I'm going to message Andy and have him send a team up to Redding to wipe down the truck before it gets returned to Penske."

Andy is second in command in the IT Department and devoted to his job. Richard considered for a moment.

"It must be really hidden if Jake didn't find it when he was looking for the prototype. We may need special electronic equipment. I'll ask Andy to go, himself."

I turned to our mother, being uncharacteristically quiet. "The police didn't impound the truck, did they, Lila? It's still at the storage unit, isn't it?" I prodded further since I didn't get an answer. "Lila? Jake did the usual procedure and rented a car to be delivered to the motel, right? The police don't know about the storage unit or the yellow truck?" I touched her shoulder with my hand. "Mom?"

Her head snapped around at my touch and she looked at me. "In all the years we've been in business, we've never lost an operative in the line of duty. It is a very sad day for us."

"I know, Mom. And I'm sorry," I sat, covering one of her hands with mine. "But we need to get to the bottom of it. We can't let it rest like this."

"I agree with Lee, Mom," said Richard. "We need to find out what happened."

He reached out and took her other hand. She inhaled a deep breath, held it for several seconds then released it slowly.

114

"You're right, children. We must take action. Time for mourning later. As to your questions, Liana, I don't believe Jacob would ever break protocol. He was instructed to hide the truck in the unit at the storage company, and I'm sure that's where it will be." Mom paused then added, "Unless someone took it."

"Richard, have Andy call first to make sure it's still there." I didn't mean for my words to sound so much like an order, but they did. "And here's a question to both of you. Who told you the chips and tester are missing?"

Neither spoke. Richard looked at our mother, who opened her handbag and extracted her cellphone. Pushing a few buttons she handed it to me. There was a text message to her from Jake. I read it aloud.

Helped load tester and boxes in black van. Couldn't stop myself. I know I did it, but don't know why. Help me. JG

"I found this message from Jacob on my phone only a short time ago, but it had been sent the night before." Mom looked away, her voice filled with regret and guilt. "I'd been involved with the birth of the baby. I didn't even think about looking at my messages. If only I'd seen it sooner, maybe I could have..." Her voice dropped off and she covered her face with her hands.

"From what I've read on the internet, Mom, the drug acts within minutes," I said. "Nobody could have gotten to him in time."

"*Hermana.*" Tío often addresses Mom as sister in Spanish in times of stress. "You have had the shock. Come to the kitchen and I will make for you herbal tea; Chamomile."

Mom nodded and rose slowly. Together they passed through the swinging door and into the kitchen. I watched them go then turned back to my brother.

"This is bad, Richard. This is so bad."

"I know. I'm still trying to absorb it."

"Maybe after you call Andy about the truck, you can do a little of your cyber magic. Find out if Sharise, Collier's ex-wife,

115

came into the country from Germany two days earlier than her schedule says."

"What?" Richard was clearly taken aback. "If you're asking me to go into Homeland Security and check on her official comings and goings into this country, I can't do that. Do you have any idea how tight Homeland Security is now? I can't get into their systems the way I used to." He paused. "It might take me days."

"We don't have days."

"No can do." He shook his head emphatically. "There's no mercy for hackers. I've got a family to think of now. I can't take the chance..." He paused again. "You know, there is something that might work, if they haven't fixed it."

He started pounding on the keys of his laptop. Honestly, how that poor computer stays in one piece is beyond me. Of course, he does go through them like candy.

"Hold it, Richard. Before you do that I've got a better idea. Remember me telling you Sharise was staying in Frankfurt to do a lip-syncing scene to one of her songs for a movie? Maybe you can find out which film company."

"That's easy enough." He thought for a moment. "If so, maybe I can stream a copy of the scene from Germany."

"Wouldn't that mean somebody had to have pirated a copy?"

"Good chance of it; happens about ninety-eight percent of the time." Richard let out a chortle.

"Why would they do that? For money?"

"Nah." Richard was dismissive of the idea. "They do it because they can. Show off to their friends. It's all kept underground, on the Dark Web, which only certain people know about." Richard paused. "Like me. There are a couple of sites. If a studio engineer made a copy, it should show up on one of these. Let me see." The pounding on his laptop commenced again. I watched him with one raised eyebrow.

"Great...I think. You all sound pretty weird to me. While you're doing that I'll go see about making us some coffee." I stood and stretched. "I don't know about you, but I need about as much caffeine as I can get."

The kitchen door swung open and Tío entered carrying two mugs of steaming coffee.

"Tío to the rescue," I said to my uncle. "You're a lifesaver. Thanks so much." I gushed while reaching out for the life-giving brew.

"*De nada,*" He said, handing a mug to me then setting the other on the table in front of a preoccupied Richard. "I will have *el desayuno* ready in twenty minutes for all of us. You will eat the meal, *niños,* whether you think you are hungry or not. You need the strength."

"Breakfast sounds great, Tío. *Gracias,*" I said, flashing a quick smile in his direction. "How's Mom doing?"

He smiled back. "Your mama, she drinks the tea and then she goes to her room to rest. Jacob was an old friend of *sus padres*. She takes this hard, very hard, but she will be all right."

I drank down about half the coffee before Tío made it back through the swinging door. The coffee was perfect; slightly creamy, slightly sweet, just the way I like it. Tío's a marvel. I set down the half-drunk coffee on the table and picked up my phone.

"Time to call Mr. Talbot and see if I can get a copy of Collier's will.

"Good luck," Richard muttered without looking up from his keyboard.

"You ain't kidding." I dialed the number. But I did have a bit of luck. Not only was Talbot in, but free to talk to me. He came on the line within a minute.

"Liana Alvarez, dear girl, how are you? How's your mother? How's the rest of the family?" All of this was said in one jovial but run-on sentence.

"Fine, fine, Mr. Talbot; thanks for asking. I know you're a busy man --"

"Not so busy these days. I've cut my practice in half. Benjamin and Clarence have taken over the bulk of it. I'm virtually a man of leisure now. But I'm sure your own time is precious, dear girl, so what can I do for you?"

"Well, I'm hoping this is something you might know about, personally. I'm working on a case involving D. H. Collier's daughter, Skye --"

"Such shocking news," Mr. Talbot interrupted. Then he tut-tutted for all he was worth. "But you came to the right Talbot. I am still handling his affairs. He started with me about twenty-years ago and he was never a man to change horses mid-stream."

"Great, because here's the deal, I need to see Collier's last will. I can't go into specifics, but --"

He interrupted me again. For a man who had a lot of time on his hands, he didn't seem to want to let anybody complete a sentence.

"Miss Collier is your client?"

"Yes."

"Nonetheless, I can't impart any information to you; it would be breach of ethics. But, dear girl, why don't you just ask her for a copy of the will? That seems the most expedient approach to me."

"You mean the kid has a copy of her father's last will and testament?"

"Precisely. I didn't approve of such a thing, of course. But Mr. Collier insisted that his young daughter have a copy of the most recent will at all times." He went into a stage whisper. "I don't think the man trusted anyone else and he certainly didn't trust the girl's mother. He told me his ex-wife might 'try to pull a fast one'. Direct quote. Not that it was possible with the way I had drawn up the will but - and you didn't hear this from me – Mr. Collier was an unusual man with what could be called an obsessive personality. I earned my money with that one. Well, I must fly now. Anything else, dear girl?"

"Yes, did Collier have any other recent activities with your office?"

118

Mr. Talbot tut-tutted again then was silent for a time. "Now, now, Liana. If there were any impending lawsuits, do you think I would be able to tell you about them?"

"No, no, of course not. I --"

"In that case," he interrupted me again, "I shall bid you adieu."

He disconnected before I could say thank you. Bless his dear little lawyer heart. Without breaking any of his ethics – almost - he managed to hint there was a pending lawsuit in the air. Was it against Rameen Patel, as the CFO feared? Or Craig Eastham? According to Rameen, both of them screwed him over.

I glanced at my phone and noticed a text message from Gurn! My excited fingers brought up the message. I saw, not words, but an Emoticon, a drawing of a popped bottle of champagne. Wherever he was, he got my message about the baby and was able to respond. I held the phone against my heart, feeling it brought me a little closer to the man I loved.

"Hey, Lee, come on over here and look at this." Richard's voice brought me back. "You got to see this. It came from *Spitze Produktionen*, Frankfurt, Germany."

"You've got something already?"

"It's all over the German Underground. Sharise is hot in several European countries, as well as Latin America."

Clutching my phone, I went around the other side of my brother sitting on the couch. When I sat down, he placed his computer on the coffee table so we could both see the screen. Then he pressed a key. A second-generation video of Sharise singing and gyrating around on a stage began to play.

"Wow!" I leaned down for a better view of the small screen. "She's certainly got energy. And look at that costume."

"What there is of it. You can hardly see her face, between her hair and the hat."

"Those are her trademarks, Richard. She's known for long, curly blonde hair and red bowler hats."

"Well, most of the dudes I know aren't looking at her hat."

"Richard!" I teased. "And you the father of a brand new baby girl."

"If my daughter ever wore something like that I'd have a heart attack."

"Richard, did you hear what you just said? 'Your daughter'. It's a miracle."

I choked up looking at my kid brother, not such a kid anymore.

"It is a miracle, Lee. I'm blessed and won't forget it." He smiled, his blue eyes burning with the same intensity as our father's. "But let's get back to work. See those?"

Richard pointed to a set of small numbers at the bottom of the video.

"December twentieth at eight forty-five pm, European time. Sharise was in Germany shooting this scene for a movie last night."

"And there you are," I said, trying not to show my disappointment. "Our non-smoking gun. Skye may be right about her father, but not her mother."

"She could be a kid with a big hate on for her mother for deserting her."

"Could be."

"Okay, sis, now that we've established Sharise's alibi, what's next?"

"I asked Skye to let me have the dossier Collier collected on Sharise and her band members. We should check it out, see how accurate it is."

"That info's pretty much all over the internet, but it's nice to have it in one place. You know, she has one of the biggest and best touring companies in the world. She travels with an entourage of sixty-six."

"Sixty-six musicians?"

"She has an orchestra of twenty, plus eight backup singers, and a musical director. The rest is the backstage crew;

roadies, lighting, sound, costumes, advance team, and a company doctor. And I'm not including locals hired in each city to help load in, put up, and break down the sets. That number is usually more than a hundred."

"Sounds expensive."

"It is. And she's hired some legends away from other bands just to back her up. They don't come cheap and they're all top notch." He paused and looked at me. "Don't you know any of this?"

"No, and I'm surprised you don't know my taste in music better. I hate punk rock."

"Sharise started out as a punker, but graduated to pop outlandish."

"Is that anything like her graduating into the world of perfume? I only ask because the perfume called Sharise, a stinker of a smell in a guitar-shaped bottle no less, came out about two years ago."

"It seems like every well-known female has her own scent." Richard said, his voice taking on a jaded tenor. "I'm surprised you haven't come out with your own perfume line called Lee's Escapades or something like that."

Then he had the nerve to laugh. And with gusto. I tried not to be offended. Lee's Escapades, indeed.

"If I did, it wouldn't be anything like her stuff. I remember going into a department store, being sprayed with a sample, and almost becoming asphyxiated. I could not get rid of the smell. How something can be exotic, spicy, and yet cloyingly sweet all at the same time is beyond me."

"I take it you don't wear the scent...and yes, I'm being sarcastic."

"Not a first for you. But back to her music."

"Back to her music." My brother barely managed to contain a smile. "Some of the songs Sharise does are her own compositions; they're okay, but she does a lot of other artists' work. Touches on every style and has a good voice. What really makes her shows work is the quality of musicianship between her and her band. That's one of the reasons she's had so much success. Although, lately I've been seeing less of her. I hear her record deal got cancelled."

"Well, I had no idea. When I find a minute, I'll go on itunes and get one or two of her songs and listen to them. Meanwhile, I've got a list of fourteen – no, sixteen – names I have to check out at Read-Out while I'm still supposedly employed there. Can you have someone in your office check out Rameen Patel and Craig Eastham's backgrounds?"

"Anything in particular you're looking for?"

"Concentrate on their finances. Just how tight was either of them for money? And Katie Hall, too. Check her out. I found out yesterday Skye is her ward for the next four years. That means Katie has access to millions if not billions of dollars in the interim. It's a strong motive for murder."

"But how would any of them get their hands on Devil's Breath? We'll need to find out just how impossible it is to come by in the states."

"And let's not forget, we have to find the tester and computer chips, a task which might jump to the number one spot. Jesus, we could lose everything, Richard."

Richard ran a hand over his tired face. "I know."

"This isn't Read-Out's loss now. It's D. I.'s. That means if we don't recover them, Read-Out's going to put in an insurance claim against us for fifteen million dollars."

"Plus if word gets out, we can kiss the company's reputation goodbye. There's no telling how far-reaching the effect would be, Lee."

High level depression sucked us both down. I let out a sigh.

"Do you think any of this has dawned yet on Lila?"

"Not much gets by Our Lady."

"Under ordinary circumstances, Lila would be chomping at the bit to go with me to Redding, but between dealing with the wedding and Jake's death…" I broke off.

Neither of us said anything for several seconds. Richard weighed his words with care.

"Lee, I'm usually more office bound on these investigations as a rule, but how about if I tag along with you? I've always wondered what goes on in the field." He reached out and touched my shoulder. "What do you say?"

"I say let's have some breakfast and head up to Redding. I want to talk to the clerk on duty. But first, we'll need to check out the storage unit. Maybe we can learn something."

If the Ivy League was the breeding ground
for the elites of the American Century,
Stanford is the farm system for Silicon Valley.
Ken Auletta

Chapter Sixteen

The two hundred and forty-five mile trip to Redding took a little over four hours. Richard slept the entire way, which was good. Somebody needed to be rested when we arrived. If Gurn had been here, he could have flown us in his Cessna in under an hour. The thought depressed me. I was doing a lot of thinking as I drove up I-5. And not one single thought was of the upbeat variety.

We arrived in Redding shortly before four pm and drove straight to Wannamaker's Storage Units. It was crucial to get there before dark and with the shorter days of winter, we only had about a half hour of daylight left.

The yellow truck was parked directly outside unit number 53, cargo end open and empty. Andy was sitting in the driver's seat typing furiously into his iPad.

Andy is a small lad, even by geek standards. He's probably around five foot four and if he weighs more than ninety pounds I'd be surprised. Next to him, Richard at five seven and a half, looks like an athlete. But what Andy does have is big brainpower and a devotion to any cause D. I. comes up with.

He heard our footsteps crunching on the gravel, turned and gave Richard a preoccupied smile.

"Hey, Rich."

He noticed me and his face lit up. It's no secret Andy has a crush on me and thinks I'm simply the cat's meow.

"Looking good, Lee."

"Thank you, Andy," I said. "What have you got?"

"I was just sending you both an email with an image of the tracking device."

"So the truck was bugged," I said, before Richard could speak up.

"We found it inside the radiator," Andy answered. "Heat resistant. If you need specifics on its other capabilities, I've got them right here. It was a favored one of the FBI. About six-years old but a good product."

"FBI? Don't tell me you think the FBI is in on this." My voice echoed the incredulity I felt.

"No," Andy and Rich said in unison.

"The FBI uses certain equipment," said Andy.

Richard picked up the conversation. "Therefore, you know it does the job. The thieves probably went on the internet and bought it."

"If you know where to go, you can buy whatever you need," said Andy.

"Where's that?"

"Tor," they said; their voices in unison again.

"It's an underground internet service, an untraceable gateway to anything," Andy said. "You can buy whatever you want, legal or illegal."

I didn't offer up just how scary the thought of that was. They probably knew better than I did what horrors lurked there. Speaking of scary, I had another idea.

"Could you buy 'Devil's Breath' on this Tor?"

Both guys shook their heads.

"Nope," said Richard. "I scoped it out and there's nothing there."

"I couldn't find it, either," said Andy. "I did find some Scopolamine --"

125

Richard interrupted, "But apparently in its natural state. And such an insignificant amount, you couldn't do more with it than cure your seasickness."

"Right," said Andy.

I turned to my brother. "I thought you were sleeping in the backseat of the car, Richard. When did you do all this research?"

"I woke up about an hour ago, somewhere around Chico," he said.

"Funny, I didn't hear you banging on the laptop."

"How could you," he asked, "when you had the radio blasting ABBA's greatest hits?"

Andy suppressed a chortle, which I chose to ignore.

"Let's get back to Devil's Breath," I said. "Why can't you buy it on this underground thingie, Tor?" My question seemed sane to me. "You just said you could buy anything there."

"Here's what occurred to me," said Andy. "The government can't check everything sold on the internet, but they are on high alert for a handful of things, say like plutonium. It's possible Devil's Breath is listed in the same category.

"I'm thinking along those lines, too," said Richard. "The FDA does monitor the most deadly. If you buy it, they may not find you right away, but they'll find you. People surfing the Dark Web know that."

"But that might not be the reason," said Andy looking directly at Richard. "The sellers might have temporarily run out of a supply."

"No stock to sell. That could be it," added Richard, nodding his head in agreement.

"Gentlemen," I said. "We need to know exactly why Devil's Breath isn't available on the Dark Web."

"Sometimes that's easier said than done." Andy pondered. "But I'll find the reason, eventually."

"Not eventually, Andy, ASAP," said Richard. "Put it ahead of anything else. Learn what you can about the drug. People are dying."

Andy gulped then nodded. I did a little gulping, myself.

"Where's the rest of the team?" I asked, looking around me. "And did you put the truck where it is now or did you find it that way?"

"We left everything exactly as we found it. And once we did a clean sweep of the truck, Richard told them to go back to D. I. with the results," Andy said. "You probably passed them on your way here."

I turned to Richard. "You've been busy in that backseat."

Andy looked at his boss for further instructions. Richard turned and looked at me in the same manner.

"So what now, Lee?"

"Okay," I said, thinking. "The truck's already been checked out. I'll look inside the unit; see what I can find. Meanwhile Richard, why don't you go to the front office and see if they keep security tapes of this place? Andy, keep researching Devil's Breath. A question, is there any way to find out who bought tracking devices like the one you have in your hand?"

Richard hooted out loud. "No way. There are thousands of them out there. We'd never find who bought this."

"Okay, so that's a dead end," I said. "There was a forklift. Is it here, Andy?"

"Inside," he answered.

"Boys, let's all do our thing and meet back here in fifteen. How's that?"

Wordless, we split up. I headed for storage unit number 53, one of the larger ones, and capable of holding a small truck. The garage-type door was open so I went right in. I snapped on my small flashlight and looked around. The cement floor was clean and looked like it had been recently swept.

Great, I thought, a neat as a pin killer. That's all we need.

127

I sat down on the seat of the small forklift and swept the light over every part of it. Clean, clean, clean. With a sigh, I turned on the motor. It revved right up with a racket that hurt my ears. The electric ones are pretty silent, but the gas models are loud and noisy. Edging the machine forward, the space it sat on was revealed. I shut the engine off, stepped out, and splayed the light on the floor. Nothing.

Ever hopeful, I trotted back to my car, popped the trunk, and took out my hand-held Dust Buster. I gave the floor, corners, and edges a sweep. Five-minutes later found me with an aching back from being hunched over, and not much to show for my efforts other than dust, cobwebs, and the skeletons of two spiders. I looked closer. Something else.

I went outside and separated the handful of crud. Between the fading light, and the strong, LED flashlight I found something so small, it was almost indefinable. But I recognized it from the shiny clusters of small, decorative glass sewn on many of my mother's evening gowns. A blue bead.

I put the bead inside a small, clear plastic bag and cleaned my hands with one of my alcohol wipes. By then Richard returned. Andy saw him and sauntered back to me. We both looked at my brother.

"I had some luck, Lee, but I don't know how to pursue it," Richard said, his face showing the ambivalence he felt. "They don't run surveillance tapes until after they close, which is nine o'clock, but the one pointed at unit 53 didn't work last night."

"How convenient," I said. "Did he check to see what's wrong with it?"

"He said the wind or something knocked it over. You can see it from here."

Richard pointed to the rooftop across from the unit in question. I turned and saw an older, large video camera lying on its side, lens now aimed skyward. Richard went on.

"Here's something that might be more important. The man in charge said he saw someone when he was walking

128

through the yard around six pm. He won't tell me anything; says he's too busy."

"What does he know, Andy? Jake died at the motel, not here. Does he wonder why all of us are wandering around on his property?"

"We told him the Penske truck was taken from D. I. and we were trying to find out who did it," said Andy. "He wasn't interested in anything more, although I had to show him identification. Very uncommunicative."

"Maybe I can get something out of him," I said. "We could use a break. Let's go talk to him."

"Oooo," said Andy. "Are you going to seduce him with your charms? Can I watch?"

But before I could answer, Richard turned to his assistant.

"Andy, this is a waste of your time. Lee and I can take care of this. Why don't you get back to learning about Devil's Breath? Then head home. Send me all your findings ASAP."

"Sure thing, Rich. I'd rather do research any day than all this detective stuff. See you around, Lee. And good luck." Andy hurried back to his car, his encased laptop slung over his scrawny shoulder.

We watched him get into his Honda Civic, mentioned before as the commuter car of choice for nerds. Andy's was brand new, however, and bright red, set off by a sleek spoiler on the back. I think there are more Honda Civics in the Bay Area than in all Japan, and some have very spiffy attitudes.

We watched Andy pull out of the parking lot before we walked toward the storage company's office.

"You've become good at delegating work, Richard. Must be the new father in you."

"Speaking of which, I called Vicki and told her what was going on. I told her I'd be back to the hospital when I got there."

"And she, being the wonderful and understanding wife that she is, was okay with that?"

129

He looked at me puzzled. "Well, of course she was. This is an emergency. We've lost a man."

I sobered instantly. "You're right. I'm sorry. I didn't mean to sound flippant."

By that time we reached the office. I pulled the door open and came face to face with one Gregor Vasilyev, or at least, that's what the nameplate on the counter read.

"Ah, you are back, Mister," he said to Richard in a heavy Russian accent. "You want information? But I am busy. I don't have time for you. I need to make a living. Go away."

"You are Gregor Vasilyev?" I kept my tone level. Before we went any further, I wanted to make sure who the man was.

He grunted with a nod then returned to copying numbers into the last column of a green-bound ledger. The task seemed to require complete concentration on his part, his writing slow and laborious. Meanwhile, I studied the muscular, scrappy looking man, youthful, but bearing more than passing resemblance to a Kodiak bear.

Here was someone you wouldn't want to meet in a dark alley, although I don't think I'd have had the nerve to tell him. What was eye-catching was the thick, dark hair, not only on his head, but on much of the body not covered by his t-shirt and jeans.

He had a scar above his left eyebrow and one on his chin barely hidden by his five o'clock shadow. Another one graced the top of a wrist visible through his furriness. I'm going to go out on a limb here and say here was a young man loaded with too much testosterone, but I don't think I'd mention that to him, either.

Focusing his attention on me, Gregor gave me a look as if I had crawled out of my Dust Buster. "Who are you?"

After fumbling around, I found my ID and flashed it to him.

"So?" He stared at me waiting. "Unless you have more to show me, I am busy."

After less fumbling around, I withdrew a crisp twenty-dollar bill and placed it on the counter. Finally I spoke.

"How's this for freeing up some of your time?"

He took the bill and stuffed it in his jean pocket. "Maybe I need more, but is step in the right direction."

"Before I do a two-step," I said, "Let's hear what you've got to say. You told my associate you saw someone hanging around late yesterday. Who?"

"I come back from delivering boxes to a customer last night around six pm. He pays me well to bring them to him. Is no big deal to close the office for twenty, thirty minutes, so I do. Is my business," he added angrily, as if I'd somehow challenged him. "I can do as I wish."

"It's the American way, Gregor," I said. "Go on."

Mollified, he adjusted the t-shirt around his neck, tufts of black hair rearranging themselves under his fingertips. "I return here and drive into back driveway. I see this girl – woman - pulling on the lock at number 53. She try to force it open, so I yell to her, I yell, 'hey you, lady, stop that."

His voice rose as if he was really yelling at someone, and he gestured with a hand as if she was standing there. Impressed by his acting ability, I nonetheless brought him back to reality.

"This girl – woman - what did she look like?"

"Not so tall as you, but younger and prettier from what I could see."

"Ouch, but go on."

He was silent, pushed back from the counter and stared at me again.

"All rightie." I pulled out another twenty, and handed it over. "Let's have more, but it better be good."

"She wear sunglasses, so I not see much of her face, but she have long, red hair straight down her back."

"Wait a minute," I said. "If you didn't see much of her face, how do you know she was prettier than me?"

131

"Ah! You are vain like so many American women." He smiled at me with teeth in need of some serious cleaning.

"Not in this case. I'm just trying to see how much credibility to give your story."

"'Credibility'? What means this word?" He stared at me non-comprehendingly, dark brown eyes huge and questioning. I could see how a visit to a dentist and about a quart of Nair might make him attractive to the opposite sex.

"Reliable, believable, trustworthy," I said. "In short, that you know what you're talking about."

"I know what I talk about. But okay," Gregor shrugged. "Maybe she was no better looking, 'cause you a pretty lady, but I could tell she was younger, by how she moved." He winked at me. "And the skirt, short, so short I want to take her right then and there and --"

He pantomimed crudely what he wanted to do. I wasn't sure when I'd lost control of this conversation, but clearly I had. Before I could cast a net back over it, Richard leapt in.

"Easy, man, easy; we have a lady present."

I looked at my brother in surprise. Richard glared back at me, unyielding.

"Well, we do. That would be you." He then turned to Gregor. "Just tell us what you saw."

"Yes," I said. "And without any gestures. How was she dressed?"

He pointed a finger at me like I was suddenly smart. "That is good question. How she is dressed. It was like the Wild West, but today."

"You mean like an urban cowgirl?"

"Yes. All the girls here in America, they like the cowboys. I'm going to get a cowboy hat; meet a lot of girls that way."

"You do that. But first, give me a few more details." He stared at me. I decided to help him out. "You said the skirt was short. What color was it? Was it the same color as the rest of her outfit?"

"Color, color, color," he droned on, thinking. "The blue. Shiny blue top, the short skirt and boots all blue."

"A light blue? Dark blue? Medium blue? There's a lot of shades of blue," I said, my pulse picking up.

"A medium. My mother would say the color of the sky on clear summer day. She liked to name the colors, my mother." He gave me an honest, shy smile. I suddenly found myself liking this fellow, although I was somewhat shocked to learn he had a mother.

"You said her blouse was shiny? In what way? How?"

"It has the sparkle, but only on the swaying things hanging down here." Another gesture indicated across the bust line.

"You mean fringes? Fringes on her blouse?"

Rather than answer he shrugged, stepped back and went into his silent routine. He stared at me. I stared at him. Richard just watching.

"I'm already out forty dollars," I said. "And all we know is she's a longhaired redhead wearing blue."

"The second part is more important, but will cost you." He grinned at us stupidly and shrugged. But he wasn't stupid. I was the cash cow and he knew it.

I withdrew a fifty-dollar bill from the stash, set it down on the counter, but kept a firm hand the side of the bill closest to me. He reached out for the money, but I pulled back, tantalizingly.

He leaned in, stale cigarette breath and hot spices making my eyes smart. "She get into van, a black van --"

"Was there anyone waiting in the van?"

"Maybe. I think so, but I don't see clearly. Windows all blacked out. Then she drove away."

"This black van. Was it newish, old, what?"

"New. Like from showroom."

He put an even firmer hand on the money before saying, "And I see license plate as she drive away. I remember last four numbers because they are same as my house."

"And they were?"

He tugged on the bill. I released my grip. He smiled and tucked the money in his jeans again.

"Seven, four, two, two. California license." He studied both of us. "You see? I told you was worth the money. It was BMW, too, this black van. Expensive. You don't ask, but I tell you, anyway. I give to you." And another sweeping gesture, this one indicating his generosity.

"Thanks," I said, turning around. I gave Richard a shove and moved to the door.

"You like the cowboy?" Gregor shouted after me. "You are older but pretty enough for me."

"I'm more of an astronaut girl, myself," I said as I hurried out, followed by Richard.

"Don't you have those cowgirl boots from New Orleans, sister mine?" Richard looked at me with a smirk, as we walked side-by-side back to unit 53 and my car. "You remember the ones with the red hearts on them. I'll bet our friend would like those."

He was teasing me about a pair of cowgirl boots I'd had to buy real fast after I lost my shoes in a chase. It was another story, another time, but it still rankled. Six hundred dollars for a pair of boots I wouldn't be caught wearing dead in a ditch.

"They've been donated to Goodwill, brother mine, and I will thank you not to bring them up again."

Richard held his hands up in mock surrender. "Okay, okay, whatever you say. Where to now?"

We arrived at the Chevy and I turned to my brother abruptly. "We should call Penske about the truck, now that it's been checked over." We both opened the front doors of my car simultaneously, me at the driver's side.

"The company is set to pick it up from here in about an hour," Richard said. "They're just glad to get it back. We had some paperwork to fill out, but Andy took care of it."

"You find out who rented it?" I swung myself in the seat and started up the motor.

134

"Complete dead end. Rented over a month ago. Phony ID and stolen credit card. All we know is it was a man."

Chapter Seventeen

Richard slammed the door shut after those cryptic words and turned to me in frustration. I, in turn, struck my hand against the steering wheel in a like emotion.

"Damn! We just cannot get a break, Richard. We have to find those chips and tester or we might lose D. I."

"You'll get them back. Finding stuff after the fact is your specialty," he added.

"Oh, great. No pressure there." I pulled out onto the street.

"I'm giving you positive feedback. It's supposed to keep workers motivated."

"I see you've been taking management classes again."

Richard laughed. "Only when forced. But seriously, you know it's not totally up to you. We'll all do our part. Meanwhile, the chips haven't been offered for sale on the internet. I've had the team looking."

"That's something, at least."

"Of course, they could go to a private buyer."

"Oh, yippee. Here's a thought. Maybe the thieves will contact Read-Out and try to sell them back."

"You think they might have been stolen to hold for ransom? Wouldn't Rameen Patel have heard something by now?"

"Yes, but would he tell us? He's hiding something. As far as I'm concerned, he might have engineered the theft, himself. He knows a lot more than he says unless he's pressed against the proverbial wall. For instance, he knew Collier was coming back five days earlier from Switzerland, and he was one of the few people who did."

"Did he now?" I could almost hear the wheels in Richard's head turning. "That's a biggie."

"I still think the stolen booty and Collier's murder are linked. And that means Patel, Eastham, and Read-Out are very likely a part of it. But Rameen Patel is the front runner. He has a temper and a keen sense of entitlement. But let's put that on a back burner for the moment."

"Okay. Where are we headed now?"

"Best Choice Motel, about half a mile from here. Where Jake died. He walked to there from here, because his rental car was delivered to the motel."

"What do you think happened, Lee? Give us one of your past scenarios."

"This had to have been planned for awhile. The thieves rented the truck a month ago with phony documents, probably hiding it in the Fremont garage the entire time. So someone not only knew Collier owned the house, but also that he didn't check on it with any regularity. Maybe he never did; just another piece of property he owned in a long succession.

"So it was the perfect place to hide the truck, especially as he was in Switzerland for over two weeks."

"Another thing they seemed to know, Richard. Yesterday they hired two stupid kids to drive the truck to Sunnyvale, steal the chips and tester then drive back to the Fremont house with the stash and stay there. Because the truck was bugged, they knew its whereabouts at all times. As long as it went to where they sent it or remained in the Fremont garage, they were safe. They stayed in the background and waited."

"Waited for what?"

I shook my head. "I don't know yet. There's a lot of missing pieces."

We came to one of those long red lights that appear out of nowhere for nonexistent traffic. Richard continued our conversation as we sat idling, the only car within sight.

"So once you took the truck, Lee, they had a way of tracking it, no matter what maneuvers you or Jake did."

"And they came out of hiding, which means they have to be fairly close by, in the East Bay or the Peninsula."

The Peninsula is what Bay Area people call any place south of San Francisco and north of San Jose. I don't know why, we just do.

Richard looked at me in appreciation. "I hadn't thought of that."

"They probably didn't try to get the truck from our house because too many workers were milling around. When Jake headed for Redding, though, they followed him."

The light finally changed to green and we continued on our journey.

"You keep saying 'they', Lee, but so far the only one we know about is a redheaded woman."

"Not true, Richard. You just told me the truck was rented a month ago by a man. And our Russian friend mentioned someone waiting in the car for the blue cowgirl. Besides, everything seems too complex for one person to manage."

"I'll buy that."

"Here's what I think happened yesterday. Jake was followed to Wannamaker's Storage. They watched him hide the truck in the storage unit, and lock up. Then they followed him while he walked to the motel, in case they needed his help later on. Remember, they've no doubt got the drug with them, so they can make him do whatever they want."

Richard nodded. "Devil's Breath."

"Once they knew where he was and what room he was staying in, they returned to Wannamaker's. They tried to break in; not realizing it was locked with one of D. I.'s special locks."

Richard shook his head. "Man, they don't know our locks. They don't break for nothing."

"I'm thinking Gregor was on his errand when the truck first arrived and, to our killers, it looked like nobody was watching the place. Once our Russian friend returned, however, and the redhead almost got caught, they had to wait until Gregor left for the night. You said that was around nine o'clock, right?"

Richard nodded.

"Okay, they disarm the video cams, but not the same way they did with the ones in Sunnyvale."

"What do you mean?"

"In Sunnyvale they used digital equipment to redirect the images. Here, they climbed onto the roof and probably used a hammer. Whatever they used, it had no hi-tech understanding."

"Why?" Richard looked at me questioningly.

"I wish I knew, brother mine. But to continue, they soon discover they can't get into the unit without the combination to the lock. They wait until Gregor closes up for the night then go back to the motel. Using the blue cowgirl as bait, she or they knock on Jake's door."

"He always went for a pretty face," Richard interjected with sadness.

"He opens the door. She either blows the drug in his face or asks him to read something from a piece of paper treated with the stuff. Maybe she even talks him into having a drink with her."

"So when the drug takes effect, they take him back to Wannamaker's?"

"Where they not only make him open the lock, but help load the chips into the black van. But something went wrong or maybe they planned on killing him the whole time."

"So why are we going to the motel, Lee?"

139

"I'm hoping the desk clerk saw something. We have to go there, anyway. The police released the room about an hour ago. Lila called the motel, paid for another night, and told them we'd be picking up Jake's personal effects."

"After that we need to get back." Richard looked anxious. "I'd like to see Vicki and the baby soon."

"*Como no.* And we're here," I said, pulling into the driveway of Best Choice Motel. I stopped under the overhang with the blinking Office Open sign. "We'll get this over with as soon as possible, and head back to Palo Alto."

The Best Choice Motel was a fairly new motel, three stories high with both outside stairs and elevators to the upper floors. It was hard to tell what the light-colored paint specifically was, as it was already dark, but there was landscaping and the place seemed well kept up.

I took out my phone and read the text from Lila again. The clerk's name was Mrs. Annette Dowis, and she'd been the one on duty the night before.

Mrs. Dowis was a chubby, middle-aged black woman. She wore her hair so short it looked like it had been shorn, but it suited her. She looked up from her computer when the bell announced our entrance, with a pleasant smile and intelligent eyes.

"Good evening. How may I help you?"

"Mrs. Dowis?" She nodded. "My name is Lee Alvarez. I'm here --"

"Oh, yes," she interrupted, her friendly demeanor overcome by sympathy. "Mrs. Alvarez called to say you would be coming by to pick up the gentleman's things. My deepest condolences for your loss."

"Thank you," I said, realizing I was feeling a sense of loss. I squashed it back down again.

"Thanks," echoed Richard. His voice carried the same sentiment. I tried to bring us back to business.

"The room hasn't been cleaned, has it?" I was concerned any clues might have found their way to a mopper's demise.

"Oh, no, Miss Alvarez. Your mother was explicit in her request that we didn't clean the room until after you came by for his things. I was in there, but didn't touch anything. Of course, the police were there, too, and dirtied up the surfaces with their fingerprinting kits, but other than that, they left it neat enough. Such a sad thing."

"Yes, it was. Can you tell me what happened, Mrs. Dowis?" I gave her a smile, which she returned fleetingly, her eyes filled with tears.

"I tried to help him, but I've never seen anything like it. He was flailing around the room and he was so disoriented nothing he said made any sense. Then he just fell over and never got up. I called the medics then sat holding his hand until they came." She brushed away a tear.

"Thank you for being with him. I can see it was hard," I said.

She nodded and took a deep breath, obviously distressed by the memory. I pushed her nonetheless.

"You said nothing he said made any sense, Mrs. Dowis. What did he say?"

She thought for a moment. I stood watching her, aware of my heartbeat.

"He muttered something about a tire." Mrs. Dowis looked at me.

"A tire?" I repeated the words. "Like a car's tire?"

She nodded. "He said it again and again. But I couldn't make head nor tail of it."

"Was that all?"

"Yes. The rest was just gibberish. I couldn't understand any words."

Richard entered the conversation. "Did you see anyone suspicious loitering around, Mrs. Dowis? You know, more weird-looking than you usually get?" His attempt at sleuthing was commendable, if not a little wanting.

Somewhat taken aback, Mrs. Dowis stuttered a denial with a shake of her head.

141

"Maybe you could tell me," I said, shooting Richard a quick 'shut up' look. "If our friend...ah...Vivian visited him? You may have seen her, a redheaded girl, a little shorter than me, dressed like a cowgirl?"

Mrs. Dowis jumped right in. "I think I did see your friend. It was pretty late, and I only saw her from across the parking lot. Over there."

She pointed a finger ending with a long, lacquered nail painted with pink flowers. Richard and I turned and looked through the plate glass window at the parking lot catty-corner to the office.

"Can't swear about the colors, because the yellow lights in the parking lot distort things. Her hair could have been red, but it was real long, almost down to the bottom of her short skirt."

She leaned over the counter, her demeanor taking on a conspiratorial bend. I leaned in, also, encouraging her with my body language to conspire away. Mrs. Dowis went on.

"At the time, I remembered thinking just who in the world she was going to see in that outfit, especially in this weather. I hoped it wasn't for...well...you know. A motel can get some pretty unsavory characters late at night even though we try to discourage that sort of thing."

She gave me a knowing look. I gave her a knowing look. Richard, just watching.

"Did you happen to see what time that was? It's important," I said.

"A little before ten, maybe nine-thirty. I can't remember exactly. But that's when I think it was. I work until two AM. I see a lot at night." She gave me another knowing look.

"I'll bet," I said. "We'll just go and check it out. May I have the keycard?"

I reached out my hand. She gave it to me with a smile.

"I'd go with you, but I have about thirty people arriving in about ten minutes, The American Taffy Union. I have to be here in case they need anything. Here's a map of the room numbers, though. I've circled the poor man's room." She handed us a paper that when unfolded was about the size of a placemat. It had a drawing of the hotel's numbered rooms with one circled number.

"No worries," I said. "We'll find it."

"Thank you," Richard said to Mrs. Dowis, opening the door to the hallway. I stepped over the transom.

"If you could just let me know when you've finished," Mrs. Dowis' voice stopped us. "I'll get the girl in there to clean up, if that's all right."

"Sure thing," I said. "We'll let you know."

The room was on the third floor and in a corner as far away from prying eyes as you could get. Unless you were followed a short time before and they knew exactly where you were.

I used the keycard and we entered a room done in rusts and browns, but managing to be bland at the same time. Jake's suitcase, like the one most investigators kept packed and in the trunk of our car for such times, sat open on the small desk against the wall. It looked pilfered through. Whether it was the lady in blue or the cops, I had no way of knowing.

Jake's car flashed in my mind. It still sat in our driveway. We'd have to do something about that, and his apartment, too. His mother was in a nursing home in Liverpool and that was all the family he had.

A wave of emotions overcame me and I sat down on the bed. Jake Gold had been peripherally in the family's life for decades. Maybe more than I'd realized.

"Lee, you all right?" Richard's voice brought me back.

I couldn't speak right away; my throat hot and tight. I cleared it once or twice and found my voice.

"I was just thinking about a Christmas decades ago, when Dad invited Jake for dinner."

Richard sat down on the bed next to me and put an arm around my shoulders. "I remember that Christmas."

"He brought me a doll for a present. It was really cute, but I was thirteen at the time, feeling all grown up." I let out a soft laugh. "I mean, here I was a teenager and somebody gives me a doll, like I'm a little kid. Anyway, I tried to look appreciative, but I guess it showed on my face. He opened his wallet, pulled out a twenty dollar bill, gave it to me, and took back the doll. He said Jews didn't celebrate Christmas, he didn't know much about kids, and for me to forgive him. It was really very sweet."

I stopped talking. My brother squeezed my shoulders then turned and angled himself so he could look directly at me.

"He gave me a pocket knife. The minute he left that night Mom took it away. I never saw it again. At least you got twenty bucks. I got nothing."

He leaned forward and butted his forehead against mine, trying to cajole me into a lighter mood. I gathered up a smile from somewhere, and gave it to him. We sat for a moment in silence, but my mind was racing. Finally, I spoke again.

"Richard, remember how I told you finding the chips and the tester was easy peezy?"

"Yeah."

"Well, maybe it was set up that way. Maybe someone wanted me to find them. Maybe it was supposed to be me in this room, and not Jake."

"Jesus Christ, Lee, don't scare me like that." He got up from the bed and crossed to the dresser. He turned and looked down at me, folding his arms against his chest. "Why do you say that?"

"Think about how Devil's Breath works. I hadn't realized this before, but a big drawback to using it is you have to be in close physical proximity to the victim."

"You mean blow it on them, touch them with it, or put it in a drink of theirs."

"Yes. I'm hard to get to. I'm either with my family or Gurn or working. Most hours of the day or night others surround me. I'm hardly ever alone. Now with all the workmen at home, it's like parade city."

"Why would someone want to 'get to you'? Isn't that being a little paranoid?" Richard wrinkled his nose the way he does when not following something.

"I'm sure this revolves around my investigations at Read-Out. Maybe I was getting too close to something."

"Like what?" Richard's question was quick and sharp.

"Duh. If I knew that, we wouldn't be having this conversation. But maybe if I had driven the truck to Redding, I would be the one in the morgue right now."

"You think you were the intended victim? All this was to get to you?" His arms opened wide and he gestured to our surroundings.

"When you say it like that, it does sound paranoid." I roused myself and began to look around. "We'll find out soon enough. Let's shelve it for now. Why don't you check out the bathroom? See if anything is there that shouldn't be."

My brother nodded and went into the small bathroom. I checked out the dresser drawers – empty - and looked under the bed. Two glasses seemed to be missing from a tray next to the water pitcher, only dried water rings remaining. Richard came out of the bathroom and leaned against the door frame.

"If Mrs. Dowis didn't let a maid come in to straighten out then he didn't use the bathroom, Lee. It's still setup for new guests."

"Did you find any water glasses in the bathroom?"

Richard shook his head.

"We'll double check with her. If the glasses should be here, that means our killer had a drink with Jake and removed the evidence. And the cover on the bed's been straightened up but underneath the sheets are mussed," I said. "It looks like he lay down either alone…or with someone."

I clicked on my small flashlight. I gave the dark rug a once over, but didn't catch anything the first time. Then I pulled out the Dust Buster from my bag and gave the rug a thorough

145

going over. Spreading the contents out on top of the bureau, Richard helped me go through the mess. *Nada* but food crumbs.

"Wait a minute," I said.

It was so small, at first glance I thought my eyes were playing tricks on me. But no, there was a tiny glint of something blue adhered to some piece of food. I didn't want to think about what that food was or how long it had been on the floor.

I separated the two with my fingernail, and pressed my forefinger against the blue glint. My eyes crossed as I brought up and focused on a single, blue bead.

"Eureka."

"What have you got, Lee?" Richard's eyes burned into mine when I turned to look at him.

"Another one; a bead from the shiny blue fringe on the redhead's blouse. A knot must have loosened from one of her fringes and she didn't notice. The beads seem to be steadily dropping off."

"You sure?"

"As sure as I am of anything at this stage. But what are the odds there would be one at the storage unit and one in this room?" Richard opened his mouth to answer. "It was a rhetorical question. You needn't compute it for me."

I pulled the same plastic baggie out I'd store the first bead in. I stowed the second one inside, and slid my fingers along the locking system.

"Let's grab Jake's stuff, Richard, and head out. We'll decide what to do with it later. We have a long drive ahead of us."

Richard nodded, but didn't say anything. I think he was feeling just as overwhelmed as I was.

Silicon Valley is like Tasmania or Madagascar.
It's developed different life-forms than anywhere else.
Steven John

Chapter Eighteen

I don't remember the trip back. Richard offered to drive and I crawled into the back seat and passed out. The next thing I knew, I awoke with a start when Richard reached back, grabbed an ankle, and shook it.

"Wake up, Lee. We're here," he said.

"Where is here? Stanford Hospital?"

"Yup."

I sat up, looked around, yawned, and stretched. Reaching for the handle, I opened the door in an awkward motion, struggling to get out of the backseat of a two-door car and move into the passenger's seat.

The cold damp hit me in the face. It had started raining again, a light rain, what I like to call California Spitting. An ominous fog had also descended, making the night nasty, nasty. I shivered and drew my coat tighter to me.

"Wow. I seem to have slept the whole ride back. Sorry about that."

Richard removed his ear buds and looked at me with a half-smile. "You needed it. You've practically had no sleep for the past two nights."

"What's up? You look worried. It can't be about me not getting my forty winks."

"Before I go in to see Vicki and the baby I have to tell you something. Andy sent me his report on Devil's Breath. I've been listening to it on the drive here. And by the way, we really need to wire your car's system to accept your phone. This Bluetooth thing is so archaic."

"Feel free to rewire my car anytime. What did you learn about Devil's Breath?"

"It's a derivative of Scopolamine, right?" I nodded. "But that's where the similarity ends. It's made by crushing the pods of the borrachero tree and then using certain chemicals to enhance their zombie-like properties. Here's why you don't find it anywhere on the black internet. It's even more volatile than nitroglycerin."

"You mean it can explode?"

"No, no, I was only using that as an example of something with unstable properties. Around three weeks, Devil's Breath either loses all potency or becomes so deadly, it can kill whoever touches, inhales, or digests even a miniscule amount. At that point, the criminal has no idea what the effect will be on their victim. Or them."

"Lifeless or deadly?" Richard nodded as the import of that fact sunk into my tired brain. "And that's at about three weeks?"

"Correct. The watchword there is *about* three weeks. It's different in every case. It could happen as early as seventeen days, or as late as twenty-five. After a certain time, Devil's Breath is a completely unstable and potentially lethal drug, even for the ones using it on their victims. In certain areas of Colombia, like Bogotá, they have access to new pods all the time, so they make fresh batches at least every two weeks."

"Could someone have a store of pods and make Devil's Breath whenever and wherever they need it?"

"No. Once the pod drops off or is taken from the tree, it begins to die and lose its potency. There's a window of only a few days to process it into the drug. After that, it's dead. And you can't freeze the pods, Lee, I checked. Freezing kills the pod instantly."

"So you need to be near the source, a mother tree."

"Somewhere that has a 'tropical monsoon climate', which is a rare and special environment. The closest one to the United States is a small region of Colombia where the conditions are right for the plant to grow. It's within the vicinity of Bogotá."

"That means we need to find out who travels back and forth to Colombia or has friends who do."

Richard nodded imperceptibly, lost in his own thoughts. Finally he spoke.

"Not so easy. You could have a network of people bringing the drug into the states on a continual basis. A lot of Colombian nationals go back and forth to their country all the time."

"Okay, okay. We've done enough for one day. Let's put this on the back burner for now, Richard. Go see your wife and daughter."

A smile lit up his face. I smiled back at him.

"We'll start all this again tomorrow. Oh, before you go." I reached in the back seat for my tote bag and pulled out the phone I took from the biker while he was up-chucking on the Dumbarton Bridge. "This came from one of the two kids that stole the chips and tester. His name is Jerome Hastings. He was told to erase the message from the man who set up the robbery a couple of days ago, but maybe you can resurrect it."

Richard took the phone from my hand, all professional now. "An I-5. If the ghost isn't on the phone itself, I'll go to the cloud and get it. Jerome Hastings?" He looked at me for verification he'd gotten the name right.

"Yes, one of the part-timers at Read-Out. Think you can do it?"

"Piece of cake. I've got a sweet program that uncovers passwords. As long as I've got their phone and name, I'm good to go. Shouldn't take me more than a couple of hours. I'll start the program tonight while I play with Stephanie."

He gave me that soft smile again; the one that happened when he mentioned his new daughter's name.

"You do that. Now get out of my car and go see your family." His smile turned into an all out grin as he leapt out of my car.

* * * *

I pulled out of the parking lot of the hospital and headed for home, maybe ten minutes away. I was exhausted, so I started singing *You Were On My Mind* to keep me awake. I may have many virtues but singing is not one of them. My loud, flat voice has been known to clear many a room. Nonetheless, as it was just me, I belted full out.

After the first stanza I stopped. The song was too close to the truth. I became silent, having depressed myself like nobody's business. Thoughts raced through my mind.

I'm starring in my own wedding in less than a week. I should be happy. Why aren't I happy? Maybe it's because my groom is on a covert mission in a foreign country. That can cause grey hairs aplenty. At the rate I'm going, Clairol and I will soon be fast friends.

Fear washed over me.

I could become a widow before I become a bride. All I have is an emoticon to suggest Gurn is alive and well.

I mentally slapped myself across the face.

Then go there, stupid. He's fine; he'll be back, just like he has countless times before. It's his job. Get over yourself.

I took a deep breath.

Okay, on to problem number two. Fifteen million dollars worth of property was stolen from a client on D. I.'s watch. Why didn't I just bring the truck back to Rameen when he demanded I do so?

Looking back on it, I wish I had. However, no PI worth his or her salt would have done that; part of the job is to protect the client's best interests. So pass the shaker and sprinkle me liberally.

I let out a noisy sigh.

150

If we get sued by Read-Out or word of this theft gets out, it could be the finish of D. I.

I swallowed hard.

It's the family business, not only uniting us but my dad's legacy. It's something I thought would always be a constant in my life.

I felt tears fill my eyes.

But saddest of all, two men are dead and I have no idea why. One was a valued member of the business and will be missed by us on a personal level. The other man, one of Silicon Valley's superstars, was just as valued to all the people who knew him.

Or was he?

It turns out D. H. Collier was a control freak who wanted everything his way, no matter what the cost. Aside from a daughter who loved him the way kids usually do, not many others seemed to have liked the man.

Does that include Katie Hall? Now that he's dead, the nanny became his daughter's legal guardian. She'll have virtual control over millions if not billions of dollars, at least until Skye is of legal age. A crackerjack motive if ever there was one.

Why oh why, did I agree to look into his death? Oh, that's right. I'm a schnook. Moving on.

This stupid IPO. Millions in the making; suspects in the making. I need to have a chat with the Read-Out people who stand to lose if it doesn't go through. That is, if Rameen Patel will let me in the door. I'll bet he's royally pissed. And with good reason. Here I tell him D. I. is going to keep the chips and tester so they can't get stolen again and whammo! Taken right from under our noses.

No matter how I look at it, I'm in such deep doo-doo. Could this day have been any worse? Oh, yeah. It could have been me in that motel in Redding. There is that. Time to go home, get the cats, go to bed, and pull the covers over my head. Unless there's a Barbara Stanwyck movie on TCM; I'll stay up for that.

I ran out of thoughts just as I hit the driveway of the old homestead. I rounded the drive heading toward the garage.

Even in the fog, I saw a flash of something small, orange and white caught in the headlights. It ran under the brush and disappeared. It only took a split second for me to connect the dots.

Tugger! Somehow my boy had gotten out, even under Tío's watchful eye!

I panicked. I am not a believer in cats being outdoors, except possibly on a leash. Too many bad things can happen. Putting aside fleas, ticks, and such, there were raccoons that can slice them open with one swipe, other cats, vicious dogs, and predators that come down from the mountains at night looking for small prey. That's not even mentioning fast traveling road vehicles. No animal is a match for a car, bus or a truck.

I slammed on the brakes, shut off the motor, and jumped out of the car into the drizzle, calling out Tugger's name. I forgot about being cold. I forgot about being wet. I ran to the last place I'd seen the cat disappear and called again and again. Nothing. After a few moments of that, I decided I needed help in rounding him up.

I nearly ripped the backdoor off the hinges in my haste to get inside. I ran through the darkened kitchen and slammed open the swinging door. Racing into the family room, I saw both cats and my uncle in the Barcalounger watching CNN news, Tío's favorite pastime.

Baba was sleeping in Tío's lap and Tugger was in a meatloaf-like position on the armrest. I'd made such a racket entering the room, three heads swiveled and stared at me in astonishment. My uncle leaned forward in his chair.

"What is it, sobrina? What is wrong? ¿Que pasa?"

"Dios mio, Tío." I took a moment to try and catch my breath. "I thought Tugger got out. But he's here, he's here!"

152

Shaking, I ran to the lounger and picked up Tugger, crushing him unto my soggy bosom. He struggled, obviously more comfortable where he'd been. Being crushed was not his thing.

Holding onto a sleepy Baba, Tío pushed himself out of his lounger and stood looking at me, not quite sure what to say. I felt like an idiot, and not for the first time that day.

Overload. I'm on overload.

I looked at my uncle. "I'm so sorry, Tío, for making such an entrance. I thought…I just saw…at least, I thought I saw…"

"Ah! *Entiendo.*"

"You understand?"

"*Si.* You see the neighbor's new cat, Ralph. They have him for several days now. A rescue cat, so they do a good thing. Still, I wish they did not let him out in the night, especially on a night like this, but what can you do? I talk to him about the dangers, the new owner. He is very nice. But people do what they believe." Tío shrugged, with the knowledge he couldn't control how other people dealt with the perceived freedom of their animals.

Tugger let out a cry, and fought to be put down. I never heard more of an "unhand me, you cur" expressed in one yowl in my life. I set him back on the armrest and he immediately began cleaning himself where my hands had touched him. Thank you, oh, loyal companion.

"Wait a minute, Tío. Let me get this straight. You're saying there is another cat that looks like my Tugger now living in the neighborhood?"

"Not really like your Tugger," Tío said, trying to hide a smile. "Not as *guapo.*"

"Not as handsome? I should think not." I heard the peevishness in my voice, but couldn't help myself. "Now that I think about it, the other cat looked bulkier, not nearly as svelte, or regal-looking. It's just that I only saw him for a moment and I was sure it was Tugger."

"*Sí*, upon inspection, there is a difference," Tío agreed, grinning full out now. "As you say, Ralph is more the sturdy; but a very nice cat."

I took off my wet coat, and hung it on the hat rack, while I digested all of this. Then I threw myself down on the sofa, burrowed the back of my head into a cushion, and sighed.

"Well, I'm glad we got that straightened out. Tío, the cat sighting was the last straw of one of the worst days of my life. I don't even know if I have the strength to walk up the stairs to my apartment."

I threw my left arm over my eyes in a dramatic gesture and groaned. I heard Tío's laughter.

"Come, come. Put your coat back on. I will carry the cats and walk you to your home. You will be more comfortable in your own bed, *sobrina*.

"I guess you're right," I said in my best Sarah Bernhardt voice. I struggled to stand. "Where's Mom?"

"She is asleep, as you should be. You both have very little the past few days."

I came to attention, giving my uncle, no longer a young man, the once-over. "What about you, Tío? Have you been getting enough rest?"

"I have the catnaps with Baba and Tugger. Together, we sleep most of the evening. Ricardo, he calls a few minutes ago to tell me you are on your way. I only now watch the news. Soon I will go to bed. Now come."

He took me by the arm and pushed me to the door. "Are you not hungry, Liana?"

I finally paid attention to my growling stomach. But before I could answer, he continued.

"I make the roast chicken with rice for me and your mama. There is plenty left. I will give you some and you can heat it up in your *cocina*."

He emphasized the word 'your' and moved toward his kitchen, leaving the swinging door open. I lumbered behind, snatching at my coat. By the time I entered his foodie fiefdom,

154

he'd already opened the refrigerator and was rooting around inside. I watched for a moment.

"Well, I've been thrown out of better places than this, Tío. Give me the food and my cats, and I'll be on my way."

Tío turned away from the opened fridge, handed me a Tupperware container, and planted a kiss on my forehead. While I stood there in a stupor, my uncle picked up and unfurled an umbrella from the stand by the door, handed it to me, and called to the cats. They came running. One in each arm, Tío crossed to the backdoor, and looked at me. I hurried forward. Under the protection of the umbrella, we both went outside, and toward my apartment.

As we walked the short span to my garage apartment, I realized I'd had enough of the world and all its shenanigans. All I wanted was to eat something, snuggle with my cats, and go to sleep. Oh, yeah. And pull the covers over my head.

Chapter Nineteen

It's amazing what a good night's sleep can do. I woke up early raring to go and feeling the glass was half-full instead of half-empty. I fed the cats after sharing a cuddle with them. I even managed to do a morning barre, and the ballet maven in me applauded. I hadn't been able to do my usual 45-minute morning barre for two days, and was feeling stiff and off-center from the lack.

When Gurn and I decided to stay in the two bedroom garage apartment, we knew there was no way I was going to be able to share the second bedroom, turned into my office/dance studio, with others. Not that I was unwilling, but beside my lone desk tucked away in one corner and the full-length mirrors running along one wall, the twenty-foot square room is empty.

Ballet dancing is exuberant and big; at least mine is. One hearty *soubresaut* or leap in the air followed by a *grande jeté*, jumping to the other foot, and anything around is likely to get steamrollered. Gurn knew it and I knew it. Even the cats knew it, fleeing the second I put my workout music on.

Converting one of the empty downstairs car stalls into Gurn's office was better for all concerned. Aside from giving each of us personal space, it would enable him to include a small gym, as well.

I decided to wear my burnt orange wool bouclé coat with the matching scarf to offset the gloom of the day. Picked up at a vintage clothing store, just wearing it made me feel happy. Determined to have a good day despite the continuing light sprinkle, chill in the air, and low cloud cover, I bounded down the stairs around seven am with an armful of cats. At least the fog had lifted. After handing off the two felines to Tío, but before heading to Read-Out, I stuck my head into renovation territory.

This is usually a place I avoided like the plague. I hate the entire process of renovating with all its noise, dust, and inconvenience. Left up to me, I'd move or burn the place to the ground. Okay, a little extreme, but listen up, Property Brothers. You'd both be working on the Food Channel if everyone thought like me. But Gurn had his heart set on doing the reno, I had my heart set on Gurn, so doing it we were.

The contractor, a nice guy who wore his forty-plus years better than his no-matter-what-the-weather Bermuda shorts, assured me the wallboard was going up that day followed by the crown molding and painting. The work would be finished within a day or two, he said. I looked around at protruding wires, non-existent light fixtures, stacked wallboard, ladders, and paint cans, but chose to believe him. Sometimes you need to go on pure faith.

Once in the car, I stuffed the Bluetooth in my ear and pulled out my phone with the intention of calling Katie about Skye's copy of her father's will. I figured with the kid going to school, both of them would be up preparing for the day.

I looked at my messages. Stunned, I saw another text message from Gurn. There were no words, but an emoticon of a heart. Just one lone heart sent thousands of miles sometime in the middle of the night. I pulled over to the side of the road and took a moment to smile at the very good start of a new day. Then I got on with my job.

Katie Hall's call went directly into voice mail. I left a cryptic message about wanting to read Collier's will, and asked her to call me back. I pulled into Read-Out, curious about how I would be greeted.

With no problem signing in, I went directly to Rameen Patel's office. I would have knocked on the door, but there wasn't one and he wasn't there, anyway. I changed my mind about finding him and cruised in the direction of my small cubicle, shedding my coat and scarf. On the way to my desk, I got double takes from most of my former co-workers at my celadon print Naeem Kahn dress, Jimmy Choo heels, makeup, and jewelry. I could tell they weren't sure who I was, me looking more like Ms. Successful Executive rather than Granny Gooch.

I dropped my tote bag and coat on my desk and sent a message to Rameen advising him I was onsite. Then I took out my list, and proceeded to the first name for interrogation. This was a twenty-one year old MIT dropout, who wound up giving me a big nothing.

Even though he was wearing a faded and too small Gap t-shirt, here was a guy who was a trust-fund baby and drove a Jaguar. To hear him tell it, money was of no concern. In fact, he had a disdain for it that only people who have buckets of the green stuff can afford to have. Furthermore, he worshipped the ground D. H. Collier walked upon, practically genuflecting each time he said Collier's name. If the CEO had told him to jump off a cliff holding a 1984 IBM PC Junior, he would have done it.

I was on my way to suspect number two, when Rameen Patel marched up behind me. I didn't think he'd be happy to see me, but the expression on his face was more like he'd eaten rusty nails for breakfast and was about to follow the meal up with me.

"Lee Alvarez," he said, with a pinched expression on his face. I didn't even bother smiling. There are times when you know being civil is completely out of line. This was one of them. Gnashing his teeth in between words, he went on. He gnashed quite well and it helped keep the mood going.

"Craig Eastham and I would like to see you in his office immediately. Follow me, if you please."

He spun around and tromped to the CTO's office, apparently sure I was fast on his heels. I wasn't. My phone rang and I saw it was Richard.

"I'll be right with you, Rameen," I called out, as I changed direction and went into the his/hers restroom. "Make it fast, Richard. I've got a fire-breathing CFO to deal with."

"Those two nerds, the ones who stole the chips and tester --"

He paused for a moment, obviously collecting himself. I was in a hurry, so I tried to prompt him to keep talking.

"Ronnie and Jerome. What about them?"

"Lee....they're dead."

"What?"

My voice had no emotion whatsoever, but it felt like my legs weighed three-hundred pounds. I sat down on the john, glad someone had lowered the lid. It didn't always happen in a male-dominated atmosphere.

"Say that again. Richard. I'm hoping I didn't hear you right."

"The Fremont Police found them about an hour ago. One of the boys, Ronnie Epstein, managed to dial 9-1-1 before he died."

"Where were they?"

"Back at the house in Fremont. Ronnie was in the hallway. Jerome was found sitting in a chair with a Superman comic book in his hands."

"Sweet Jesus. How did you find all this out?"

"Frank called. Both guys had the chemically altered Scopolamine in their system. The company doctor monitors everyone with the implanted chips twice a day, morning and evening. But he says once the stats came in this morning, it was already too late; the drug is so fast acting. With this new information, the cause of Collier's death has been ruled as possible murder. Bulletins on Devil's Breath are being sent to

159

every law enforcement agency in the Bay Area now. California is a very nervous state."

"Oh, my God. Richard, that's four men dead in less than 48-hours."

"I know. I talked to Lila. She wants you to call her."

"Later. I'm about to take a meeting with Patel and Eastham."

There was a pounding on the door then Rameen's stern voice. "Miss Alvarez, we're waiting."

"I've got to go, Richard."

More pounding on the door, followed by a jiggling of the doorknob. I lifted the phone away from my mouth.

"Keep your shirt on, Rameen," I shouted. "I'll be right out." I lowered the phone and my voice again. "Were you able to get that erased message back from Jerome's phone?"

"Almost," Richard said. "We found something, but barely audible. We're using audio enhancing software on it right now. I should know more within the next hour or so."

"Any clue as to whose phone sent it?"

"All we know is it's a six-five-oh exchange. We've got data running. I found out something else you should know. About that --"

The pounding resumed. I flung open the door, and said into the phone at the same time, "We'll have to talk later, Richard."

Hanging up, I glowered at a taken aback but hostile Rameen Patel. I pointed a finger in his face.

"You! Don't you know it's rude to interrupt a lady in the restroom?" He gasped, but said nothing. I went on. "Craig Eastham's office. So you say. Right now."

I pushed him out of the way and moved with Paul Bunyan-like strides. I beat Rameen to the CTO's office by about ten seconds. Enough to see Craig Eastham sitting behind his desk looking like he'd swallowed a pint of apple cider vinegar.

Rameen entered the room and came to stand next to the seated CTO. Both gave me a superior, disdainful look. I put both hands on his desk and leaned in on Craig Eastham, who pulled back at my aggressive gesture.

"Please sit down, Lee," the CTO said nonetheless, in his best administrative tone. He was angry but contained.

I glared from one to the other. My anger was not contained.

"I will not sit down. And a pox on your fifteen million dollars worth of missing crap."

I think like a Silicon Valley entrepreneur.
Failure is a great teacher.
Tadashi Yanai

Chapter Twenty

It took a moment for the men to get over their shock. Then both Rameen Patel and Craig Eastham tried to speak at the same time. But I would not be interrupted. I waved them away like I was directing a bad philharmonic orchestra.

"You two shut up and listen to me. Four men are dead and their deaths are directly linked to Read-Out. Try convincing the police you're not involved in this, 'cause I'm not buying it. With any luck, they'll be here any minute and throw you and your illustrious board in the hoosegow."

They looked at one another with genuine fear on their faces. Jaw slack, Eastham turned back to me and tried to speak, but I was on a roll.

"So do your worst. You want to sue the pants off Discretionary Inquiries? Be my guest. We're insured and it's only money. But, I repeat, four men are dead. That supersedes any of your idiotic IPOs." I spun around and headed for the door.

"Wait, Lee," Rameen's voice was loud enough to stop me. I stood at the doorway and folded my arms across my chest. He gestured for me to take a seat. I did not. His voice took a begging tone. "Please, sit down and let's discuss this."

I walked closer to Craig Eastham's desk. That was as much compromise as I was willing to give. Eastham looked at me with true puzzlement on his face.

"You've thrown me, Lee," said Craig Eastham. "What are these other deaths you've mention? What three other men? I don't understand any of this. David's suicide is the only death I knew about."

"Rameen didn't tell you that yesterday one of our agents, Jake Gold, died while guarding Read-Out's chips and tester?" I gave Rameen a hard stare. "It seems you like to keep mum about a lot of things."

While I glared at Rameen Patel, Eastham turned to him open-mouth. But the CFO only swallowed and was mute. I went on.

"And this morning, two young men by the names of Jerome Hastings and Ronnie Epstein, who worked for this place as independent contractors, were also found dead from the same cause."

Eastham sat stock still, but I could see he was thinking. He finally spoke. "You're saying that four men are dead and their deaths are related to Read-Out?"

"Well, you're slow on the uptake, but yes. Three had your chip implanted in them and the fourth, one of our operatives, was trying to protect those chips. Coincidence? I don't think so. I'd lawyer up if I were you."

"Oh, no," said Rameen. He let out a groan. "This can't be happening. This could be the end. We could lose everything."

"That's all you care about?" My voice rose in pitch. "This company? Four men are dead!"

"No, no, of course it's not." Rameen protested, but it was weak. All Eastham could do was work his jaw back and forth.

I was about to say more when I heard a ping-ping from my phone that meant I had a message. I decided to stop talking. It had all headed south, anyway.

"We'll have to continue this conversation later, gents. Make no mistake, I will find out if either or both of you are involved in these deaths. If so, you're going down. Consider yourselves on notice." I opened my phone and reading the message, headed out the door slamming it behind me.

Call me immediately. Urgent. R

Before I returned my brother's call, I stood outside Eastham's office trying to pull myself together. I was glad the CTO had a door for me to slam closed. I like dramatic exits - that's the Latina in me - but I have to admit I don't ordinarily do that type of confrontation. There's not much percentage in it. I like to keep the element of surprise on my side, not alert people I'm going after them.

If Patel and Eastham were involved in those two kids' deaths, maybe alerting them would cause them to get nervous and make a mistake. That is, if they were guilty of more than just being insensitive, selfish louts. Besides, the element of surprise was long gone. Things were spiraling down at a deadly speed.

Richard answered in the middle of the first ring. His voice was anxious.

"Lee, I don't know what you're doing, but it can't be more important than what I found out. The black van belongs to Ty Deavers, Sharise's band manager. It was reported stolen three days ago by his housekeeper. Here's the latest, both he and Sharise landed at SFO from Germany not fifteen minutes ago."

Richard managed to say everything with one breath, but now inhaled a much needed lungful. I took the opportunity to speak.

"He may not have been in the country, but he could have hired someone to steal the chips. Our woman in blue. We've got to find her, Richard."

"Uh-uh." I could feel him shaking his head. "We should drop all this in Frank's lap, Lee. Things are too dangerous. I don't want someone blowing Devil's Breath in your face. I think that's what Lila wants to talk to you about. If not her then me."

Now this is the point when a big sister wants to smack her baby brother on the behind. Or maybe even kick him.

164

"Richard, I realize you are now the proud father of a baby girl, but that does not give you the right to tell me how or when to do my job."

"Lee --"

"The only way I am going to stop looking into Collier's death --"

"Lee -"

"Is if his daughter tells me. Otherwise, I have an ethical obligation to continue -"

"Liana!"

"Excuse me, Richard! But do you know how much you sound like Mom right now?"

I could hear the indignation in my voice. Nothing could be worse, my kid brother and I told each other countless times, than to be compared to Mom. He did not rise to the bait. His voice was cool and matter-of-fact.

"I am my mother's son, Banana Breath, as you are her daughter. But we're all grown up now and have to pay attention to what we're doing."

His voice was soft, as he spoke an old childhood nickname of mine, just between him and me. He'd dared me to eat as many bananas as I could; I did, and became sick as a dog, much to his eight-year old glee. He knew how to play me then; he knows how to do it now. I thought for a moment and climbed down from Mount Superior.

"Right you are, Richard, and I apologize. We three need to take a meeting, calmly and rationally." I looked at my watch. "I should be done here in a couple of hours, if the first suspect on my list is any indication. Why don't we meet back at the office at three o'clock? How's that?"

I heard a beep beep - it's amazing all the different sounds a phone can have for its various communications - and saw Katie's name. "I've got to go, Richard."

"Three pm," my brother repeated. "The office. I'll let Lila know."

"Check. Love to Vicki and the baby."

165

"I'll tell her."

"And apologies again, brother mine."

"Sometimes that Latina blood gets the better of us." I felt Richard's smile over the airwaves. We'd ended on a better note. That was good.

What created Silicon Valley was a culture of openness,
and there is no future to Silicon Valley without it.
Sarah Lacy

Chapter Twenty-one

I moved away from Eastham's office, as I answered the phone. "Good morning, Katie."

"Good morning, Ms. Alvarez."

"Call me Lee."

"Right, I forgot. Lee. Do you have some news for us? Skye is anxious to know what you've learned."

I didn't answer the question, but asked one of my own. "Did you get my message about the will?"

"Yes, I have a copy here to show you. Skye gave it to me before she went to school."

I mused for a moment. A teenager has to find her father's last will and testament for a detective investigating his death before heading off to school. How sad is that?

"It's very sad, Lee."

I hadn't said my thoughts aloud. I was sure of it. Was Katie psychic? For sure, I didn't know as much about her as I should. I let it go for the moment and looked at my watch again.

"May I drop by around eleven, eleven-thirty to see it?"

"Why don't I fax you a copy? It might save you time from coming here."

"Thanks, but I was hoping you'd let me check out David's home office. He does have one, doesn't he?"

"Looking out over his own private rainforest. What is it you're searching for, Lee?"

"Just want to know the man a little better." I didn't feel like telling her about the black ring box, but a good exploration of his home on the chance it was there was called for.

"See you around eleven then. Skye should be home from school. She has a short day on Tuesdays."

"How's she doing?"

"It comes in waves. But she wanted to go to school today, so I let her. A special project. I'll tell you about it later."

Katie disconnected and I went to the second name on the list. Phil Spector, not to be confused with the record producer. Phil was an anomaly at six-foot four and weighing in at three hundred pounds. His glance in my direction was cursory at best, his attention then returning to his monitor. It was obvious he didn't recognize me in my getup any more than the rest did around here. I pushed aside some candy wrappers and sat on the edge of his desk.

Phil was very forthcoming, even offered me a Milky Way bar, which I declined. I'd have to cut back on those as it was, if I didn't want to wind up looking like Phil. Unfortunately, Phil didn't know squat, but I suspected as much. I tore through the rest of the list in just over an hour, because they didn't know squat, either.

That left the board members, not so easy to corral. I'd have Richard and his gang do a background check on each before I tackled the board in person. Which led me to thinking about what my brother had found out about the CFO and CTO. I'd know more at our afternoon meeting.

* * * *

I arrived at the entrance to the Collier compound around eleven-fifteen. A wide asphalt drive served as roadway to the private and heavily guarded five-acre complex.

The day was developing into a windy and moist one, where an umbrella did you no good at all. Even a hat was useless against the unpleasant gusts arising when least expected. My hair was one big ball of frizz, despite the use of every hair product known to man.

I took my foot off the accelerator and tapped the brake repeatedly, inching my way through the hoards of television reporters milling around the fifteen-foot high wrought iron gate. I've never met a reporter yet who was bothered by inclement weather; job requirement.

On each side of the driveway vans holding their equipment sat ready to transmit anything the reporters deemed newsworthy. Hopefully, I'd refrain from running over one of them so the transmission wouldn't be about me.

A pushy woman from KTFO banged on my window incessantly, microphone in hand. I ignored her and continued to crawl toward the small gatehouse where two uniformed guards waited. I wondered how I would be able to roll down the window to let them know who I was without having Her Pushiness shove the mic in my face.

I needn't have worried. The guards must have been on the lookout for me, because one beefy looking guard bounded out of the gatehouse attached to a large and snarling German shepherd. Wagging his tail at about a hundred miles an hour, I sensed a canine love of job that would have sent me packing if he was coming after me. Fortunately, he wasn't, but headed straight for Her Pushiness. She went packing big time.

Satisfied with a job well done, the dog barked his head off at the remaining ring of reporters. After spraying them with his saliva – good boy – they, too, withdrew in a hurry to the safety of their designated vans. With a smile on my face, I pulled up to the gatehouse and rolled down my window. The second pumped up guard wearing a sidearm – but no dog - came out. He stuck his head in the window.

"Identification, please."

I showed my ID and the guard scrutinized it with great care.

"Keep it to under ten miles an hour, please, Ms. Alvarez."

He touched his cap in a slight salute and hit a remote clicker twice. The front gate slowly opened. One of the reporters behind me must have stepped out of his van, because the dog started his snarling, snapping, and barking routine, barely controlled by the first guard. The second guard gestured for me to drive through. I edged forward feeling like I was going into a top-secret military base instead of the home of a whackadoodle techie who made good.

I followed the drive speckled with Royal Palm trees for probably half a mile. On the way a peacock took his time crossing the road while displaying gorgeous fan-shaped tail feathers. Off to the side, several flamingos and ducks frolicked in a large pond fed by a dancing waterfall.

Another uniformed man, dressed more like a custodian or groundskeeper, followed wild Canada geese around with a rake and shovel cleaning up after them. He looked up when he heard my car and gave me a friendly wave. I waved back feeling like Dorothy in the *Wizard of Oz*.

"Toto, I don't think we're in Kansas anymore," I muttered.

I swung around to the end of the drive. There stood a three-story glass and cement-colored structure, vaguely reminiscent of Frank Lloyd Wright's work. Balcony railings dripped with green foliage. Behind them, sliding glass doors or plate glass windows offset what could have been an austere building. Large and imposing, it managed to look light and airy even in the gloom of a wintry California day.

A smiling but anxious Katie was waiting for me at the top of the front entrance's polished cement steps. I got out of the car and gave the façade another once over.

"Wow," was all I could say. "This is some place."

"That's what most people say when they first come here. And the entire structure inside and out is built from cement. Wait 'til you see."

Katie continued to smile, but I could see it was an effort. Eyes red from crying, she carried an icepack in one hand. She opened one of the two front doors adorned with white and silver Christmas wreaths, and stepped aside.

Unbuttoning my coat, I took a few steps inside then froze in place. Katie followed me and reached out a hand for my coat, all the while watching my reaction to the billionaire's home.

Before me was the grandest three-story high living room I've ever seen. The ninety foot or more square room was decorated with a few select larger-than-life pieces. Masterfully arranged, your eye was drawn from the entrance to the other side, where a chrome and glass fireplace climbed to the top of the high ceiling. To the right of the fireplace a majestic white Christmas tree, decorated with bronze, silver, and crystal ornaments sparkled under pin spots of lighting.

A hand-blown glass Chihuly chandelier, in shades of yellow and orange, hung mid-center of the room. Cascading down from the ceiling at nearly twenty feet, it was nearly half again as wide. It was the largest chandelier of Chihuly's I'd ever seen, and I'm including his museum works. I have one of his small lamps. I cancelled a vacation to New York City to buy it.

My eyes went to the perimeter glass wall. At the base, an outside pond continued into the living room. Winding its way inside, the water lapped at stone edgings. On the other side of the glass, the tropical rainforest I'd heard about shimmered in lush shades of green. Encased in a ceilinged structure that reached up to the sky, ferns, plants, and mature trees seemed to thrive. Colorful and exotic birds and flowers dotted the panorama making it more dreamlike than real. And what a contrast to the weather outside.

Several Lucite or Plexiglas chairs stood by matching tables in conversational patterns. They encouraged you to sit down, relax, and admire the amazing scene for the living work of art it was. I turned to Katie.

"Did David Collier make the furniture? I understand he worked in the art form. And what is it? Lucite or Plexiglas?"

"Both names are applicable, Lucite or Plexiglas. It just means a higher quality of acrylic. And yes, David made those. It was his hobby. He has...had...a workshop in back with all the latest equipment, and an assistant to help him. He did the acrylic furniture throughout the house. He felt it was superior to glass in its lack of breakage. Another reason is that it weighs half as much as glass and can be cut and glued more easily, allowing more possibilities in design."

She paused and let out a small laugh. "I sound like an ad, I know, but he often talked of nothing else but his Plexiglas projects and computer chips." Katie paused again without the laugh. "I'll miss that."

"Was he working on a project now?"

"He was always working on one thing or another in his spare time, but I don't remember him mentioning any specific project." She looked past me to the rainforest. "He and his assistant made all the Plexiglas in front of the rainforest. It may look like glass, but it's not. The same with the floor. It's a highly polished, textured cement, not granite."

"Really? So this is a house where nothing is as it seems."

"Well, I guess you could say that, Lee. It sounds a little more sinister than I like."

I smiled at her. "Then we won't say it."

I took the two steps down into the living room, my heels echoing on the hard surface of the floor. I turned back to Katie as she pressed the small icepack against first one eye and then the other. When she noticed me noticing her, she gave out a small chuckle.

"I didn't have any cucumbers and I don't like tea." Katie waved the pack. "So this is it."

172

"Ice is best, anyway." I paused. "Sorry for your loss."

She looked down and nodded. "Skye is waiting for you in David's library. She got home from school about ten minutes ago and went directly in there."

"I was surprised when you told me she went to school today," I said, brushing my hands off into the pond. Two white and gold Koi came scurrying, but left disappointed.

Seemingly eager to talk about something other than D. H. Collier's death, Katie rushed on. "She's working with three other students on a light refraction element for fly fishing. If it succeeds, you wouldn't need any real lures on the end of your line. You could digitally change the size, shape, and color to whatever attracts the specific fish you're trying to catch."

"Does she take after her father in that?"

"She does, but Skye's more of a team player. The team is hoping to win this year's competition. She didn't want to let them down. The deadline is next week." She moved to the other side of the living room toward a hallway. "If you'll come with me, I'll show you where David's office is."

I followed, observing her as I trailed behind. Today she wore a mustard-colored dress, too baggy and long. Mustard is a hard color to wear and not for the majority of us. I wouldn't be caught dead in it, myself. But then I have been trained since birth by a maternal fashionista to look on that sort of thing as a disregard of one's duty to the world at large. From bad to worse, on Katie's feet a pair of hideous soft-soled UGGs moved silently atop the hard surfaced floor. I'd never be caught dead in a pair of UGGs, either. Oh gawd, I am my mother's daughter.

"I hope you don't mind." Katie threw the words over her shoulder, bringing me out of my usual mental wanderings. "But I'm going to leave you two alone. Skye wants to talk to you without me present."

In the adjacent hallway the cement wall color changed to off-white, done in an almost marbleized effect. The floors remained the same as the living room's, polished to a rich, gleaming grey. I usually hate the color grey as witnessed by D. I.'s color palette, but this was beautifully alive. I've read the use of cement today is so sophisticated it can be made to look like any stone or texture desired. I had to believe it; I saw it with my own eyes.

The hall was lit by what had to be indirect lighting, bathing the walls and floor in a soft glow. It looked natural, but I didn't see a window anywhere.

After many yards, we came to a large circular area. The outer, curved 'u' shaped glass wall displayed another spectacular view of the rainforest. The inner right of the circle allowed you to either continue walking down the hall or veer off in one of two separate directions.

Katie stopped and turned around to me. "I know it seems confusing, but it's really quite simple to navigate. This hall continues to David's office, the library, and further on to the indoor/outdoor pool and tennis courts. The middle hall goes to a staircase, which leads up to the bedrooms; there are eight of them. The far right hall angles back to the kitchen and dining room then out to the garage where the cars are kept."

"Cars? How many did Collier have?"

"Nine. He didn't drive them so much as he liked to collect them. He left the driving and maintenance up to Marty. The latest addition is a Tesla. See that first door ahead on the left?"

I nodded and she went on.

"That's David's office. His has – had - a magnificent view of the rainforest. He sometimes went out and fed the birds and small animals. He loved the forest. He spent as much time in it as he could."

Her voice sounded so sad, her face looked so pained; I knew instantly theirs was more than an employee/employer relationship. Katie had been in love with D. H. Collier. I don't know why I hadn't seen it before.

Of all the inventions of humans, the computer is going to rank near or at the top as history unfolds and we look back. It is the most awesome tool that we have ever invented. I feel incredibly lucky to be at exactly the right place in Silicon Valley, at exactly the right time, historically, where this invention has taken form.
Steve Jobs

Chapter Twenty-two

I knocked on a smooth, faux marble door without a knob. It slid open silent and fast, reminding me of futuristic sci-fi movies. I stepped inside a huge angular room with eighteen-foot ceilings and recessed lighting. Three grey-black walls showcased shelves filled with books, older computers, monitors, and TV screens from every era displayed almost like a museum. Maps of the world in various sizes, antique and modern, hung from dowels in between. On the wall opposite a mammoth desk was a line of up-to-date monitors, now turned off.

The fourth wall was glass or Plexiglas, showing another outstanding view of the lush rainforest. In one corner a door gave access to the outside. I'd been wondering how anyone got out there from the house.

Inside the forest, a gentle rain began to fall. I heard nothing, but lavender and white orchids, green-grey ferns, and small limbs of trees, bobbed in tempo with the soft droplets of water. A small blue and yellow bird fluttered across the landscape. Unreal.

"Daddy has it rain every hour on the half hour for ten minutes."

I turned to the sound of Skye's voice. The high back chair spun around to reveal the girl. The enormous desk chair with its padded arms and neck rest, made her look small and very, very young. Her voice droned on without any inflection.

"Computerized days and nights mimic a real rainforest to the minute. Sometimes I like to hear the rain falling." She reached out and touched a switch on the desk. The soothing sound of a soft rain filled the room.

"It's also kept at a constant temperature of eighty degrees Fahrenheit, with an eighty percent humidity level. It comprises a total of two acres and costs three thousand dollars a day to maintain. That's not including the costs of the maintenance crew or the vets and scientists who come in twice a month to check on the small animals, birds and butterflies. Ten monitors cover breeding nests and dens. Daddy liked to see how they were doing."

Skye pointed to the row of blank monitors across from the desk and flipped another switch on the desktop. The monitors came to life, showing different close up shots of the rainforest.

"Daddy wanted to bring in predators; have as much of the eco system as he could in there. I asked him not to. I didn't want to see a snake eating one of those beautiful birds. The world is too filled with violence." She looked up at me, tearless eyes devoid of any expression. "Don't you think?"

I had a momentary urge to tell her of the coroner's findings on her father; of how he didn't die from a broken neck or asphyxiation but by chemically altered Scopolamine. But putting aside my promise to Frank, the news might send her over the edge.

"Skye, have you talked to anyone? A counselor? Someone who can help you through this?"

My tone was easy, but inside my heart was pounding. Here was a child in the deepest kind of shock. She, in turn, asked a question of her own.

"Katie said you wanted to look through Daddy's office for something. What is that?"

"Not sure until I find it." My answer was deliberately vague.

"Then go for it." Skye jumped up from the chair in one awkward move. She crossed to the glass wall, hands clasped behind her back, staring out into the rainforest, talking all the while.

"Have you wondered why the Plexiglas doesn't fog over with all the heat and moisture from in there? It's not just the glass being double tempered, there are, like, drying elements shooting up from above and below. The air currents help keep the birds from flying into the glass and hurting themselves. Sometimes the mice come up and sniff at it. So cool. Daddy said that if the world keeps going the way it's going, these private rainforests will be all that are left. This one's Brazilian."

I crossed to the window and stood alongside her. "Skye, did your father have an inventory made of the flora and fauna in the rainforest?"

"Daddy inventoried everything. Why?"

"Just looking for a certain tree, so if you could let me see the inventory, it would be great."

"Sure, I can send you a copy."

"Thanks."

I pivoted away and went back to the desk. Skye turned to watch me, but didn't move. Her manner was shy.

"I wish you'd tell me what you're looking for. Maybe I can help you. Daddy was always losing things, like his keys and wallet. He had his own locating system, chips attached to nearly everything he owned."

"Is that similar to ones you can get on the internet? You know, you clap to find?"

"No." She let out a mocking laugh. "His are far more sophisticated and much smaller; tied to a satellite. They have no range limitation. He called them a locator chip. He said soon there'll be all kinds of service chips saving mankind from needless hours spent on mundane things. He believed they'd free up society, much the same as robotics did. Any single function performed by a machine or a living being can be performed by one of these; that's what he said. We'll depend on chips for everything one of these days."

She pulled back her sweater and pointed to her upper arm. I strained to see a small white dot on the skin.

"I have one of the Read-Out chips implanted in my arm. It's, like, more sophisticated than the locator chips. It lets me know if one of my migraines is coming on. I have a lot of those, but now I know when to take the medication beforehand so they're not so bad."

She paused. "I'm talking too much, aren't I? I can't seem to help myself. If I just sit around, all I do is think. I hate it." Her body trembled with her final words.

"You know, now that I think of it, I could use some help." I went to the ebony desk and pulled open a drawer at random. "I'm looking for a small black box, about the size of a ring box."

She smiled and rallied. "Do you think he chipped it?"

"He might have. What was inside was worth a lot of money."

Once again, Skye didn't allow space for her size. She rushed to the desk, her body glancing off mine. I tried to back up, but stumbled and fell into the chair. She wheeled around and the surprised look on her face made me laugh. She was contrition itself.

"Oh, I'm so sorry, Miss Alvarez."

"If you're going to be knocking me around, you'd better call me Lee."

I winked at her and her face reddened. She reached out a hand to help me out of the chair.

"Katie says it's because I've grown four inches taller in the last six months. I'm nearly five seven now."

"Growth spurts can be hard." I took her hand and pulled myself up from the deep, cushioned chair. "I remember the summer when I grew nearly three inches. Nothing in the house was safe from me."

She smiled and looked at her feet. "Thank you for trying to make me feel better."

"Why don't we see if we can find that black box, Skye? Any suggestions on how we go about it?"

She sat at the desk, and pressed one of six buttons in a console at the edge of the desk. A section of the desk slid open and a keyboard and monitor slowly rose from below. Once it had stopped, Skye leaned in, peering into the monitor.

"This is Daddy's computer. I know how to get into all his programs," she added with pride. "The program we want is called Bloodhound."

Graceful tapping on the keyboard brought up a screen with blinking dots. Most of the dots were in a clump near the bottom of the screen. As she clicked on each dot, short names appeared with a number behind it, such as key1, hat2, glasses3 and so forth. Even Collier's jackets were numbered.

"Where is this mass?" I pointed a finger to the clump of continuously blinking dots.

"They're in Daddy's bedroom. When the police returned his things, Katie put them there. Except for this dot here." She brought the cursor to a single dot on the side that read 'flashlight 3'.

"Where is it? Can you tell that?"

"Sure. He could track anything no matter where it was. He linked the program not only to existing cell towers, but also to one of our satellites circling the earth. This way if a chip gets out of cellular range, the dish can pick it up. If you double click on the dot it gives you longitude, latitude, and the physical address." She tapped the mouse twice and another screen popped up.

"This URL shows the current location of each of the chips. There's our address. And if you right click the mouse on the dot, it will even give you a Google map visual." She demonstrated as she spoke and a long shot of a rooftop appeared. "See that? The flashlight location chip is in his car in the garage."

"That's amazing, but how do you find small, possibly hidden things?"

"You either use an app on your cellphone or one of these remotes." She opened a drawer containing several small gizmos that looked like a small TV remote control.

"With something like keys, once you find the approximate location, you put in the corresponding name of the chip, and scan the area. Either your phone or the remote locks onto it and makes a pinging sound that becomes faster the closer you get. The chips are very thin and no bigger than a baby aspirin. They stick on anything, even glasses or jewelry. The life span is like forever. They use solar power. He helped his friend design them. He says...said... they're child's play."

The pride in her father's work came forward. For a moment her eyes sparkled.

"A couple of years ago, he attached a chip to one of Sharise's handbags. He thought he knew where she was every minute of every day until he found out she gave the bag to her stand in." Skye laughed lightly. "That was, like, funny."

"Is the locator chip anything like the Read-Out chip?"

"Oh, no. They're only good for one thing, pinging where they are. And they do need to be out in the sun now and then to recharge the solar battery. If not, after a year they're dead." She sobered at using the word 'dead'. I saw her spirit fade before my eyes.

"Skye, is there a way to tell how many locator chips he had working?"

She perked up a bit. "Oh, sure." She brought her cursor to the bottom of the screen where a small icon of a bloodhound sniffing the ground.

"Your father had a sense of humor." I was suddenly seeing another side of the controversial man.

"He did," Skye agreed, but never took her eyes of the screen. "If you click on the bloodhound, it brings you to another page and you can see how many locator chips are active at the moment."

She took a moment to read the results. "There are fifty-two. Fifty are inside the compound. I can find out what they are attached to just by clicking on them. Daddy named them all." After clicking through each, Skye remarked, "I didn't realize he had so many hats."

"What about the other two? Does that mean they're outside the perimeter?"

"Let's see." She sat down in the chair and pulled in closer to the desk. After a brief search she looked up at me. "One labeled 'W' is located in the Sunnyvale Police Department. I can tell because when I right click on it, it automatically goes to a Google map of the building."

"That's more than likely his last will and testament. I know they have it. What about the other one? Where is it?"

"Let's see," she said, reading the data from the last three chips. "It also isn't clearly labeled. It says 'P', nothing else. The address is in Palo Alto."

"Do you recognize the address, Skye?"

"No. I wonder what it means?"

I was pretty sure I knew what it meant. 'P' for prototype, but I kept the revelation to myself.

"If you give me the location, and loan me one of your pingers, I'll try to find out."

Skye chuckled and tapped in a few keystrokes. "I've never heard it called a pinger before. I like it." She pointed to the open drawer. "Take whichever one you like; they're all the same. Oh, and I just sent the address to your phone."

"Thank you. Now, Katie said you wanted to talk to me privately, Skye. What about?"

She turned and looked at me, unmasked fear coming into her eyes.

"Daddy's will. Why do you want to see it? What are you hoping to find?" Before I could answer, her words went on, fast and staccato. "You want to know who might have had a reason to kill Daddy. But he left money to everybody, everybody, but most of it to me. But why would I kill him? I loved my father."

Her outburst threw me.

"Skye, nobody's accusing you of anything. I think reading his will might give me a better impression of the --"

"It's Katie then, isn't it?" She interrupted in a shrill, almost hysterical voice. "I read Daddy's will again last night. For every year she stays with me, she gets a million dollars. But that's not why she's here. She's here because she loves me. Not everything is about money."

She fairly spat the last words out before squeezing her eyes shut. Her lips became taut and thin, so much so it was difficult for me to understand her next uttering.

"It's not Katie."

"I never said it was."

"Besides, Daddy gave her a bunch of money while he was alive. He told me. He used to say, 'throw money at people up front, right away. Then if they stay it's because they want to.' You should see what he pays Marty and Theresa, too. And Mr. Gonzales, the groundskeeper. Even the security guards. Nobody wanted him to die. Besides, Katie loves me!"

I reached out with my hand and touched her on an arm, which shook beneath my fingertips. "I'm sure she does, Skye. I can see that she does. I just wanted to read it for my own understanding. That's all. But if you don't want me to, I won't."

She was somewhat mollified and gave me a weak smile. Doing a one hundred and eighty degree turn, she said, "No, no, that's okay. You can read it right now if you want."

She reached for her knapsack, unzipped it, and pulled out a rolled-up will contained by a rubber band. She slid the rubber band off the blue bound document and it popped open to reveal a thick set of papers. Skye set the will before me in a casual way, but I could still see fear in her eyes.

"Here you go. But I already know that when Daddy died, Sharise got a million dollars a month or twelve million dollars a year for the rest of her life. It's set up in some sort of trust. And then there's Mr. Eastham. He gets all of Daddy's stocks in Read-Out. Daddy once told me they would be worth over a billion dollars one day. And Mr. Patel..." She paused, a puzzled look covering her face. "Daddy said he knew a secret about him. That's why he made Mr. Patel quit his job back east and move to California to work for him."

"Rameen Patel has a secret? What is it?"

"I don't know." She shook her head and leaned back.

"Tell you what, Skye, why don't you play a video game or something and give me a half hour, forty-five minutes to speed read the will myself. We can talk after that."

"Did you want me to leave the room?"

"Not unless you want to. Up to you." I smiled at her and picked up the blue bound document, one I pretty much know the ins and outs of. Crossing to a comfy leather chair on the front side of the desk, I sat down and started to read.

The first part of the will was pretty straight forward. Part One, Personal Information. *I, David Harold Collier, a resident of the State of California, Santa Clara County, declare that this is my will.* Part Two, Revocation of Previous Wills. *I revoke all wills and codicils that I have previously made.* Part Three. Marital Status. *I am legally divorced from Mary Louise Fitzhugh also known as Sharise. Divorce decree attached.* Part Four. Distribution of Wealth and Holdings. *The enclosed two-acre rainforest, my home in Palo Alto, and the surrounding grounds, are to be left as is and in perpetuity to the State of California, for the purposes of research only, with the proviso that my daughter, Skye, be allowed to live there until such time as she chooses to vacate.*

I was stunned. Putting aside he seemed to fear the State of California might turn the house into a bed and breakfast unless he stipulated otherwise, he gave away the family home.

True, Skye could remain there, but it wasn't really hers. For me, it wasn't a financial thing, because the kid was as rich as Croesus, but a sense of continuity, family, and belonging. Okay, another visit to Planet Weird, as far as I was concerned.

I took a deep breath and read on. The yearly sum of eight million dollars was to be taken out of the D. H. Collier Trust and used for maintenance of the rainforest, house and grounds. Apparently, that sum was the known annual running costs of the compound.

The heftier part of the will was the bulk of his estate and left to his one daughter, Skye Collier. The list of holdings and assets went on for three, two-columned, typewritten pages. Croesus would have to take a backseat to Skye. I could see where she'd never have to worry about paying rent anywhere in the world. She could even buy a country if she wanted. But still. Kicked out of your own home.

Reading further, the kid had been right about Craig Eastham. He had a standard 'right of survivorship clause' regarding any upcoming stocks in Read-Out, meaning that if one should predecease the other, their share of stocks would revert to the surviving partner. When Read-Out went public, Eastham would make millions, if not billions, and no longer splitting it with his co-founder.

Two things struck me as I read his other beneficiaries. One, he only left ten thousand dollars to each of his employees no matter how long they'd been with him. For a billionaire, I thought that was on the chintzy side. Then I remembered Skye's remark about how Collier liked to give money up front. I'm sure he paid exorbitant salaries. Probably with his passing, the people who worked for him went into mourning on a couple of levels. I'd run it by Collier's business manager, just to make sure I was right.

The second thing was the mention of Darlene and Phillip Fitzhugh being left one of the Fiji Islands in the Pacific on which they currently lived, an island valued at fifteen million, six-hundred thousand dollars. It took me a moment to realize they must be Sharise's parents and Skye's grandparents.

I knew Collier's parents were dead, both having died in their eighties. But Sharise's parents were much younger, probably only in their late fifties, early sixties. No one had mentioned them yet, certainly not Skye, and I wondered if they chose to live so far away from their only granddaughter. Or were they in an enforced exile? Knowing a little of how Collier operated, the latter was entirely possible. I'd check on that, too.

After I read his charities and bequeaths, of which there were enough to call him a generous and honorable man, I looked up and tried to keep my voice gentle.

"I see your grandparents, the Fitzhughs, are in the will. Are you close to them?"

"Not hardly. Like, I don't even know them. They left for their Polynesian vacation right after I was born and never came back."

"Do you know why?"

"Who cares?" Her tone was dismissive, hardness returning to her face, taut mouth relaying brittle words. "They like the island life. Good for them. Who needs them, anyway? Daddy said we were better off with them in the middle of the Pacific."

Before I could react to this, Skye went on.

"But you can see other people had better motives than Katie. I mean, the Fitzhughs get some island worth millions. Besides, Katie would never hurt Daddy. She was..." Skye broke off, pinching her lips together again.

"She was in love with him," I finished for her.

Skye didn't answer, but nodded. She inhaled a long breath sprinkled with small, unspent sobs.

"Yes. Once I thought he loved her, too. For a while, I thought maybe they would get married. Sometimes I'd see him sneak into her room when he thought I was asleep."

185

She broke off in a self-deprecating laugh then looked away.

"But that stopped. He met Tanya, a Vogue model. That was followed by Allison the actress, and then somebody I can't even remember." She sighed. "He went with a lot of women, but he only loved one." She paused. "Sharise."

"Ah…Skye…did you know Sharise's plane landed at SFO a short time ago?"

"It's on the calendar. She already left two messages and texted me a few minutes ago."

"You might have to see her, with what's happened."

"I know." Her voice sounded resigned.

"If you don't want to, talk to your father's lawyer about an injunction."

She shook her head. "No, it's better to meet her and get it over with. I know what she wants. She wants me to live with her now, especially now that he gave this place away. I inherited most of Daddy's money. She wants to get her hands on it, but Daddy was prepared for that. If she, like, tries anything, the terms of the will take away everything he left her. His lawyers made sure of it." She looked at me, her expression way too hard and knowing for someone fourteen years old. With a curled lip, she added,

"So eat it, bitch."

I just think people from Silicon Valley can do anything.
Elon Musk

Chapter Twenty-three

I adjusted the rearview mirror of the car to see fully what I was leaving behind. Hoards of reporters still milled around the gates. A guard was having an argument with Miss Pushy Reporter, who'd broken free again. She'd banged on my windshield as I inched my car out the gate until the German shepherd growled her into submission. Now she was paying for it.

The Collier compound; I was glad to be free of it.

Craig Eastham answered on the first ring. One good thing about being their hired PI, I had access to everyone's personal information, including their private cellphone numbers.

"Yes? What do you want, Lee?"

"I need to speak with you. Now and preferably away from the office."

"I'm not at the office. I'm home in Portola Valley."

"I don't think you want me to come there."

I heard an intake of breath. Then an exhale. "Why not?"

"I don't think we want to chance being overheard."

Just when I thought he would hang up, he spoke again. "Where then?"

"How about the Highland Inn Beer Garden? I could use a burger."

"When?"

"Fifteen minutes?"

"Fifteen minutes."

Neither one of us said goodbye. We just hung up.

I arrived early, Eastham was late. There'd been a long line and I wasn't even halfway through one of the Inn's hamburgers, known far and wide for their yumminess. They were so good the place was still packed with Stanford students at one-thirty pm.

The Highland Inn is one of the oldest businesses on the Peninsula, dating back over one hundred and fifty years. It's a rustic, roadside spot with an outdoor picnic area offering simply beers & burgers.

When I was a student, I often came here for lunch, eschewing the beer. I had to return to my classes and I didn't need a buzz on or to be falling asleep at my desk. This day I eschewed the beer because I needed my wits about me.

No one was sitting outside due to the inclement weather. Thus, the inside tables were crammed. Loud, noisy, and sitting in groups, the students made me question if I'd ever been that young or carefree. Depressing though the thought was, I smiled as I watched them.

Burger and coke in hand, I leaned against one of the walls, and kept an eye out on the door. Craig Eastham didn't see me at first. I took the opportunity to study the man as he entered, not as a Silicon Valley giant, but just as a man.

I compared Eastham's to Collier's persona, and found him lacking. Collier had been tall, slender, and fit. The CEO's hair had been a well-tended and shiny silver; an elegant shock of white running through the top. D. H. Collier exuded the look of a modern-day, successful man loaded with style and panache.

Craig Eastham was no such thing. In his mid to late forties, he was on the short side and could lose a few pounds. His salt and pepper hair was wild and unkempt, too long for the wildness of the curls crowning his low forehead. Like a lot of techies, he had a soft, paunchy look about him from sitting in front of a computer fourteen, fifteen hours a day. The only deviation to the norm was instead of the pallid skin tone of a brainy nerd, Eastham was tan. Maybe taking care of llamas in the California sun had an extra bonus.

Eastham finally saw me and waved, an anxious look crossing his face. Pushing his way through the throng, he came to my side.

"Sorry I'm late. I had to finish up feeding the llamas." He looked around him. "This doesn't look like a good place to talk."

"No, it doesn't," I said, reluctantly throwing the last half of my burger into a nearby trashcan. "Bad choice. Why don't we go sit in my car?" I slurped the remaining coke out of the paper cup and threw that in the trashcan, as well.

A sharp wind cut through my coat as we opened the door and left the restaurant. I was sorry I hadn't worn a sweater underneath, even though the coat was lined wool. Sometimes a wet cold goes right through anything.

I beeped the car doors open and we slid inside the warmth of the Chevy. Neither one of us said anything for a full ten seconds. I had a feeling we could sit there all day like that, but I had other things to do.

I turned in my seat toward the CTO, the leather making a crunching, crackling noise as I moved. Eastham looked mighty uncomfortable. Couldn't be the car seats; these were special order and as comfy as sitting on your couch in the living room.

"Why don't you tell me about your wife and David Collier?" I made my voice as gentle as possible, given the question.

He scooted up and down in the seat, nervous, antsy, whatever, the leather echoing his movements, as they had mine. "I don't know what you're talking about."

"Oh please, Craig. Don't ever try your hand at acting. You have no talent for it."

He sat perfectly still and looked straight ahead. I prodded.

"You may as well tell me. Even if you don't think so, people always leave a trail somewhere."

He ran a quick, pudgy hand over his face then let out a choked sigh. "How did you know?" He still wouldn't look in my direction.

I decided to be honest. Not a first for me and it often lands me in a bucket of trouble. But there you are.

"I didn't, not really, until now. I suspected it this morning, but I wanted to make sure."

"You tricked me." He let out a sound half way between a laugh and a snort.

"Sorry, but it might be important to the case. Tell me about the affair. It if means nothing we'll never mention it again, I promise."

Beads of sweat appeared above his mouth. He swiped at them with a jerking motion before speaking.

"My wife, Carol, is a good woman, a good wife and mother to our two boys. They're eleven and sixteen. I work long, impossible hours. Always have. But it seemed to be all right. We've always been..." He broke off and shrugged, thinking of the right word. "Comfortable. That's the word, comfortable. And then things started happening; maybe a couple of years ago."

He turned and looked at me for the first time.

"Carol is bipolar, did you know that?"

I shook my head.

"It started with the online gambling. Thousands and thousands of dollars every week. Even our eldest boy got hooked. Then a few months ago she changed her hair color. Dyed it blonde, and bought some new clothes. I didn't think anything of it at the time. Women have a right to change their looks, right?"

He turned to me for agreement. I didn't say anything, so he faced front again and went on.

"Anyway, shortly after that I found her in the bathtub, wrists slit, blood everywhere."

His voice cracked and he fought back tears. It broke my heart and I reached out and touched him on the shoulder. I

190

don't think he was aware of the gesture. Suddenly he burst out in a near shout.

"That son of a bitch, David Collier! He could have any woman in the world. He did have any woman in the world. Why did he have to go after Carol? She nearly died. It was horrible." The last words were hardly more than a broken whisper.

"When was that, Craig?"

"Three months ago. Three long, long months ago."

"Did Collier know about Carol's attempted suicide?"

Craig shook his head. "No, we kept it very quiet. Even the boys don't know. We told them she was in the hospital because she needed an adjustment to her meds; it's happened before. Fortunately, I found her in time. She was in the hospital only two nights, but she's still in therapy. I guess you could say something good has come out of it. It's helping with her gambling problem. My son's, too."

He stared straight ahead then buried his face in his hands, sobbing for a solid minute. I was silent and let him cry it out. When he was done, he took out Kleenex from his pocket and wiped his eyes. I reached out and gave him another, one I pulled from my stash. For the first time, he smiled at me.

"I'm sorry," he stuttered. "Sorry about this."

"Don't be. I'm sorry I had to put you through it again."

"Should I tell you the truth? I'm glad David's dead, that miserable egomaniac. She told me he pursued her for months only to drop her after two weeks. She was so guilt-ridden, not just for me, but for the boys, that she tried to kill herself."

He wiped at his nose before going on.

"And you know why he did it?" He turned to me, eyes burning into mine.

"Because he could." I didn't even need to think about the answer.

"That's exactly the kind of sick son of a bitch he was. Another notch on his belt. Never mind our friendship, our business relationship, that she was a married woman. Oh, hell." He turned to me again. "But I didn't kill him. If I had, I would have run him through with a saber, face to face."

I thought for a moment. "I believe that's your style, Craig. Defending a woman's honor."

"I'll bet you're wondering why I'm still at Read-Out after I found out, after he nearly killed my wife. Well, it's simple. We need the money. We are flat broke. And the business is as much mine as it is his…was his. If this IPO doesn't go through and soon, I'll probably have to declare bankruptcy."

He leaned back into the cushions, seemingly spent. He didn't look in my direction. He opened his mouth to say something, but paused first, maybe thinking it through. Finally he looked at me, his voice filled with resignation.

"So what now? Are you turning me in to the police? Is this going to be in the papers? I'm thinking of my boys."

"No. It'll be like we never spoke. I just needed to know. No one's going to learn of this from me or anyone at D. I. unless it's pertinent to the case. One thing, what happens to Collier's share of stocks now that he's dead?" I watched his reaction carefully.

"Well, I hope they come to me," he said with a shrug. "We each signed a Right of Survivorship agreement and there's supposed to be a clause to that effect in each of our wills, put there for the sake of expedience. There's a clause in my will, and I'll have to change that now. But being who we're dealing with, maybe David left them to some stripper in Las Vegas. I wouldn't put it past him."

His bitterness was almost palpable, but I didn't allay his fears about what I'd read in Collier's will. Not my place.

"Why don't you go home, Craig, before it starts to rain again? And unless something else comes to light, our conversation will never be mentioned again. You have my word on it. Thanks for coming."

He took a deep, almost cleansing breath, nodded to me, opened the car door, and stepped out.

*Silicon Valley has evolved a critical mass of engineers
and venture capitalists and all the support structure –
the law firms, the real estate, all that - that are all actually
geared toward being accepting of startups.*
Elon Musk

Chapter Twenty-four

I'd turned off 280 South and onto Sand Hill Road, where I pulled over to the side of the road and made a call. I let the car idle, not environmentally correct, but sometimes it's just the right thing to do. With a sigh, I pressed the speed dial again and put the phone to my ear. If the amount of phone calls I'd been making kept up, I would soon have a cauliflower ear. But that's just me griping.

My brother took his sweet time about answering. I hate that. Whoops. Still griping.

"Richard, what's the address you have for Sharise's manager?"

"Ty Deavers?"

"Yes."

"Give me a minute." I did. "Found it. 1543 San Carlos Drive, Palo Alto."

I looked into my phone at one of the addresses Skye messaged. "That's what I thought. Same address. I think the prototype is there, Richard. And maybe the rest of the booty, too."

"You don't use words like 'booty' around Lila, do you? I mean, she's hard enough to handle as it is."

I ignored my brother's comment about our illustrious leader, and recounted my conversation with Skye in detail. I have a form of memory retention that allows me to remember and repeat conversations verbatim, at least for a time. I chose to hit only the salient points about Eastham. Richard was impressed.

"You've been busy."

"I have."

"What's on the agenda now, Lee? Sounds like you have a plan."

"Well, for one thing, I'm skipping our three pm meeting. I've got yet another stop to make."

"I hope it's not going to Ty Deavers' place to try to get the prototype back by yourself. Our Lady will not be happy. Neither will I."

"I promise not to break in, but I already called Frank and he's meeting me there with a search warrant. He thinks he can get one with probable cause, based on Collier's locator chip pinging in Ty Deavers' house. It has no reason to be there other than theft. But I promise not to do any B and E...at the moment."

"That makes me feel so much better."

Richard had a sarcastic edge to his voice. In fact, the whole conversation had been strained. I struggled to understand why. I said I wasn't going to break into Sharise's manager's house by myself and I meant it...sort of. But brothers, who can explain them; who can tell you why.

"By the way, Richard, Skye sent me a list of all the plants and animals contained in the rainforest, which I forwarded on to Frank. A borrachero tree is not on it, but I'm sure Frank is going to look at the rainforest with a magnifying glass. Do you have any updates for me?"

I pulled out onto Sand Hill Road again only to be stopped by a red light. Shoving the Bluetooth in my ear, I listened to my brother's findings.

"All the high rollers you think of as being loaded aren't. Sharise has spent more than she's made for the last two years. I had no idea what it costs to mount a touring rock concert, especially one as jazzy as hers. After seeing her expenditures, she could use twelve million dollars a year."

"Too bad she was in Germany, Richard."

"Hired an assassin?"

"Too vindictive for a professional; they would have just shot him."

"Okay. Craig Eastham. His finances are major shocking. His wife is a closet gambler and a bad one, at that. She spends a lot of her time online losing tens of thousands every week. Their eldest son has the same problem. Between the two of them, they've gone through millions."

"So he told me, but I'm glad to have it confirmed. Craig also told me Collier dumped his wife shortly after he bedded her. That's why she tried to commit suicide."

"Sounds like a good motive to me." Richard cleared his throat. "Katie Hall. She and Collier had a thing about three years ago. Then he moved on. Rumor has it she didn't take it well. Katie kept nosing around in his love life, writing nasty notes to women he was dating and stuff like that."

"Really?"

"Collier threatened to fire her if she didn't stop. The only reason he hadn't up 'til then was Skye liked her so much. I guess hell hath no fury like a woman scorned."

"I wish people would stop saying that. It's so sexist. Women aren't any more scornful about being dumped than men, Richard."

"Maybe more creative?"

"Not even. But Collier's codicil does make her a rich woman, so she's on the short list. What about Patel?"

Richard's voice became slow and thoughtful. "There's something. But it happened when he was underage, so it's locked up in his juvie record."

"He has a juvenile record?"

"Yeah, and I can't get into those, no matter what I do. Even I have my limitations."

"I never thought I'd hear those words, brother mine."

"You're hearing them now." He paused. "Although...." His voice tapered off.

"Although?"

"I have a friend in Barstow. And he has a friend with a research job at City Hall. Let me see what I can do."

"Keep working your magic, Richard. Meanwhile, I should be in Palo Alto in a few minutes."

"Before you hang up, Mom told me to remind you of your four o'clock fitting, something about your wedding dress."

"Yikes! It's the last fitting, too. I'd better show up."

"If you know what's good for you. And Jake's funeral is tomorrow. The Coroner's Office has released the body. As you know, Jewish tradition is to bury people within forty-eight hours. He has a plot in Colma. We're supposed to be there for the service at nine AM in the morning."

I felt the tightness in my throat again. "Sure thing. Is there anything I can do to help?"

"In your spare time? I don't think so. Patti is making most of the arrangements. His car and all his belongings are being donated to the International Rhino Foundation. He stipulated that in his will."

"Too many readings of wills right now, Richard. I don't like any of it."

"No."

We were silent for a moment then I cleared my throat and changed the subject. I hoped my voice came out sounding anything like normal.

"Where's Mom right now?"

"She's with Vicki and the baby now --"

"Ahhhh. I need to swing by for some baby time. How is everyone doing?"

"Fine, but be on the alert. When Lila finds out where you'll be instead of at the meeting today, she'll be livid. You know what she's like then."

"Howling at the moon, splitting logs with her bare teeth, setting fires in a single glance? She don't scare me none."

"Oh yeah? Try having her drive to Ty Deavers' and creating a scene in front of Frank. I wouldn't put it past her."

"*Dios Mio*! Don't give her the address, Richard."

"Too late."

"Okay, tell Mom I'll be at the fitting for sure. But let her know I'm trying to find and return the tester and chips to Read-Out, so we don't lose D. I. in a lawsuit. That's the only reason I'm not going to be at the meeting."

"Hold on. I've got a call coming in. Well, what do you know? It's Mom." His voice took a gleeful turn. I, on the other hand, was terrified.

"Goodbye; I'm hanging up."

I did so and threw the phone in the back seat. I arrived at the address in Palo Alto, slowing down to a crawl to assess the layout.

The house was a stucco mini-MacMansion, showing the standard 1980's tan color in places where it wasn't covered with green ivy. Pretty, but ivy can so destroy stucco it surprises me when people let it take over.

Frank's squad car was already there, as well as backup. He was outside on the well-manicured lawn having an intense conversation with one of his lackeys. I gave a short toot of the horn, waved, drove down the street and parked, figuring I would wait for Frank to hike over to me with an update. Seconds later a coroner's wagon showed up followed by another police car, lights flashing but no sirens.

197

I was in Bangalore, India, the Silicon Valley of India,
when I realized that the world was flat.
Thomas Friedman

Chapter Twenty-five

I didn't like this turn of events at all, so I hopped out of the car and walked back to the stucco house. If Ty Deavers was needing a coroner's wagon, there went one of my suspects.

The rain had stopped and the sun peeked out from a few passing clouds raising the temperature to a tolerable degree. A gust of wind, cold and damp, showed us who was boss, though. Winter was amongst us, and I drew the scarf tighter around my neck. Passing one of the officers, I waved a greeting. He recognized me and let me through. Frank was pacing in the driveway, deep in thought.

"What's going on, Frank?" He didn't answer right away, but grabbed one of my arms and pushed me back in the direction of my car.

"You're lucky you didn't do anything stupid. If you had been inside, I might have had to arrest you. Or it might have been worse."

It was more of a growl than words. I pulled my arm out of his grasp, but didn't move.

"What's happened?"

"A woman is dead. Lying on the floor of the living room. We saw her through the window when we came up to the place with the search warrant. We didn't know she was dead at the time, but it gave us probably cause to break down the door."

I drew in a breath of air, but said nothing. Neither did Frank. We stared at each other. I was the first to break the silence.

"Devil's Breath?"

"She has the same look as those two boys in Fremont, so I wouldn't rule it out. We won't know for sure until the autopsy, but that could take some time."

"Is Ty Deavers in there?"

He shook his head. "No, but his van is in the garage. We don't know where he is yet. His plane landed hours ago. We've got an APB out on him."

"Who's the dead woman?"

"Don't know that either. But we'll do the usual things. We'll find out."

"Does she have long red hair?"

"No."

"Wearing a blue cowgirl outfit?"

"No. You think this might be your lady in blue from Redding?"

I answered his question with a question. "So no Read-Out chip implant?"

"Not that we know of. The medical examiner didn't mention finding it and he knows what to look for." He searched my face for any revelations on my part. "Why should she have an implant? Does she have something to do with Read-Out that I don't know about?"

I shrugged.

"Don't give me that shrug. What are you keeping from me? Five people are dead. If you know something, you should tell me."

"Frank, one of Collier's chips is here. That's what this locator says." I pulled the remote-like gizmo out of my pocket. "That means Ty Deavers has something to do with this, even if he was out of the country at the time. Let's go in and see if we can find what's in there."

"I thought you already knew what you were looking for. The prototype."

"Then let's go find it."

Frank made a snatch at the remote. I whipped it out of his reach.

"No, no. This is mine."

"Stop playing around, Lee. This is serious."

"If you want to use it without handing me an injunction, you'll have to let me go in with you."

I walked around him and toward Ty Deavers' house. When he didn't follow, I turned back to him.

"Coming, Frank?"

He hesitated then followed, muttering as he walked. "Sometimes I think your father let you get away with too much."

"Funny, Mom says the same thing. So Deavers' van is in his garage? I thought it was stolen."

"Yes, but it's miraculously reappeared and is being impounded as we speak."

"Mind if I look inside it? I won't touch anything, I promise."

"No, you can't. Besides, I've already looked inside."

"You have?" I stopped and turned back to him. "Well?"

"Well, what?"

He continued walking and passed me, but said no more. After a beat I called out.

"Okay, you win, Frank."

My voice made him stop, turn, and face me. I tossed the gizmo to him. He caught it without taking his eyes off me. I smiled in what I hoped was a winning manner. Actually, it was mostly an idiot grin, all teeth, little substance.

"If I show you how to use the remote, will you tell me what you found inside the van? Please?"

He let a trace of a smile cross his lips. "All right. It contains a strange looking kitchen cabinet; I think it's your chip tester, and cardboard boxes. I opened up one of the boxes and the chips you've been looking for are there. Once Evidence checks them out, I'll return the lot to Read-Out. Satisfied?"

"That means D. I. won't get sued for fifteen million dollars or be badmouthed throughout the Bay Area."

My voice shook. I hadn't realized until that moment how frazzled I'd been over the loss of the tester and chips. Not to mention the impact its loss would have had on D. I.'s reputation.

"Lee honey, I would have told you that whether or not you gave me the remote control. But it's better you did. You should have as little to do with this as possible."

"But I'm the reason you're here in the first place. I let you know what was going on."

"And I'll convey your part in it to Read-Out's CFO when we return the stolen materials."

I thought for a moment. "I guess that does free me up to find D. H. Collier's killer."

"Good God." He shook his head. "Don't you ever quit?"

"No," I replied. "If the prototype is inside, who will you return that to?"

"Rameen Patel has filed a missing report on it, so it's officially Read-Out's property."

"Officially, it's not. He didn't pay Collier for it yet. It belongs to the estate."

"Then I'll ask him for a bill of sale. We'll see where it goes from there."

He gave me a grin, not idiotic like mine, but warm and friendly. We both relaxed a little. I started to say something. He stuck out a hand to stop me, so I kept my mouth shut and let him speak.

"And don't worry. I'll tell whoever it belongs to your part in the recovery of it."

"I wasn't thinking about that, Frank. But thanks. I'm wondering if the prototype is here, after all. I think whoever killed Collier – or is that whomever?" I interrupted myself and looked at Frank.

"Don't get stuck on those kinds of things; this isn't an English test. Go on, Lee. I want to hear what's going on in that furtive thing you call a mind."

"No, on second thought, I think I'll keep thinking about this. A lot of the puzzle is still missing."

I turned to walk back to my car. He shouted after me.

"I don't have to tell you this is not a parlor game."

I waved over my shoulder still walking straight ahead. "And I don't have to tell you this is not over yet."

Perhaps the strongest thread that runs through the Valley's past and present is the drive to 'play' with novel technology, which, when bolstered by an advanced engineering degree and channeled by astute management, has done much to create the industrial powerhouse we see in the Valley today.
Timothy J. Sturgeon

Chapter Twenty-six

I opened the car door to get in just as my phone rang. I looked at the incoming call and though I didn't recognize the number, it had a D.C. area code.

"Hello?"

"Miss Alvarez, this is Vice Admiral Saks."

I sucked in air, so noisy and quick, my chest hurt from the effort. "What's happened? Is Gurn --"

"Easy, Miss Alvarez. Lt. Commander Hanson is just fine."

"He is? You're sure?"

"Yes. He's delayed, that's all. He asked me to call you as a favor; he didn't want you to worry. I don't ordinarily do this sort of thing, far from it, but I understand you two are getting married upon his return. And he once helped my son with a problem." His gruff voice softened on the last sentence then picked up the same formal, no nonsense tone again. "He'll be a day later than expected. Goodbye, Miss Alvarez. Try not to worry," he added, disconnecting before I could respond.

"Goodbye," I said to dead air. "And I'll try not to worry." I put my head down on the steering wheel. "I can't take much more. Too much is going on. And I never have a minute to just sit and think."

As if to make sure I knew that, my phone rang again. I looked at the number. Other than the 415 area code, I was clueless. I answered, anyway, instead of letting it go into voicemail. It was that kind of day.

"Hello?"

"Ms. Alvarez?" The voice sounded musical and vaguely familiar. "This is Sharise. I understand you're looking for me. At least, that's what my daughter said before she hung up on me."

"I am hoping to converse with you, yes. And call me Lee. You know D. H. Collier is dead, right?"

"It's been all over the news and in the German papers, even if Skye hadn't screamed over the phone repeatedly of how I was responsible."

"And are you?"

A lilting laughter filled the airwaves. "Now how could I be? I just flew back from my European tour."

"When did you get in, Sharise?"

"We cleared customs about five hours ago. I'm home now."

"Is your manager with you?"

"Ty? I last saw him at the airport. One of his friends has a gig there for the holidays. Ty likes to play the drums, so he was sitting in when I left."

"SFO, right?"

"Why all the questions about Ty, Ms. Alvarez…ah…Ms. Lee?"

"Just Lee."

"Of course. I thought, Lee, I was the one you wanted to talk to."

"I'm hoping you and I can meet soon."

"That sounds lovely. How about now?"

I looked at my watch. Three-thirty. If I didn't show up for the final fitting, I would be one dead bride, courtesy of my mother.

"How about six?"

"Any time you say. Do you know where I live?"

"2752 Mar East Street, Tiburon."

"Very good. Oh, and Lee, my daughter is a bit of a drama queen. I hope you haven't taken any of her accusations seriously."

A melodic laughter filled the airwaves again. I hate callous, insensitive people, even if they are world famous rock musicians. My voice was even colder than I meant it to be.

"Her father is dead. Dramatics work very well in times like these."

"As you say; my apologies. Six o'clock then, Lee."

"Six it is, Sharise. And thanks."

She didn't reply and we disconnected. Before I called Frank to tell him of Ty Deavers possibly being at the airport, I unlocked the glove compartment to make sure my Beretta Tomcat was there and fully loaded. It was.

Silicon Valley is completely different:
people here really live on the edge.
Linus Torvalds

Chapter Twenty-seven

The fitting at Angela's Fitting Room went fast. I was in no mood to admire my reflection while spinning around with acres of silk velvet twirling at my feet. Thank God Mom wasn't there or I might have twirled my brains out, just to keep her happy. The upshot was the wedding dress had to be taken in again. The key to losing weight is having your fiancé on a secret mission, people dying left and right, and running around looking for a killer. But I don't think Weight Watchers would approve of the method.

While at Angie's I received a text from my mother, telling me to wait for her. Love her though I do, that info hurried my departure. I leapt into my car around four-fifteen, leaving Angie holding the gown and the proverbial bag. Let her deal with a mad-as-a-hornet mother; we were paying her enough.

Accompanied by steady rain and the dinging of incoming messages, I was still on 101 at six-ten, barely having reached South San Francisco. Tiburon is nearly fifty miles from Palo Alto, and I'd hoped to make it in an easy hour and forty-five minutes. But between the heavy rain and Bay Area rush hour traffic, it may as well have been five thousand miles away.

In the interim, Frank kept me updated. No prototype chip. The gizmo directed them to an empty black ring box sitting on the floor of the garage, but nothing inside. Bummer.

Ty Deavers had been found banging on drums at the San Francisco Airport and having a fine time. His passport read today's date for entry into the good ol' U.S. of A. Furthermore, about twenty witnesses said he never left the bandstand once he got off the plane from Germany, collected his luggage, and cleared customs. Another bummer.

Deavers had no idea why there should be a dead woman in his house, who she was, or why his van – which was reported stolen by his housekeeper three days before – was found back in his garage. Frank was still working on the identity of the woman. Not to repeat myself, but I was so bummed.

I hit speed dial. Frank answered before it rang once. It was like he was on speed pickup.

"Good timing for your call. I've got an update. Rameen Patel has been arrested for Collier's murder."

"What?" I nearly drove off the road in shock. "Are you kidding me?"

"No. Broas has something. Just what, he's not sharing. But it has to do with Patel's past."

I thought about what Richard just told me about Patel's juvenile record. And then there was the tense relationship between him and Collier. Secrets everywhere, but did any of them lead to murder?

"And what about the other deaths, Frank? Does Chief Broas think Patel did those?"

"He's not saying, Lee, and it's not in my jurisdiction. But the woman's death is, and we think we know who she is."

"Really, who?"

"Sharise's stand-in and Ty Deavers girlfriend, June Mitchell. Her fingerprints aren't on file, but she fits the description; five foot six, brunette, mid to late twenties. She flew back to the states a couple of days ago. Her landlady says she hasn't seen her since last night."

"No pictures of her?"

"Not that we can find."

207

"A girl in show business, Frank? No headshots? No selfies? What are the odds?"

"Before she met Sharise, she worked in a drugstore. That's where the singer found her and offered her the job as her stand-in. Only time she's been on camera that we know of is in costume as Sharise's stand in. Deavers gave us a picture of June from his phone, but it's out of focus; hard to see her features."

"Where is Deavers now?"

"At the morgue, identifying or not identifying the body. I'll know any minute. He's cooperating, for all the good it's doing us. We can't get him on a thing yet. But he knows something. I don't know what it is, but he's terrified."

"Frank, one thing about being stuck in traffic is that in between swearing my head off and giving rude drivers the finger, I've had time to think."

"I don't like the sound of that. And I don't care for the finger idea, either."

"You need to get another warrant, hire yourself an arborist expert in deadly tropical trees, and give Collier's private, two-acre rainforest a going over. I'll bet you a pair of Christian Louboutin shoes you're going to find a borrachero scopolamine tree, even if it's not on Collier's inventory."

"I don't know who this Louboutin is, but I'm getting all too familiar with the borrachero trees. You really think one of those trees is there?"

"Yeah, I do. The answer to all of this is that one of those trees is here in the Bay Area, hidden in plain sight. *Hijo de perro!*" A car cut me off, almost forcing me into the next lane. My tires slid against the wet pavement for a moment then straightened out. Meanwhile, Frank was yelling.

"Hey, watch your language. I know what that means in English."

"You should be here on 101 arresting some of these reckless drivers. Where's a cop when you need one?"

"Avoiding you."

"Ha ha. And check on the employees. You might find somebody very unlikely working in that compound."

"I've already done that. But I will try to find that tree. I'll set it up for tomorrow. It's pitch black outside now."

"And raining. Here's a thought, you might want to send a couple of officers to the Collier Compound. Get someone to stay with Skye Collier and Katie Hall tonight. I'd feel better if someone's with them."

He paused. I could hear his hesitation over the phone. "What's going on you're not telling me?"

"Let's just err on the side of precaution. We don't know everything there is to know yet."

"That's for sure. I've got a better idea. I'll take them into protective custody. Put them up in a hotel, incommunicado. A possibility of one of those trees being on the premises gives me enough reason, at least for twenty-four hours."

"Have to hang up, Frank. I need to call a lady about why I'm late."

"What are you late for? Where are you going?"

"Can't hear you, Frank. Every other word is cutting out." I disconnected. Gawd, I love these cell phones.

Sharise answered on the eighth ring, just when I thought it would go into her voicemail.

"Yes?" Her voice still sounded musical but on the bored side.

"Sharise, it's me, Lee Alvarez. I've hit a little traffic – actually a lot – and I'm still on the south side of San Francisco. Sorry. If it's too late, maybe we can make it tomorrow. I'm sure you're dealing with jetlag."

"No, I'm fine, Lee. I'm looking forward to meeting you."

"And I, you."

"I tell you what, Lee. Why don't we meet at a little restaurant I know in San Francisco? Split the difference? There's a place on Post called The Oceania. Ever heard of it?"

"I've been in a couple of times for drinks."

"I'll call and make a reservation for seven-thirty for two. They know me there."

"Glad you don't mind braving the rain. By the way, do you have any pictures of your stand-in, June Mitchell?"

"June? I think I have one either on my phone or my IPad that we took at a party in the south of France. Why?"

"Could you bring it along? I'd like to see what she looks like."

There was a pause. "I'll look for it."

"Thanks. See you at seven-thirty."

I disconnected, stared out at the pouring rain, and the bumper to bumper cars. This was going to be a most interesting night.

Something new will always be the source
of growth in Silicon Valley.
Steve Jurvetson

Chapter Twenty-eight

I arrived at The Oceania Restaurant around seven-twenty. I opted to leave the car with the curb valet service even though it cost twenty dollars plus tip. Rain, wind, and chilly though it was, there was a festive air in the City. Holiday lights were everywhere, sparkling in the heavy downpour.

A soggy Santa tried to stay dry under a nearby building's overhang, while ringing his bell for donations. Wrapping my coat about me, I slung the tote bag over my shoulder, popped up my umbrella, and hurried to him. I dropped a twenty into the bucket. If I had that much to spend on valet parking, I had it for charity, as well.

Santa gave me a surprised but pleased look and renewed his vigor with the bell. He was a small man, not quite as tall as me. His hands were red and chapped from the weather. The one holding the bell was white at the knuckles. I pulled off my lined black leather gloves.

"Hey, Santa, you look like you could use these."

I proffered them to him and watched his face light up. He had very twinkling blue eyes. No wonder he was picked for a Santa.

"Lady, I sure could. It's freezing out here."

"Then here you go." I dropped them into his outstretched hand. He laughed a phlegmy laugh and I smelled a bit of holiday cheer on his breath.

"Thank you, Miss. Merry Christmas."

"You're welcome, Santa. And backatcha."

Despite the weather, the streets were bustling with cars and sidewalks were filled with merry-making people. Christmas was just four days away. Standing under Oceania's awning and oiling my now naked hands, I wished I felt more in tune with the season. But them's the breaks, kid. Ho, ho, ho.

I turned around and looked at the three huge wreaths wearing plum and lime green ornaments hanging in the plate glass windows of the restaurant. Somewhat cheered, I opened the door and pushed my way through revelers to the maître d' podium, and waited in a short line.

Happy hour at The Oceania is a good deal. I've taken advantage of it myself a couple of times when in the City. Dozens of men and women at the bar and surrounding small tables were doing the mating call, while drinking specialties of the house and eating yummy appetizers. I remembered the last time Gurn and I ate, drank, and laughed at one of the tables. I felt a pang of longing, as I followed the man's directions to Sharise's table.

The singer was waiting for me at a table for two in the corner of the room, next to a Christmas tree, also decorated in the plum and lime theme. Facing me, she gave a wave as I approached. I didn't think she knew what I looked like, but that's the internet for you. There's nobody who isn't on it if you know where to look for them. Except for June Mitchell. Interesting, that.

As I maneuvered the last few feet of the room, I took the opportunity to appraise the woman. She was amazingly beautiful and very young looking. I did a quick recap and remembered she gave birth to Skye when she was barely seventeen. That made her thirty-one, three years younger than me, although she didn't look a day older than twenty-four or twenty-five. I was aging by the minute.

Sharise's pale blonde hair, usually seen in sausage curls, was straight and shiny, hanging mid-way to her waist.

Framed by long, dark lashes, turquoise colored eyes shot out at you, unusual and captivating, even from a distance. A high forehead and sculptured cheekbones completed the flawless look. Then she smiled and the wow factor went up by a hundred percent. Stunning white teeth – oh, please be capped – gleamed from between smiling, rose colored lips.

Okay, I had to face it. Here was a woman and a half compacted into one. It was like watching the winner of the Miss Universe pageant, only up close and personal.

"Hello, Lee." Within those two words warmth, friendship, and sincerity exuded. Swept up by it all, I was surprised she didn't continue with, 'And if I could do one thing during my reign, it would be to bring peace and goodwill to all. And to become a brain surgeon'.

"Hello, Sharise." I smiled back at her, radiating I hoped, at least two-watts of personality compared to her stadium lighting. I shorted out.

My nose twitched as the scent of her signature perfume wafted from across the table toward me. Even in the relatively open space of the restaurant, my eyes started to water. The scent, like her, was over the top. It came to me then that I hadn't smelled the perfume on anyone else in many months.

Long fingers ending with rose-colored nails gestured for me to sit across from her. I removed my coat, handed it off a waiter who showed up out of nowhere, and sat down. Before I could say anything she gave me an appreciative stare.

"My goodness, Lee, no one told me how beautiful you are in person. Online photos don't do you justice. If I didn't know you were a private detective, I would have said you were a model." She continued to gush. "And those eyes! Are they really lavender? Or are you wearing contacts?"

"No, they're mine." I have to admit, I stuttered under the excessive brown-nosing. "I don't wear contacts."

"Well, I'm jealous." She leaned forward, almost conspiratorially. "You see, I do wear them. My natural eye color is really just plain old blue, but don't tell anyone."

213

"If the subject ever comes up, I promise to be mum."

I tried to smile winningly. She smiled at me as if I was her new BFF.

On the table before me was a small picture of a brunette. Anxious to get back to familiar territory, I picked it up and scrutinized it.

"I take it this is a picture of June Mitchell. She doesn't look much like you."

"With a stand-in it's more the total package. She and I are the same height and body structure. When she wears my wigs and costumes, we look enough alike for lighting calls and blocking, a very time consuming thing. I prefer to be writing or practicing the piano in my dressing room."

I studied the picture again. "She does sort of have your smile. Not as much voltage, but similar. May I keep this?"

Without waiting for an answer, I slipped it into the pocket of my skirt. Resting my hands in my lap, I pretended I was the proper lady I hope someday to be.

"Of course," Sharise said after the fact. "I printed it out for you. I took the liberty of ordering us champagne cocktails. They make a good one here."

She raised a hand and the waiter came to the table with two champagne flutes filled with pink, bubbling liquid. He must have been standing nearby waiting for her signal. A tall, angular man of middle age, he looked at Sharise adoringly. He set one of the festive glasses in front of me, never taking his eyes off her. He placed Sharise's before her as if it were the Silver Chalice.

"Thank you, Mason. We'll order in a minute."

She gave him a dazzling smile. I thought he was going to faint. He nodded and left as Sharise turned to me, lifted her glass in a toast, never missing a beat.

"Merry Christmas."

I lifted my glass, returning the toast. "The same to you." I took a sip and felt an instant buzz. "Wow, I need to be careful. I should have some food in my stomach."

"We'll order in a minute." She, too, took a sip then paused, smiling at me. "So what is it you want to know about David and me?"

"When was the last time you saw him?"

She set down her glass, turning her mind to deep thinking. "I'm not sure. Maybe five or six years. I can't even remember the last time I saw him in person."

"And yet he kept scrupulous notes on where you were all the time, even to your current tour in Europe." I watched her carefully.

"His was a different type of personality." She shrugged. "His mind went in that direction. He had the ability to keep tabs on people and so he did."

"That didn't bother you?"

"Of course it did." Her answer was sharp, taking on an indignant tone, which she backed off of immediately. "I was used to him getting into my personal space. I didn't like it, but there wasn't much I could do about it."

She paused, twirling the fluted drink on the table. She picked it up and took a healthy slug then looked at me.

"You know, he raped me. Not just once, but many times."

I was a little taken aback by the abruptness of the statement. "David Collier raped you?"

"My father worked for Laser One, David's first big financial success. I was sixteen. It was this time of year, a Christmas party. I went with my parents. David saw me. He was forty-one. My father fawned over him; his big, important boss. And I was hardly more than a kid. It was the first time I ever had any alcohol other than a little wine."

She took a longer drink. "Anyway, to make a long story short, David took me home and I woke up the next morning in his bed. He admitted to me years later he'd given me Rohypnol. You know what that is?"

"A date rape drug."

215

She looked at me. "And it wasn't the only time. You need to do some catching up," she said, gesturing to my barely touched cocktail. "Drink up."

I obeyed.

Sharise raised her hand again and Mason showed up out of nowhere.

"I'll order you another one."

"I really shouldn't. I have a long drive back to Palo Alto."

"Don't be silly. Champagne cocktails are nothing more than sugar and Angostura bitters."

"All right. But I should have some food."

"Mason, bring us two more of these and some caviar. You know the one I like, Royal Osetra. And your seafood bisque." She looked at me. "Have you had their bisque?" I shook my head. "You'll love it."

Mason said nothing but nodded obsequiously before leaving. Sharise turned back to me, her smile fading.

"My father was promoted the next day. My mother bought herself a new BMW, the one she'd always wanted. Now don't get me wrong, I was flattered at first. David took me to Paris the following weekend and bought me an entire wardrobe. He wined and dined me. I got to ride around in his chauffeur driven limousine. But after about a month, I wanted to be with kids my own age, you know? Meanwhile, I got pregnant. When I told my parents, suddenly I was getting married to a man the same age as my father. I never even finished high school."

Sharise took a healthy slug of the drink. After what she'd told me, so did I. She went on, her voice quiet but razor-sharp.

"Even at sixteen I knew the man was obsessed with me. He had to know where I went, what I did, every minute of every day. I couldn't have any friends or social life. Being an inventor, he used things to track my movements, even when I was as big as a house with Skye. I thought I'd kill myself."

Sharise stopped talking when Mason arrived with the caviar sitting amidst crushed ice in a blue bowl. On his heels, another waiter set down a silver platter containing a dish of tiny pancakes. He was followed by a third waiter with smaller bowls of chopped hard boiled eggs, lemon wedges, diced white onions, and crème fraîche. When you pay nearly three hundred dollars for fish eggs, I guess they deliver it with a lot of pomp and circumstance. Everything but the king's men blowing trumpets.

"Help yourself," Sharise said, with the gracious gesture of a caring hostess.

Starving, I picked up a pancake, slathered it with cream and dropped some chopped egg on it.

"Don't you like caviar?" Sharise looked into my face with concern.

"Not really. It's a little salty for me."

"Try this. You'll see Osetra isn't very salty at all. It's quite tasty. Put some on your blini then squeeze lemon on top."

I did so. She watched me then followed suit. We both took large bites of the pancakes at the same time, almost eating them in one bite. Sharise smiled at me.

"Delicious, isn't it?"

I nodded and took the last bite, finishing off the small pancake. So did Sharise. We both reached for another blini and began the ritual again.

"How do you feel?" Sharise leaned in, studying my every move.

"Feel?"

She nodded.

"I feel...I feel...I don't know, okay, I guess."

Sharise sat back, grinning. "You know, Lee, when we finish the caviar, why don't we skip dinner? We should go back to my house. Tiburon's not too far from here. We can have an uninterrupted conversation. I think you would like that."

"Yes, if you want me to."

"Good." She turned to Mason, who had been hovering nearby holding the champagne cocktails. "Thank you, Mason, but please cancel the bisque."

"Yes, ma'am." The waiter set the two flutes in front of each of us. Sharise opened her bag, pulled out a credit card, and handed it to him.

"Here's my card. Charge whatever to it. And give yourself a thirty percent tip. Merry Christmas to you and your family."

His face lit up. "Thank you, Madame, and Merry Christmas to you, too." After he bowed and scraped a little more, he left the table. Sharise returned her attention to me.

"Where's your car, Lee?"

"Right outside. I left it with the valet service."

"Finish up your drink and the food. Then we'll go. You'll follow me to Tiburon in your car."

"All right."

I slathered another pancake with caviar and crème fraîche and popped it into my mouth. Then my coat appeared as mysteriously as it had vanished. I slipped into it with the help of the second waiter, who also handed me my umbrella. Sharise's jacket was being held for her, a bright red wool, with large gold buttons. On her it looked smashing. On me, I would have looked like one of Santa's taller elves.

The rain had become little more than a heavy mist. After handing the valet both car checks, Sharise turned to me. A smile coated her face like soft wax.

"Now, Lee, you are to follow me home. I'll drive slow. Did you put the address into your GPS as I instructed?"

"Yes."

"Let me see." I offered her the phone and she checked it over. "Good. Then you won't get lost, will you?"

"No."

"And you are to stay on the phone with me the entire time, understand?"

"Yes."

"If another call comes in, don't answer it, understand?"

"Yes."

"And don't stop your car for any reason, understand?"

"Yes."

"Then let's go, Lee Alvarez. You're mine now."

Running a real business is exacting, daunting, repetitive work. Even in Silicon Valley.
Ben Stein

Chapter Twenty-nine

2752 Mar East Street was a one-of-a-kind modern four bedroom, five bath, bay front home on Mar East in Tiburon. Massive dollar signs, please.

The skies had cleared considerably during the forty-minute trip to Tiburon, as they often do this time of year. I got out of my car to see panoramic views of Angel Island, San Francisco, and the Golden Gate Bridge lighting up the sky. I stood for a moment, listening to water lapping at a dock on the bay side of the house.

"Come on, Lee." Sharise called to me from the entrance to the house. "You'll get a better view from inside the house."

I stepped over the threshold, both hands in my coat pockets, and past the waiting Sharise. She held out her hand.

"Give me your phone."

I complied. Drawn to an unobstructed view of the San Francisco Bay and the City skyline seen through floor to ceiling windows, I crossed into the large living room. To the left was a hallway leading to the bedrooms. To the right was a six-sided, enclosed terrarium where several medium sized trees were flourishing. Sharise's voice caused me to turn around and face her.

"Now I'm going to make you a nice little drink. Wouldn't you like that?"

"Another dose of Devil's Breath? Lethal enough to make me take a long walk off that short pier out there?" Before she could answer, I walked over to the enclosure. "This must be where the borrachero scopolamine tree hangs out."

"What? Sorry?" She stuttered in her surprise. "What's that you said?"

"At first I thought it was in Collier's rainforest, but it occurred to me his is overseen by a barrage of caretakers. They'd have spotted it in a hot minute. At the very least it would be on the inventory list. I'll bet you know how to take care of your tree. Everything seems to be doing just fine in there."

"I thought you --"

"You thought I was under the spell of Devil's Breath, courtesy of June's photo? No, no. I figured it would be chancy in a public restaurant if you dropped a dose in a drink or blew some in my face. You might be overseen. But slathering a photo with some beforehand? Now there's the ticket. So I covered my hands with Vaseline right before I came into the restaurant. Petroleum jelly; impenetrable. And after I touched June's photo, I used a hand sanitizer from my bag, just to be on the safe side."

I walked toward her, displaying my hands as I talked.

"I was hoping you'd do something like that. That's why I asked you for the photo. The cops are going to love what's on it, I'm sure. What was the plan, Sharise? Bring me here to drown me in the bay? Or have me jump off the Golden Gate Bridge before they put the preventive netting up? That's supposed to happen any day now."

After a brief hesitation, Sharise made a quick move to run away. I made a quicker one and withdrew the revolver from the pocket of my coat. Aiming it at her, I stepped closer, but still kept my distance. I didn't want anything blown in my face.

"Uh-uh. Stay right where you are. Don't make any more sudden moves or I'll be forced to shoot you. I know how

Devil's Breath works and five people are dead from it. You're not making it six."

Sharise froze for a moment, probably considering her options. I took the opportunity to withdraw another phone from my pocket. The rock singer stared in disbelief.

"The one I gave you was a throwaway. This is my real phone, linked to D. I.'s mainframe, as well as PAPD. Our entire conversation, since I walked into the restaurant, has been recorded. Before I came inside your house, I texted Frank to call the Marin Police Department."

I gestured with my Tomcat to one of her forest green leather chairs. "Let's sit down and wait for the police. They should be here in about five minutes."

She sat down slowly, never taking her eyes off me. I sat across from her on the matching sofa, leaned forward, and pushed a tall flower arrangement on the coffee table aside. I, too, wanted an unimpeded view of my adversary. I was taking no chances. Sharise smiled suddenly and leaned forward, as well.

"I don't know what you're talking about. We were just having a little fun, you and I."

"Killing people isn't fun. At least, not to most of us."

"And how did I kill these five people you mentioned? I was in Germany until this morning."

"No you weren't. Your stand-in was. You and June switched passports. You arrived in San Francisco three days ago, disguised as June. With a brunette wig on, you look like her or close enough for jazz. All you needed was Ty's help in making everyone believe you were still in Germany syncing the movie. But it wasn't you. It was June wearing a blonde wig, your clothes, and imitating your mannerisms. June looked and acted enough like you to fool people who'd never met the real Sharise before."

Sharise scowled at me, her features turning hard and ugly. "I see I should have taken care of you first, before David. But I had just learned about your being hired that day.

222

Unfortunately, it was all set up with David. He was so eager for me to meet him, especially as I'd returned early from Europe just to be with him." Her tone was mocking and churlish. "I'm sure you figured out by now he and I had gotten together a few times in Switzerland at my suggestion. He thought I was softening, planning to go back to him. For a smart man David could be such an idiot."

"So was it the same scenario as you tried with me?"

"Not quite. We met at the Sunnyvale house. He was in the garage working on the plastic container for some idiotic party he'd planned on sabotaging. Always trying to bend people to his will. I showed up disguised as a cowgirl."

"Ah! The red wig," I interjected.

"Yes, this time I wore the red wig. I told him I didn't want to be recognized. He thought it was exciting, having a clandestine meeting with his ex-wife dressed up like someone else. We had champagne to toast the occasion, and I put the drug in his drink when he wasn't looking; much more than I put on the photo for you. When he was under, he did what he was told."

"Which was to go to Read-Out and hang himself. With a little help from you."

"But first I made him give me the prototype and the codes to the garage so I could do the rest."

"It wasn't enough you were going to kill him, you wanted to destroy his reputation?"

"Why not? He was destroying mine. His wealth was a weapon he used to punish people he couldn't control. He told me he was going to obliterate the business he helped create, just because they dared to go against him. He didn't care about the workers or their families. All he cared about was himself. But his ego suited my purposes. It made him vulnerable. So I decided to embarrass his memory, make him look like the vicious, vindictive man he really was; a total asshole."

223

For a short breath of time a true sociopath revealed herself to me. Or maybe she was just plain nuts.

"But always in the back of my mind I knew I needed to worry about you, Lee Alvarez."

"What about me?"

"I was told you were smart. And the downside to being smart, is being cocky."

"Funny, I was about to say the same thing about you, Sharise."

She laughed. "I knew the map of the East Bay I left in David's office would eventually lead you to his parent's home."

"It did."

"I wanted to take care of you there, but you arrived sooner than I thought. I missed you by minutes. Those stupid boys, I never should have trusted them to do the job. They failed miserably." Her demeanor changed suddenly. She folded her arms. "You know, this is a form of entrapment. My lawyers --"

"Your lawyers are going to have a tough time keeping you out of jail."

"You can't prove anything. They will make your taped phone call inadmissible. So I have one of the sleeping sickness trees. So what? They're not illegal."

"No, just deadly. But your biggest mistake was killing Ty Deavers' girlfriend, June. He's really scared. Any minute he'll be talking his head off."

"His word against mine? I don't think so. I say he's lying. There's no proof of anything."

"The German police have corroborated that June's fingerprints are all over that studio."

I actually made that up. I had no idea what the Germans did or didn't do, but I went on with the lie.

"If she was supposedly here in the States, how did June's fingerprints wind up in the German movie studio? Nobody was supposed to be there but you and Ty Deavers."

Sharise sat back in the leather chair and thought for a moment. Then let out a small laugh.

"She was supposed to keep the gloves on I gave her at all times. Silly girl. So you're saying I've been foiled by modern science?"

"Not so modern. But very efficient."

She hesitated then leaned forward again. "In that case, should I tell you the truth?"

"It would be refreshing."

"June was greedy. She wanted more money, much more. And the reason I did all of this was so I could have David's money, not hand it over to someone else. So I met her at the airport when she and Ty got in this morning. When he went to play drums with his buddy, June and I changed identities back to ourselves in the ladies room. I gave her some Devil's Breath and brought her back to Ty's. Then I gave her more of the drug, enough to finish her off. I've gotten quite good at knowing just the right dosage."

"I'll bet you have."

"And a little goes a long way."

"But why kill her there?"

"I thought if she was found in Ty's house dead, he'd be accused of killing her then I'd be rid of them both. I tried to set it up that way, and I'm usually very good at these sorts of things."

"Two birds with one stone."

"I didn't count on him not doing what I told him. Imagine, sitting in on a gig all day and having an unbreakable alibi. And before that, stupid little June had to go and take off her gloves in the German studio." Shaking her head, she let out a self-deprecating laugh. "It just goes to show; you can't trust anybody to do what you tell them."

"Did you chemically alter the pods yourself?"

"I've turned one of my bedrooms into a lab. It's not hard. When the tour was in Bogotá, I came across some very interesting characters that were willing to help me put a lab together here in Tiburon. They even helped me smuggle in a tree."

"It sounds like you were planning this a long time. But then it must have been tough having an ex-husband so controlling and powerful."

"You have no idea." Her face lost its color. "Six-months ago he bought my contract from my producer and told me I would never perform on television again. He had already taken over my iTunes contract. Now that I'd become somebody, he was systematically destroying my career and there was nothing I could do about it."

She stared at the gun in my hand, almost as if seeing it for the first time.

"You don't know what it was like; having a man so rich he could buy and sell your life. You think people cared about what he was doing to me? All he had to do was write a check for a hundred thousand dollars, a million dollars, or threaten to put them out of business. What I wanted, my life, meant nothing to him. He had so much money. It was like a sickness. I finally realized it was him or me. Can't you see that? I had to kill him. Even giving up my child to him wasn't enough to buy my freedom!"

"But what about the others? Like Jake Gold?" My voice was harsher sounding than I intended. I reined in my feelings.

She was quiet for a moment, her face mirroring a myriad of thoughts and memories. For as much as she'd been in control before, she now lost it, bursting into tears.

"I had to do it. It was the price for being free. Don't you see? Can't you see? It was David's fault. The man was a monster."

Screaming, her arms flailed in the air in tune with her emotions. She ranted on.

"And I needed the money. Thanks to him, I'm losing money with the tour. It's all so expensive. He wouldn't stop no matter how much I begged him. He was strangling me, cutting off my contacts and money sources. I needed to be free. It was like I couldn't breathe!"

She covered her hands with her face, sobbing into them. I watched her in stunned silence. The next thing happened so fast, I wasn't prepared for it.

She uncovered her face and there was a small blowgun in her mouth. Maybe she had it on her the whole time; maybe it was hidden in the pillows of the chair. She leaned forward and blew a dart straight at my face.

I've probably failed more often than anybody else in
Silicon Valley. Those don't matter. I don't remember the
failures. You remember the big successes.
Vinod Khosla

Chapter Thirty

More of a reaction than conscious thought, I moved my head to the side. The dart landed in my hair, a puff of white powder releasing on impact. I could feel some on my neck and cheek.

Sharise, meanwhile, bolted from the house. I sprang up and found the kitchen, ducking the powdered side of my head under rushing water from the sink. How much was absorbed in the few seconds before I located the kitchen, I had no idea.

I raced outside. Sharise's car was still in the driveway, but there were noises on the dimly lit deck leading out to a small dock. I headed for it, stumbling in the unfamiliar terrain, trying to avoid what small amount of light there was. It's a good thing I did.

A shot rang out close enough for me to feel the spray of dirt when the bullet hit the ground. I crouched down behind a railing and took the safety off my gun. If this was the way we were going to play it, fine by me.

A motor started. I took a chance and looked through the railing toward the sounds at the end of the dock. There was the silhouette of a sailboat, mast reaching up to a dark sky, backlit by the lights of the Golden Gate Bridge.

I'd been thrown by the sound of the motor, but many sailboats have them for when there's no wind. A moving figure was casting off. It had to be Sharise.

"Oh, great," I muttered. "Another boat. Why do all my cases involve people on boats? I hate boats. And where are the stupid police?"

I put the safety back on the Tomcat, shoved it in my coat pocket, screwed my courage to the sticking place – wherever that is - and ran for all I was worth. Even when the dock ended, I kept running. I flung myself at Sharise, Superman style, and we crashed to the floor of the cockpit in a tussle.

The small sailboat dipped and swayed under our weight. Sharise gave me a push away and the strength of it surprised me. The small of my back hit something that nearly knocked the wind out of me. I'd read somewhere Sharise was a Pilates fiend. Time to be respectful of her craft.

The moon came out suddenly from behind rainclouds. It was like someone had thrown a spotlight on the entire bay. I saw the boat drifting away from the dock, as much from the wind and water currents, as the putt-putt of the motor. I also saw Sharise reaching for her gun lying on a cushioned seat.

I stood, trying to shift my weight for a maneuver to kick the gun out of her hand, Karate style. Impeded by my coat, wet surfaces, wind, and the up and down motion of the boat, I couldn't seem to get it going. They say a poor carpenter always blames his tools, but I said to hell with it. I pulled my arm back, while lunging forward. Then I punched Sharise on the jaw as hard as I could.

When writer Ian Fleming puts 007 in a brawl, he never alludes to what the punch does to the puncher as well as the punchee. Yes, Sharise fell to the deck like a rock. But I almost dropped to the deck myself. My right hand felt like I'd broken every bone in it. The sharpness of the pain was so intense I'd have paid more attention to it, if had it not been for the boom coming right at me. Now who was the idiot who untied that?

In the Internet world, especially in Silicon Valley, everyone is at the ready all the time, and turnaround is relatively short, if not instant.
Chad Hurley

Chapter Thirty-one

One thing I've learned about a sailboat, other than to avoid them like the plague, is don't think you're going to outmatch a boom. Even on a small seventeen footer like this turkey, booms are one powerful thing. When they start moving, they're not stopping for nobody, no how.

The boom rammed me midsection, carrying me out over the water. My Jimmy Choos, which I had just broken in, thank you, came off with the impact. Feeling the salty spray of San Francisco Bay beneath my bare feet, I wondered if it was too late to become a nurse. This detective stuff was getting old.

My alacrity for swinging my legs up and over, and straddling the boom was second to none. Even I was impressed with my agility. As I hung over the water on the boom, the boat tilted precariously toward me. Let's face it. I still weighed around a hundred and thirty pounds. Between the wind, waves, and being off-balance, the boat could capsize at any minute. And it was fr-fr-freezing.

On a positive note, I had changed to slacks at the fitters so at least I wasn't dealing with a skirt. I scooted in, while the boom bobbed and bounced like a bucking bronco. I lost my grip once and toppled to the side.

Hugging the boom, my new best friend, I tried to catch my breath. I wrapped my legs around it and hand over hand, continued underneath toward the relative safety of the boat.

The whole thing probably took less than two minutes but felt like an eternity.

All the while I was waiting for Sharise to wake up and shoot me or some enterprising shark to break water for a late evening snack. After all, the island isn't called Tiburon for nothing, named in honor of the Great Whites patrolling its waters.

A maverick wave hit just as I slid off the boom and onto the deck. Thrown off balance, my foot landed on one of the many metal cleats that live there, and I heard or felt a snap in my ankle.

I dropped to the floor of the cockpit in a crouching position with a screech. The boom grazed my head as it passed over. No matter how much pain I was in, the first thing I had to do was tie the boom down or it was going to continue its wild ride over and around the boat.

It's called securing the boom to a preventer, but I'm just showing off. I learned this jargon and how to do it from a guy I used to date who loved sailboats more than life itself. In fact, he's sailing somewhere off the shores of Tahiti, currently with a girl young enough to be his daughter. I dodged a bullet on that one.

Fortunately, the moon was still out and at least I could see. My right hand throbbed like crazy, and my left ankle felt like someone was prodding at it with a hot poker.

I ignored them both as I waited for the boom to rock and roll itself close enough so I could secure the preventer to the block. Miraculously, the winds died down for a second, the boom was in position and I secured it...or gybed it...or something.

I heard Sharise moan. Was she waking up? I remembered her gun, crawled on my hands and knees to find it on a cushion, and threw it overboard. Maybe I should have saved it for evidence, but I had no idea how to put the safety on and was a little busy. I tried not to worry about how hard I'd hit

Sharise. Although she still hadn't moved, the moaning gave me hope she would be okay.

I looked up to see we were heading directly for one of the many buoys in the bay. Minding its own business, it blinked little warning lights about its location telling you to Stay Away Or Else.

Oh, come on, guys; it's just one thing after another with a boat. That's why I hate them.

I hobbled to the tiller and turned the rudder starboard. I think. I'm never sure about my left and right on a boat. But we were no longer on a collision course with the buoy. Finally, I found the running lights and throttle.

Thank you, ex-boyfriend, for teaching me the basics of boating.

In the distance I heard police sirens. The sounds became louder and louder as I steered us back to Sharise's dock. Within minutes four policemen ran onto the dock guns drawn, looking toward the boat. I couldn't wait to get this tub back to shore and hand off Sharise to them. I was tired, drenched, and body parts were killing me. I'd had this Captain Ahab routine up to the gills.

Out of the blue, I felt a shove in the middle of my back that sent me sprawling onto the deck. I rolled over and managed to rise to a squat position. Lit by the ever-nearing deck lights, I saw Sharise's face, furious and deadly, looking down at me. At the same time both she and I noticed a long handled grabbing hook, used to haul tie lines out of the water, clamped beside the seat cushions.

We both lunged for it, but Sharise got there first. I tried to stay upright, but it was dicey with only my one good foot to support me. I fell backward and grabbed at the tiller to stay upright. Meanwhile, I could hear one of the policemen shouting something. I couldn't understand the words but the tone sure meant business.

Unfortunately, I was too preoccupied to reply. Sharise stood before me holding the grabbing hook like it was a baseball bat. And she was looking at me like my head was the ball, and she was about to make a home run.

I shrank back as far from her as I could on the small boat. I'd like to say I commended my soul to God, but actually I thought about Gurn and Tugger, not necessarily in that order.

"Stop! Drop the weapon immediately or I'll shoot."

The commanding words of one of the policemen reverberated in the air, clear and concise. He stood, along with the other officers, on the deck at the waterline, now not more than ten feet away.

"This is the Tiburon Police Department. Drop the weapon."

He was an older man, large and imposing, and carried the weight of his years and position with him. He aimed his firearm directly at Sharise. I could have kissed him.

"I mean business, lady. Put the weapon down or I'll shoot. This is the Tiburon Police Department," he repeated.

Sharise looked in the officer's direction then back at me, deciding what to do. Meanwhile, my mind raced. Was he going to shoot her or was she going to cream me?

Please, please, please shoot the bitch.

Just when I thought I was a goner, she dropped the metal hook, which clattered with a metallic sound to the deck. Before I could breathe a sigh of relief, the singer dove over the side of the boat into the dark water, disappearing into its murky depth.

We who work in technology have nurtured an especially rare gift:
the opportunity to effect change at an unprecedented scale and rate.
Technology, community, and capitalism combine to make
Silicon Valley the potential epicenter of vast positive change.
Justin Rosenstein

Chapter Thirty-two

At four-thirty in the morning I awoke to the noise of someone entering the apartment. What with police reports, trips to the Emergency Room, yada yada, I didn't get home until midnight. Helped upstairs by Tío and Mom, I collapsed on the bed and was asleep at twelve-oh-five.

I didn't need someone breaking in during the early hours of the morning. Putting aside the fact that I'd had it, I was in no shape for battling a burglar. One hand was swollen to the size of a catcher's mitt and my sprained ankle could only be stood upon with the help of support wrap, crutches, and Advil®.

I turned on the light with my good hand then reached under the pillow for the Tomcat. Releasing the safety, I aimed the gun at the door, and yelled out.

"Listen, if you are Sharise or anyone else, fair warning. I have a gun. And the mood I'm in, I'm going to shoot first and ask questions later. So just turn around and leave, please. Save us both a lot of trouble."

"Lee, darling, it's me," someone said from outside the bedroom door. "Don't shoot. It's me."

"Gurn?"

I sat upright, paralyzed by the familiar voice. Gurn appeared in the doorway, still dressed in fatigues. He dropped his canvas bag on the floor and took off his cap. His face was scratched and his right eye was multi-colored and puffy. Over his right eyebrow was a cut, closed with a butterfly clamp. He smiled his beautiful lopsided smile, as he limped toward the bed, took the revolver from my frozen hand, and set it on the nightstand. Then we both spoke simultaneously, as we reached for each other.

"*Dios mio*, what happened to you?"

"What happened to your hand, darling?"

We went into an embrace. I felt his warmth and love, and began to cry in the crook of his neck.

"Darling, darling Lee. Don't cry. I told you I'd be back. Shhh, darling, shhh. Don't cry."

"I can't help it," I sobbed. "I'm so happy."

"I'm happy, too."

We broke free and covered one another's faces with kisses. I heard plaintive meowing at our side. Baba and Tugger were vying for attention. Gurn leaned over and picked up a cat in each hand.

"Come here, you two." He hugged both cats, set Tugger down, and rubbed the side of his face free of scratches against Baba. "How's my second best girl?"

I could hear her purring a response in his arms. I did some purring of my own, while I looked at him. I reached out and touched one of the scratches with my fingertips.

"Your face. Your handsome, beautiful face. What happened?"

He didn't brush my question off the way he usually did. "Fortunes of War. Got a bruised heel, black eye, and several cuts out of it. Could have been a lot worse. I didn't lose any men. Who's this Sharise?"

"An escaped murderess. She's killed five people and when the police tried to apprehend her, she jumped into the Bay off Tiburon. That was several hours ago. Oh, yeah, and she tried to kill me, too, but that's another story."

235

He dropped Baba to the bed, his face taking on a look of surprise and appreciation. "You do get around, don't you?"

I gave him the highlights of the past few days then reached out for a long and lingering kiss. "You're here. You're really here. But you're back earlier than the admiral said. How did that happen? I can't believe it. Merry Christmas to me!"

Gurn laughed and stroked my cheek. "I got lucky. It went better than planned. Then there was a transporter that had space for one more and was leaving in fifteen minutes. I think Vice Admiral Saks had something to do with it. I didn't even have time to change or take a shower. But I only wanted to get back to you."

I wrapped my arms around him. "Thank you. Bless you. Bless him. I was...worried."

"I know. We'll talk about that later. There's been a development." He looked first at my swollen, black and blue hand then down at my bound ankle. "Your own fortunes of war?"

I nodded. "Sprained ankle. And the hand, well, no breaks but significant bruising. How about I give you the blow by blow when you come out of the shower?"

"Am I taking a shower?"

"A nice, long one."

"Do I smell that bad?"

"Yes."

He got up, turned away, and stripped off his jacket then his shirt. On his back were several big bruises of his own, some turning yellowish. I thought about the bruise on my back from being thrown on the metal cleat by Sharise. I suppressed the urge to laugh. Gurn turned back to me with a grin on his face.

"What?"

"Just look at the two of us. And we're walking down the aisle day after tomorrow. What a couple." I laughed again then sobered. "Actually, don't take too long a shower. Jake's funeral starts at nine. You know about that?"

"Yes, I read about it on the plane. Damn shame."

"Your parents arrive a few hours later. And in between there's something I need to do."

"Sounds like a full day."

"And then some. We should try to get some sleep."

He took off his pants and stood in his jockey shorts observing me for a time. Both cats stared up at me, as well. Gurn dropped the last of his fatigues on the floor before he spoke.

"Whatever you're involved in; it's not over yet, is it?"

"No."

"Are you going to let me help you?"

"Yes."

"I'll be out in ten minutes."

"Make it five."

I waggled my eyebrows at him. Gurn waggled his eyebrows at me. Cats, just watching.

Seed investing is the status symbol of Silicon Valley. Most people don't want Ferraris, they want a winning seed investment.
Sam Altman

Chapter Thirty-three

The next thing I knew there was a pounding on the front door. My mother called out repeatedly.

"Liana! Liana! Wake up! Something dreadful has happened."

We heard the front door open and her high heels clomping down the hallway, which was unusual. My mother is not a clomper by nature. A moment later the door to the bedroom burst open. Stiff and sore, Gurn and I untwined ourselves from each other, tried to sit up, and gaped at Mom. She stood in the doorway gaping back. She seemed so shocked, she could say nothing. Gurn spoke up.

"Good morning, Lila. What time is it?"

"Gurn, you're back. It's seven-thirty," Mom stuttered. Another first.

"Yes, ma'am. I got in early this morning."

Mom's shocked expression turned to pleasure then concern. She moved to the foot of the bed, scrutinizing Gurn like he was a flawed diamond.

"Welcome back, dear boy, but what has happened to your face?"

"Hi, Mom," I said meekly. I think I waved with my good hand.

"Just a little run in with barbed wire. I lost."

"Other than that, you are well, Gurn?"

"Yes, ma'am."

"Hi, Mom," I repeated.

"Although, you look frightful."

"Yes, ma'am."

"Not that it matters now. Nothing matters."

Mom let out a huge sigh, and sank down at the foot of the bed, disrupting Tugger and Baba's snoozing. Being the smart animals they were, they jumped off and scurried under the bed.

I looked at Mom in surprise. Since she'd entered the room her behavior was highly unusual for the Lila Hamilton Alvarez I knew. Here was a lady who believed proper etiquette was the thirteenth commandment. For her to be so overwrought as to sit down on a bed in front of a gentleman who wasn't her husband meant something beyond awful had happened. Dare I say it? Catastrophic.

"Mom, you're scaring me. What's wrong?"

"Oh, there you are, Liana." Another deep sigh exuded from the woman. "Well, I don't know any other way to tell you both. The wedding is off." She then repeated in a softer tone, "The wedding is off."

"Our wedding?"

"Yes, Liana. It's off." She held her face in her hands emitting yet another sigh.

"Excuse me," I said, turning to Gurn. "Did you call the wedding off?"

He shook his head. "Did you?"

I shook my head. We turned back to Mom.

"The bride and groom did not call the wedding off, Mom. So who did?"

And then my mother, Miss Aristocratic Palo Alto Blueblood, also known as the Ice Princess, burst into tears so strong, the bed shook. Between sobs she said,

"The church burned down!"

One of the nice things about living in Silicon Valley is that I end up at all these conferences and things, and I get to listen in on the zeitgeist.
Rick Smolan

Chapter Thirty-four

I sat back, dumbfounded. Gurn threw back the covers, thankfully wearing pajamas because that's not always the case. He hobbled to comfort my mother at the end of the bed.

"It'll be all right Lila. We'll make this all right."

Mom looked down. "What happened to your leg?"

"Bruised heel. It'll be all right in a couple of days."

I got out of bed, snatched my crutch, and limped toward my mother and husband-to-be. Mom was watching me out of the corner of her eye.

"Oh, my God. This just gets worse and worse." She turned from me to Gurn, horror written on her usually placid features. "You have scratches all over your face and a black eye --"

"Did it turn black now? I was afraid it was going to do that."

"And Liana has a black and blue hand."

"Yes, ma'am."

"And you both are lame."

"Yes, ma'am."

She looked at him. She looked at me. Then she turned her face up to the heavens.

"Why is this happening to me? Why does everything happen to me?"

240

I don't think Job could have said it better.

"We can make this all right, Mom," I said. "Just wait and see. The worst is over."

"No, it's not," she countered.

"Maybe not, but everything's going to wind up fine," I chirped.

Gurn sat down beside her and gave her a big hug. I sat down on the other side of my mother and followed suit. My crutch fell to the floor with a thud. I ignored it.

"Exactly," said Gurn, copying my chirp. "In a couple of weeks, we'll both be fine."

"That does me no good at all," Mom said. "The wedding is day after tomorrow. You two look like you should be in a hospital, not walking down the aisle, if there was an aisle to walk down, which there isn't, because the church has burned down. Well, not the entire church, just the interior. The wind blew over a candle and up it went. What wasn't destroyed by the fire was decimated by the water from the firemen's hoses."

She withdrew a lace hanky from her sleeve and delicately blew her nose into it. We each patted her gingerly on a shoulder. She shook us off, stood, and wheeled around to face us, anger usurping her sorrow.

"People are showing up for a wedding that isn't going to happen. And from all over the world."

"The world? Who's coming from the world, Mom?"

"The Governor General of Punjab. He was an old friend of your father's."

"The one with the elephant!" I turned to Gurn, wonderful childhood memories overtaking me. "When I was a kid and we went to India, I sat in a howdah on top of the elephant and rode him all around the courtyard. It was a great elephant; so gentle. I wish the General was bringing the elephant. We could have rides and --"

"Liana." Mom's voice was low and frosty, yet ironically tinged with hysteria. "Never mind the elephant. I don't want to hear another word about the elephant."

241

"Okay, Mom. No elephant, no rides, cool with me."

"Be quiet and let me think; I need to think."

"Sorry, Mom."

"We'll never live this down." Mom paced at the end of the bed, shaking her head and wringing her hands. "This is a catastrophe."

"Oh, that word," I muttered. "Everyone keeps using that word." I wracked what little of my brain was left to wrack. "Wait! I've got it! We'll move the wedding and reception here."

I looked at Gurn for approval. His eyes lit up. Or his one good eye lit up. The other remained swollen, black and blue.

"Of course," he said. "Why not?"

"There's not enough room for one hundred and fifty people." Mom thought for a moment. "Is there enough room?" She calmed down. "I suppose we could set up a tent, with tables and chairs, over the pool for the reception. But there isn't enough room for the ceremony there, as well. Where would we have that?"

"Inside the house, Mom! It'll be a little cramped; maybe they'll have to stand, but people will understand. We'll just call everybody and reroute the whole thing. We'll have to tell the padre - although he probably knows his church burned down - but the caterers and florist --"

"Most of the flowers went up with the church," Mom interrupted, picking up her pacing routine with vigor. "At my insistence, Gaston delivered them last night to store in the basement. I'd thought it would be better to have the potted plants on hand. All the water the firemen used to put out the fire flooded the basement. Gaston is livid. He'll never do another arrangement for me again."

Mom thought Gaston was a genius with cut flowers. I thought he was a blooming idiot.

She turned to us, arms opened wide in supplication. "Where are we going to get two hundred pots of gardenias by day after tomorrow? I secured all there were in the Bay Area. I struggled to find those two hundred."

"They don't have to be gardenias, Mom."

"Of course, they do," she said, inconsolable. "They're your favorite flower. I visualized the vestibule and chapel filled with pots and pots of gardenias, the scent of them filling the air, as you walked through the rose covered arch and down the aisle."

"Before everyone passed out from the smell," I murmured.

"Not to worry," Gurn put in, trying to override my aside and make things right. "I know a florist in D.C. He can fly some gardenias in and do last minute floral arrangements, if you want. I'll call him right now."

Gurn jumped up, or as close as he could come to jumping up in his condition, and reached for his phone. He headed for the living room, phone in hand, closing the door behind him. I looked at my mother, back to her hand wringing and pacing, now in double-time. I stood and tried to catch up with her, hopping in her direction holding my bad ankle off the floor.

"Mom, as long as I have Gurn, you, Richard, Tío, and my friends, I don't need gardenias. I'll limp along," I said pointing to my upheld ankle.

She stopped and faced me. "Oh, Liana, how brave."

She embraced me with enthusiasm, which threw me off balance. As I wobbled, I decided not to say anything. Here was a prickly woman on overload, if ever there was one. She broke out in a smile for the first time.

"You're right, dear. We must soldier on. What choice do we have, actually? I suppose this isn't the worst thing that can happen to a person."

"No, it isn't, Mom," I said, thinking of Skye who had a dead father and a mother who was probably in the digestive system of a Great White. Then I watched my mother switch gears into her Ruler Of The Universe mode. Stand back, everybody. Lila Hamilton Alvarez coming through.

243

"You have inspired me, Liana. I will not let this situation get the better of me. If only the Wedding Planner hadn't quit midstream. So unprofessional." Mom's self-righteous indignation filled the air.

"Mom, you were going behind her back and countermanding everything she did. And you kept telling her what to do with her other wedding. A groom has the right to wear a plaid cummerbund, if he wants."

With her selective listening feature in full swing, Mom didn't hear me.

"I know. I'll simply prevail upon all available staff at Discretionary to help out in this catastrophe."

"There's that the word again." I held up the forefinger of my working hand. "But that's a good idea. I know everybody at D. I. ...ah....Discretionary will help."

"We'll notify everyone attending of the change in location. I'll have to find a large tent, tables and chairs, but that should be no problem. I have the day before me. It will cost extra, of course." She let out a martyr's sigh before continuing. "But I accept my reversal of fortune with aplomb."

"Good girl," I murmured under my breath. Again not hearing me, Mom went on.

"Our kitchen should be large enough to accommodate the caterer. I'll hire extra people to help with the set up, too. We'll have to do a lot of rearranging of the living, dining, and family rooms to make way for the folding chairs. We can probably move the larger pieces of furniture into Gurn's new studio, except for the piano. The rest can go upstairs."

"Gurn's studio? I'd forgotten about that. Is it done?"

"Yes, yesterday afternoon. And thank goodness it's empty. Because we can't leave the furniture outside. It's raining again; predicted for the next three days." She looked up again at the ceiling. "Which is all I need."

Another Job moment, but she rallied.

244

"The bridesmaids could make their entrance down the grand staircase and through the rose archway, followed by you. Thank heaven the archway is still at Gaston's. I am so glad I had the stairs re-varnished last year --"

"Yes, down the grand staircase, just me and my crutches," I interrupted.

"Oh, dear." She looked me up and down. "We may have to accommodate your injuries for the ceremony."

"Gurn's, too. He's not walking much better than me. We could rent a couple of Segways." She stared at me. "You know, those two-wheeled, self-balancing, battery operated..." I broke off because she continued to stare. I stuttered on. "You stand on them and they cart you around."

"I am aware of what they are, Liana. I'm not having anything like that at my wedding." She tapped her chin with an ever-manicured finger. "Although your mobility does present a problem."

She looked at me and I looked at her. I grinned.

"The Governor General's elephant is looking pretty good right now, isn't it? He had a pretty nifty howdah."

Mom gave me an exasperated look. "I can't stand around here all day making jokes with you. Get dressed, Liana, and for heaven's sake, try to look presentable at Jacob's funeral. Please wear black."

"I don't have anything black. But I promise to look somber."

"Very well. Mr. and Mrs. Hanson arrive at three-thirty. Don't forget dinner at Evvia, seven-thirty."

"The rehearsal dinner, right?"

My mother's face took on the pained Job look I had come to know so well.

"No, dear. The rehearsal dinner comes after the rehearsal for the wedding. Thus, the name. Both of those events will take place tomorrow. Gurn's parents are hosting the rehearsal dinner. Tonight is the "welcome friends and family dinner," hosted by Vicki and Richard. Just once, Liana, I wish you would read the schedule."

She'd said the last bit through grinding teeth. Frankly, if you had asked me beforehand if it were possible to talk and grind your teeth at the same time, I would have said no. Live and learn.

"Mom, I promise to read it thoroughly before we pick up the Hansons. Pinky swear."

She gave me a what-am-I-going-to-do-with-her smile. I gave her an I'm-trying-my-best smile. We wound up hugging. Mother/daughter train back on track. Choo-choo.

"Now I must leave, Liana. I have my wedding to reinvent."

And with that, she turned on her heel and marched out of the room.

*In most parts of the world, starting a company that goes bust
is dubbed a 'failure.' In Silicon Valley, we call this 'gaining experience.'
We are willing to take the risks that are inherent for innovation.*
Sebastian Thrun

Chapter Thirty-five

"You going to finish that bear claw?" Gurn turned his head and glanced at me fifteen minutes into the trip to Colma. Riding in his Jeep Grand Cherokee, the one with initials after the name, was not what I think of when I conjure up the image of a Jeep. It had all the comforts of your living room, including a stereo system to rival Carnegie Hall's, and warmed, leather seats. I'm not sure this souped-up Jeep bore any resemblance to the one Eisenhower rode around Europe in during WWII.

My little '57 Chevy paled in comparison in every way. So I was glad to be in his SUV again with him driving. My right hand was so stiff I couldn't wrap it around a steering wheel without seeing stars. Nothing was broken, but it was painful to move, even though that was exactly what the doctor wanted me to do.

I was glad Gurn offered to drive. But not enough to hand over the rest of Tío's still warm from the oven bear claw.

"Yes, I am going to finish my bear claw, mister. I just set it down for a moment to get my phone from my bag to call Frank. So don't even think about it. I told you we should have taken another one."

"With Lila staring us down like that? I didn't want to hear again about how many calories they have, either. I think three thousand each is an exaggeration."

"Mom just doesn't want us to gain any weight before the wedding. As if everything else has been going along without a hitch."

At the mention of the word 'wedding' we both became silent, but smiled a little. I looked over at Gurn.

"I love you. I'm so glad you're back."

"I love you, too." He shot me his lopsided grin, the one that makes my heart flip-flop. Then his features took a more serious bend. "Lee, we need to talk about something. I have to tell you --"

He was interrupted by the ringing of my phone. I glanced at the incoming number.

"It's Frank. I have to take this. Can we talk later?"

His sweet smile returned. "Of course."

"Good morning, Frank. I was about to call you." I rushed on. "Wait a minute. Gurn's with me. I'm going to put you on speaker."

"Good morning, Gurn," Frank said, his voice booming throughout the car. "Welcome back."

"Good to be back, sir."

"Lila tells me you look about the same as our Lee does; a little rough around the edges."

Gurn laughed. "I met a ski run that didn't like me."

"Uh-huh," said Frank, clearly not buying it. "Well, wherever you're skiing these days, we're grateful to you."

"Thank you, sir."

"Any word yet on Sharise?" I was trying not to think about her, but I had done little else since she dove off the sail boat the night before.

"Here's something, Lee," said Frank. "They did find a woman's boot. Do you happen to remember what Sharise was wearing on her feet?"

"Prada high-heel boots, red leather, the shaft trimmed with turquoise, white, and red feathers," I said without missing a beat. "Gorgeous."

"I might have known in the midst of fighting for your life, you'd notice the lady's footwear."

He let out a light laugh. Gurn followed suit. Then Frank continued.

"Well, that sounds like what they found. The feathers don't look so good, but that's the San Francisco Bay for you."

I hesitated. "No body yet?"

"No," Frank said, "but with the strong currents in the Bay, it probably was pulled out to sea."

"You may not find it for months, if ever," added Gurn.

"Exactly," agreed Frank.

"That's if Sharise is dead, gentlemen," I said. "She could have survived. She wasn't that far off land."

"San Francisco Bay is brutal, even for a competitive swimmer," said Frank.

"If the cold or currents don't get you, there's being thrown against rocks or found by a shark," said Gurn. "I'm a strong swimmer and I'd think twice about going into the Bay in the dead of night."

"You both make a good case for it, but I don't know..." My voice tapered off.

"Time will tell, Lee," said Frank sagely. "Every available man and woman has been searching for her. So far, nothing but a boot." He cleared his throat and changed the subject. "Let's move on. Fill me in with what's going on. Where are you?"

"We're on our way to Jake Gold's funeral in Colma."

"Sad business, that," Frank said. "If Sharise is alive, she has a lot to answer for."

"According to Mom, Jake didn't want any hoopla at the service. It should be pretty short. Then we'll go to the Collier Compound. When are you going to notify the press about Sharise's disappearance and possible death?"

249

"About fifteen minutes before you get to the compound, just like you asked. You have to tell me when you're on your way."

"Will do."

"It'll play on every radio and TV station in the Bay Area when you give the word. What do you think you're going to find at the compound? Or are you telling me yet?"

I answered the question with a question. "Did you tell the guards to let us in when we arrive?"

"I did. They're expecting you in an hour or two."

"You haven't released Skye and Katie from protective custody yet, have you?"

"No, I've been stalling, although I'll have to do it soon. There's no reason to keep them. You're testing my patience on this one, Lee. What's going on?"

"I'll know more once I'm at the compound." Silence. I pushed. "Hey, I've been right so far, haven't I?"

"Well…" Frank drawled the one word, maybe reluctant to admit it. "I'll have my men right outside the gate should you need us. Still no effects from the Devil's Breath?"

"*Nada.* Maybe I got it off my skin fast enough or maybe it's because there was no one to boss me around. In any event, there was no residual amount in my system as of eleven-thirty last night. There's another call coming in. I'll keep in touch."

I disconnected then hit the accept button for my incoming call.

"Morning, Richard. Did you get my message that Gurn was back? He's with me now." I put the phone on speaker again.

"Hey, proud new papa," said Gurn.

"Hey, Huckster," said Richard, calling him by his nickname from NROTC day. "Good to hear your voice."

"Same here, Rich," Gurn replied. "Can't wait to meet the little munchkin."

"Stephanie's beautiful. You'll see her tonight at the dinner." Richard cleared his throat. "Lee, I thought you should know I think I found what Collier used to blackmail Rameen Patel into working for him."

"Has Rameen been released from jail yet?"

"Yes, thanks to your evidence and Sharise's recorded confession. But what I'm about to tell you could have been one of the reason Chief Broas arrested him in the first place."

"Then we sure don't want to have this conversation at the cemetery."

"No, someone might overhear."

"Make it fast, Richard. We're almost there."

"Okay. It isn't pretty. Vehicular manslaughter. When he was a junior in high school he took his father's car without asking permission, and plowed into three bicyclists, a mother, father, and their six-year old daughter. He killed the whole family. Said he rounded a turn, the sun was in his eyes, and he didn't see them until it was too late. He was speeding – not by much, but legally speeding - and only had his learner's permit."

Both Gurn and I shot each other stunned looks. Richard went on.

"His lawyer asked for leniency. Based on his contrition, Patel was sentenced to six months in a juvenile detention center, with his license suspended for five years. Because he was a minor his name was kept out of the papers and his file locked up. From what I understand, he's never been behind the wheel of a car since."

Gurn joined in. "I'll bet it would it be easy for someone like Collier to dig up this information if he was looking for something."

"It took me less than a day. And I didn't have any trouble finding locals that knew and remembered. If this is what Collier was threatening him with, I can see why Patel gave up his career on the East Coast and took the chancy job out here. That's not something I'd be proud for my daughter to know about me."

"Dynamite blackmail opportunity," said Gurn, quietly.

251

"By the way, Lee, Read-Out dropped the suit against D. I. And on another note, Patel's begging you to keep looking for the prototype, if you're willing. 'With apologies for my behavior.' Direct quote."

"Does Rameen know we know about his past?"

"It's not my place to tell him, sister mine. I thought I'd let you drop that bomb."

"Or not," I countered. "He probably lives with it every day of his life. Besides, he's got enough on his plate right now."

"I agree. By the way, I also spoke with Craig Eastham."

"You've been busy," I said.

"I've been the one holding down the fort. But to go on, Eastham said the board is making noises about voting to declare bankruptcy if the prototype isn't found soon. Without it, there's no business."

"Thanks for telling me, brother mine. Hanging up now. We're at the cemetery. Then we leave for the compound."

"Don't do anything foolish when you get there, okay? Watch out for her, Huckster."

I looked at Gurn, crossed my eyes, and stuck out my tongue. He gave me a wink. "Only if she'll watch out for me."

* * * *

The service went fast, almost too fast. D. I. was closed for the day and all employees, except for Richard, came to Colma to show their respects for a fellow worker. Even Stanley wore a sober tie. Jake had been cremated according to his wishes, and the ceremony was short and sweet.

Mom invited everyone back to the house for her version of cake and coffee. That would be cheese and egg soufflés, smoked salmon, cucumber sandwiches, French pastries, and flowing wine served in her best crystal goblets. Gurn and I passed on the wake and headed to the Collier Compound.

We pulled up to the gatehouse and stopped. Gurn has an air of authority about him, even out of uniform. But when the guard leaned in, and saluted smartly, I was taken aback.

252

"Lt. Commander Hanson, sir. This is a surprise, sir."

Gurn paused a moment before saying, "Midshipman Bulward, isn't it? From our NROTC days. Kurt Bulward?"

"Sir, yes sir."

"I see you're in private service, Bulward."

"Sir, yes sir. Dropped out of college, had a run of bad luck, and here I am, sir. But it pays very well."

"Glad you landed on your feet."

"Yes, sir."

Gurn turned to me. "You know Ms. Alvarez, Bulward?"

"Yes sir, from the other day. We've been expecting you, ma'am."

"Where's the German Shepherd?" I leaned over Gurn to ask the guard.

"On a break, ma'am." With a smile, he passed a clipboard through the window to me. "This is a list of the personnel inside the compound at this time, ma'am. There are seven of them. Our instructions are not to notify anyone you are entering nor let anyone out until you give the word."

"Bully, Bulward," I said, taking the clipboard from his extended hand. "I mean, thank you. You're sure no one has come out of the compound since last night?"

"No ma'am. The list of people in residence is at the bottom. After Collier's daughter and her nanny left last night under police escort, there were seven of them inside. Still are. This is the only way in or out. Mr. Collier had it set up that way. Even went as far as placing eight-foot high electronically monitored fences around the perimeter. When a bird sits on one, we know about it."

"It all sounds very San Quentin to me."

"Ma'am?" Bulward gave me a puzzled look.

Gurn looked at me and rolled his eyes. He turned back to the guard. "Just let us pass, Bulward."

"Yes, sir." Bulward saluted again and pressed a button inside the gate.

The double gate glided open and we drove through. The tropical world of the Collier Compound opened up to us, but Gurn didn't notice. He had a pensive look on his face, no doubt regarding his ex-cadet, Bulward.

"Small world, huh?" I studied Gurn's face. "Running into one of your former cadets like that."

"Not everyone makes it," he said. "I'm just a bit sad when I come across one, though." He shook off the past, and looked around him. "Is that a strutting peacock I see?"

"And flamingos, too."

We rounded a turn in the road, sided by rare tropical plants. The rain had picked up again, but still, it was dazzling.

"Several hundred feet beyond is another turn where the road is shielded from the buildings by tall bushes and trees. No one can see us. Stop the car there and get out. I should be able to drive the rest of the way by myself." I had a momentary bout of concern. "You're sure you can run with your bruised heel, if you have to?"

Gurn nodded. "As long as I keep my weight on the balls of my feet, I'm good. I can't run five or six miles, but I should be okay for what you have in mind."

"Good, because I'd rather not shoot anybody if I can avoid it."

I got lucky because my dad moved us to Silicon Valley before it really was known worldwide as an important tech hub.
Robert Scoble

Chapter Thirty-six

As I slid behind the driver's seat of the Jeep, I wondered just how daffy I was being. It was tough enough to drive a car in my current condition, let alone try to run. In fact, I could barely walk. And I was in a profession where you needed to be able to do stuff like that, especially the run part. But I'm a *coup de grace* kinda gal and had to see this through to the end.

Fortunately for me, Gurn's car was fairly silent and the rain was adding its background noise to the scene. I kept my foot off the accelerator and coasted to the end of the drive, coming to a stop in front of the one open door of the four-door garage. I sat for a moment, listening to the steady click-click of the windshield wipers. Inside the garage a sleek but dry black Tesla sat with its trunk ajar and one of its doors open, as if waiting for someone.

I got out of the Jeep, careful not to slam the car door or make any noise. Pulling the collar up on my raincoat, I hobbled into the garage with the aid of my crutch. Actually, I wasn't doing too bad. Either I had improved a lot overnight or I was getting the hang of this crutch thing.

Collier's nine cars sat tandem style, three to a row, and except for the Tesla, all were covered with tarps. Using the end of my crutch, I pushed the lid of the Tesla's trunk up. Two cardboard boxes jammed with books, clothes, and tchotchkes were inside.

Above my head there was a noise like a piece of furniture being dragged across the room. I moved to the bottom of a staircase that went to the upstairs apartment, just as I heard an overhead door blam open and close. Thudding sounds of feet descending the stairs caused me to back up against a shelf containing neat, orderly tools. I withdrew the Tomcat from my pocket and waited.

A middle-aged, tall man flew past me carrying a heavy suitcase. He stopped when he saw the Jeep blocking his exit.

"Good morning," I said. "You must be Marty, the chauffeur."

He wheeled around at the sound of my voice, and stared at me breathing heavily. Marty was a muscular man, one who probably worked out every day, judging by the bulges pushing at the seams of his clothes. Between his pumped up body, longish hair, square jaw and jutting cheekbones, he looked like a comic book villain. He certainly had a villainous air as he stared back at me.

"Who the hell are you? Get your car out of my way."

"I'm Lee Alvarez, Marty. You drove Skye and Katie to my office the other day."

"What do you want? And move your damned car before I move it myself."

He threw the suitcase inside the open car door and advanced toward me, flexing his hands, arms, and neck. Even his nose quivered. He had this menacing thing down, I'll say that for him. I raised my good hand with the revolver in it, and pointed it at him.

"Watch your manners, Marty. As to what I want, I want the prototype back. I know Sharise gave it to you and I'm here to collect it. Oh yes, and I'm taking you in as an accessory to murder. In summation, I'm not moving my car."

He stopped at the sight of the gun. I saw him assess me in an instant. Eyes searching in all directions, he hesitated. Then with a quick pivot, Marty bolted from the garage out into the rain. I hobbled after him as fast as I could and saw him running down the driveway. Just as he passed some tall brush, Gurn sprang out and tackled him.

I tucked the gun back in my pocket and moved toward the two men writhing on the ground. Gurn had his offensive/defensive moves solid, but I could see Marty did, too. He leapt on top of my man, who let out a 'whomp' sound, as air was pushed from his lungs. Gurn quickly got the upper hand, and shoved Marty off with his legs. Marty was thrown to the ground, but jumped up like a cougar. He unsheathed a small knife hidden inside one of his pockets.

Gurn jumped to his feet, as well, and together they did the crouching down, circling routine, where each man wants to get neither too close nor too far away from the other. They circled once or twice, with Marty doing a few haphazard lunges at Gurn's groin. I soon neared them, but neither man seemed to notice.

With Marty's back to me, I waited until he circled directly in front. Then I flipped my crutch over, and taking the bottom of it with both hands, pulled my arms back and swung. I let him have it, Babe Ruth style. Sharise had given me the idea the night before, and at this juncture, it was a good one. The knife clattered to the pavement in one direction while Marty tumbled in the other, rolling over once then lay still on the wet pavement.

"Thank you, sweetheart. I was hoping you'd do something like that," Gurn said, still breathing hard. "Man, he was a tough one."

"You're welcome. Here," I said as I thrust a long plastic tie at him. "I found this on one of the shelves in the garage. It should keep his hands tied."

Gurn pushed Marty on his stomach, put one of the man's wrists on top of the other, and looped the tie over the man's hands and pulled tight. I knelt down in the rain to search the man's pockets.

"What are you doing, hon? You can't do that." Gurn's face looked shocked.

"Sure I can. Before Frank gets here, I want to get the prototype back. Without it, Read-Out might go under. And that can't happen. Future generations of Alvarez women are counting on this chip. I'm pretty sure he has it on him. He wouldn't have been so quick to run away if he didn't."

"Lee, that's against the law. Tampering with evidence."

I ignored the love of my life, pulled out Marty's wallet, looked inside, and found a small, Saran wrapped, glass-cased iridescent square. "Aha! Here it is."

"If they ask me, this didn't happen," Gurn said.

"Good, because if they ask me, that's my answer, too." I returned the wallet to Marty's pants pocket and shoved the small square inside my bra, just as my phone rang. I looked at the incoming call.

"Hi, Frank, perfect timing. Where are you?" I listened for a moment. "Great. Come on in. We've got your accomplice; Marty, the chauffeur. He's the one who helped Sharise the night Collier was murdered. But I'll explain it all to you when you get here."

I disconnected and turned to Gurn. Out of the corner of my eye, I saw one of the groundskeepers, an elderly Asian man dressed in a slicker and hat, leaning on a rake and staring at us.

"There's a witness," said Gurn, waving to the man. The man hesitated then waved back. "Might have seen you ransacking Marty's pants. I'll come and visit you in jail."

"He's straining to see us, like he's nearsighted. Probably blind as a bat without his glasses."

"Maybe you need some. He's wearing glasses."

"Never mind. Here comes Frank with Skye and Katie."

Chapter Thirty-seven

"Skye's asleep."

Katie stood in the doorway of the massive stainless steel kitchen. Several dozen orange and yellow blown glass orbs, probably more Chihuly, hung at different lengths over designated areas. They gave what would have been an otherwise cold setting warmth and light. Three shelves containing cookbooks, worn and well-used, added a very human touch.

"I promised to get her up in time to meet the team and start setting up the display for the contest," Katie added.

"The digital fly-fishing," I said.

"It'll help keep her mind off what's been going on," said Katie, as she walked into the kitchen toward us.

Gurn, Frank, and I sat around a long granite island watching the Collier private chef make perfect crepes, one at a time. It was mesmerizing. Perfectly golden and round, Chef Walt would fold them in fourths, and plop them on a large platter in the warming oven. Canadian bacon sizzled on a skillet, filling the air with another mouthwatering smell. It was all I could do to keep from drooling on the counter. I turned to the approaching woman.

"How is Skye doing?"

"Better than I thought she would." Katie smiled at us, running fingers through her short, dark hair. "But I haven't told her yet about the latest developments, her mother's death."

"I hope she can get past her mother killing her father. That's a lot to handle." Frank's tone was more of a father rather than a police officer. He's a man who's never lost his heart, no matter what he's seen of the world.

"I haven't known Miss Skye long," said Chef Walt in his soft German accent, "but she strikes me as a child who is better for knowing the truth of a situation." Wearing his dress whites, he flipped another crepe.

"Regardless, I don't want to say anything until we know one way or another," said Katie. "It's all so heartbreaking."

"Yes, it is," Frank said.

"But kids can be pretty resilient," Gurn said to no one in particular, hair still damp from a recent shower. He looked at Katie. "Thanks for letting me take a shower. I was covered in gravel and wet leaves."

"My pleasure, but tell me, do you always carry a change of clothes in the trunk of your car?"

Katie smiled at Gurn. She took a seat next to him at the highly polished, white granite island, which also served as an eating counter.

"Be prepared, that's a scout's loyal creed." Gurn swiveled his chair to face Chef Walt, and then not so subtly changing the subject. "Those look delicious."

"I've discovered crepes are welcomed any time of the day." Chef Walt answered, sprinkling the crepes with powdered sugar.

He filled a second platter with the crispy bacon. Homemade strawberry and apricot jams already sat on the counter, along with a bowl of fresh cut persimmons. Aromatic coffee stayed hot in a nearby carafe. I poured myself a cup.

Katie turned to me, suddenly anxious. "Do you really think Sharise is drowned? Is this over?"

"That's what they're saying," I answered.

"Yes, but what do you think?" Katie persisted.

"Sharise's body could be found any minute now. Marty has been arrested, carted off to the hoosegow, and is already naming names. The Scopolamine tree at Sharise's house has been chopped down and all the chemically altered drugs confiscated from her property."

"And as soon as I have a few of these crepes," said Frank, "I'm off to Tiburon to make sure everything between both Marin and Santa Clara counties is nice and legal. This has all the signs of being over."

"Ladies and gentleman, brunch," said Chef Walter, bringing the two platters to the counter, and serving us family style. He joined us at the counter and 'opened the ceremony' by picking up a crepe with his fork.

We dug in, making appropriate noises. Our mood lightened noticeably. Good food can do that to a crowd, especially any crowd I hang out with.

"Chef Walt has only been with us for eighteen months, but he makes the best crepes this side of St. Louis," announced Katie, also snagging a crepe with her fork. "Everybody says so."

"Allowing for a slight exaggeration, Katie," he replied with a laugh, watching the nanny.

Chef Walt was a rotund man in his early forties, and follicly challenged, as the saying goes. But no side hairs combed over a bare pate. Bald and loving it.

Katie giggled and looked away, but not before a few sparks flew. Gurn saw it, too, and grinned at me. Maybe there would be love in this household sooner than anyone thought. Or maybe I just had romance on the brain, me getting married in two days.

Gurn shoved a forkful of crepe dripping with apricot jam into his mouth then turned to me. "So should we pick up on what we were talking about before we got distracted by food?"

"You mean how Sharise managed to be in two places at the same time?" Frank looked at me. "It's a pretty unique crime, that's for sure."

"I want every detail," Gurn said, chewing his food. "The things I miss when I'm gone. Makes me never want to leave your side again." He winked at me.

Katie took several pieces of Canadian bacon on her plate along with two more crepes. She had a healthy appetite; a perfect match for a chef. Between bites she asked, "I want every detail, too, Lee. How did you figure it out?"

I tried to lasso my mind and bring it back from the crepes. "I was always led on by Skye's certainty that Sharise committed the crime, no matter how impossible it seemed. And I kept running out of suspects. But we have Tugger to thank for showing me the way. He's my cat," I explained.

"Your cat is a detective?" Chef Walt stopped eating and looked at me in disbelief.

"Let's call him a junior detective." I said.

Gurn shook his head and laughed. "I should have known Tugger was somehow involved in this."

"There's a new cat in the neighborhood that looks enough like Tugger to be mistaken for him," I said. "That is, from a distance and if you didn't know the real deal. For several minutes I thought Ralph was Tugger."

"Tugger is the name of your cat and Ralph is the name of the other cat," said Chef Walt, trying to clarify the feline lineup.

"Exactly. And sometimes you see what you expect to see and not what...or who...is really there."

Katie and Chef Walt looked confused. Frank just laughed.

"Don't worry, folks," said Gurn, pouring himself another cup of coffee. "She'll get around to telling us how she worked it out."

The chef leaned back with a grin. Katie nodded. I cleared my throat and went on.

"You see, once I realized I'd been fooled by which cat was which, I saw that Sharise and her stand in, June Mitchell, traded places after the last concert in Germany. They were careful not to be seen by anyone but Ty Deavers, her manager, who was also in on the switch."

"So June became Sharise, and Sharise became June," said Gurn. "Pretty clever."

"How could they possibly do that?" Katie's brow furrowed in confusion.

"After their last concert the band and crew were scheduled to arrive in America the following day, Sunday, the eighteenth. All except Sharise and Ty Deavers. Those two were staying on for the lip-synching scene in a German movie and leaving Germany two days later. So June became Sharise; Sharise became June. The murder of Collier was planned for the night of the eighteenth. Ty Deavers' job was to keep people at a safe distance from the fake Sharise while June posed as the rock star back in Germany."

Frank jumped in. "Meanwhile Sharise, disguised as June, made sure she booked a seat on a flight that none of the other band members were on, which was easy to do as the rest of them lived on the East Coast."

"So as long as neither woman was around someone who knew them," said Katie, eyes wide with understanding, "they were able to trade places."

"Exactly," I said. "And with the wig and hat covering half her face, and the outlandish costumes, who was to know it was June bouncing around on the sound stage instead of Sharise? She was lip-synching to songs, anyway, not really singing, so it was perfect."

"How far ahead do you think this was planned?" Gurn speared a slice of persimmon before looking at me.

"A long time, apparently," I said.

Frank took over. "When Marty was told Sharise was dead, he broke down and admitted everything. Collier was going to be in Switzerland for some small plastic surgery at

263

the same time Sharise was to be in Germany performing. She and Collier met up a few times in Switzerland, supposedly rekindling their romance."

"Much to his delight," I added. "And due to their mutually high profiles, they kept their meetings very hush-hush. Thanks to Marty, Sharise knew Collier's plan was to secretly fly back earlier than expected to continue with his sabotage plans of Read-Out and the people he felt betrayed him."

"Let me get this straight about him and Read-Out," said Chef Walt looking from Frank to me. "Mr. Collier's intention was to make it look like he was helping to get more backers by throwing a big bash when in reality he was selling company secrets and trying to destroy the upcoming IPO?"

"In a word, yes," I said. "And it all fit right into Sharise's plans. She flew back early, too, ostensibly to continue their assignation. And not wanting the paparazzi to get wind of it, she told Collier she would come back in secret, as well."

"I guess David believed she finally returned his love. It's sad," said Katie. "But just how was Marty involved in it?"

"It was Marty who drove the tester and chips back from Nevada, per Collier's instructions," I said. "And he's the one who picked Collier up when he arrived from Switzerland five days early and brought him to the Sunnyvale house where Collier hid out. Then Marty met Sharise at the airport a few days ago and drove to her home in Tiburon to make a fresh batch of Devil's Breath. Then they both went to where Collier was waiting for her."

"Marty also was her companion in Redding." Frank's voice was somber, having known Jake for as long as the Alvarez family. "She went there disguised as the cowgirl, and together they killed Jake Gold."

"I know I probably shouldn't, but I feel sorry for David. He seems to have made so many bad choices," said Katie.

"That can happen when a talented and complicated man who wields a lot of power doesn't get what he wants," said Gurn.

"'Absolute power corrupts absolutely', as the saying goes," Frank said.

We were all silent for a moment then Katie spoke up.

"I hope Skye never learns about that side of her father."

"We'll do what we can to spare Miss Skye for as long as we can." Chef Walt's face wore a grim look, but his eyes were filled with warmth and camaraderie.

Katie threw him a grateful smile then was reflective. "I knew David was unhappy with something at Read-Out, but I had no idea what. But I'm sure he told Marty the details. He told Marty everything."

"And then Marty relayed the information to Sharise," said Chef Walt, catching on.

"You could call Marty a double agent," Gurn said.

Katie shook her head in disbelief. "Marty told us his mother was sick, and he would need time off now and then. We never thought anything of it." She turned to me. "But why did he do it? He's been with us since before Skye was born."

"You forget that Marty has known Sharise since she was not much older than Skye," I said. "They formed a bond early on. I don't know when they became lovers, but they certainly were."

"Marty said he didn't like the way Collier treated Sharise," said Frank. "Can't say as I blame him on that score."

"It does sound like David Collier was a twenty-first century stalker with high-tech tools," said Gurn.

I nodded. "True enough. Marty wanted him dead so Sharise would be free of him. For her part, once her ex- was disposed of, she would get a million dollars a month for life."

"I'm wondering if she was just using Marty," said Katie.

"It sounds like it would be within her character," said Chef Walt.

265

"Sharise was a very smart lady, smarter than people gave her credit for," Frank said.

"And she was desperate. Ty Deavers didn't know it," I said, "but he was the sacrificial goat, meant to take the blame if things started unraveling."

"Which they did," said Gurn, "Thanks to you."

"She didn't count on Read-out bringing me in to find out who was sabotaging the upcoming IPO. Me snooping around made Sharise very nervous."

Gurn smiled at me. "You were Sherlock Holmes to her Professor Moriarty."

"Something like that. First she tried to get rid of me by sending me to Fremont on the trail of the chips and tester. She hoped to meet up with me on my own and give me some Devil's Breath. But I got there sooner than expected. When she saw she missed her opportunity, she sent her motorcycle squad after me."

"Just how many people were involved in this?" Katie turned to Chef Walt before adding, "I can't keep up."

"Me, either." The chef nodded with a small laugh, and both looked at me.

"Ty Deavers and June Mitchell were part one of this elaborate scheme," I said. "They were promised a lot of money to help pull the switcheroo off in Germany. I suspect Jerome Hastings and Ronnie Epstein were afterthoughts, maybe to throw me off the track."

I shook my head and was silent for a moment. The deaths of those two kids weighed heavily on me.

"But Marty was the important California cohort; the one who helped Sharise the night Collier was killed. After he was drugged the first time, Marty and Sharise took Collier to the back stairs of Read-Out's offices. They told him to use his code card to let the three of them into the building; the one place that didn't have surveillance cameras. Once upstairs, Collier opened his Chinese puzzle desk for them and did anything else they wanted."

Frank spoke up. "Then Sharise gave him the second dose of Devil's Breath close to midnight. When he passed out, Marty admits to carrying him into the boardroom. Together they undressed him, strung up the rope, put his neck in the noose, and kicked the ladder out from underneath him. Marty being a weight lifter, he did the heavy work himself, under the careful supervision of Sharise. Then they left the way they came, by the back stairs."

"Leaving him hanging in his underwear," added Gurn. "Just to humiliate the man. Unbelievable."

"Her big mistake," I said, "was not realizing the Read-Out implant would record the Scopolamine in his body. That tipped off the police right away. But what did it for me was him being stripped of his clothes, and leaving them on the conference table. That didn't sit right. It just felt plain ghoulish."

"But why would she want to steal the prototype and computer chips?" Katie gave me a perplexed look.

"The same reason she wanted Collier to be seen half naked, hanging in the boardroom." I said. "Not only did she want him dead, she wanted to make him a laughing stock; set him up to ridicule. Plus the thefts and supposed suicide were smoke screens for what was really going on, the murder of D. H. Collier for his money."

"I'm surprised Marty knew enough to help Sharise decode the video cams on the garage in Sunnyvale," Gurn said. "He didn't strike me as the type. But, of course, I only met him briefly this morning and not under the best of conditions."

"Neither Sharise nor Marty needed to know anything," I said. "In Collier's zombie-like state, they made him program the codes into the security cameras, himself."

"Marty admitted to using a hammer on the video cam in Redding," Frank said. "And Sharise used the two computer geeks, Jerome and Ronnie, to do any technological jobs. She promised them ten thousand dollars if they helped her. Instead, she killed them."

"Those poor, stupid kids," muttered Gurn.

"I know," I said. "Sharise seemed to have had no conscience at all."

"Or maybe she was just plain insane," offered Frank.

"It's all so cold-blooded," Katie said.

"Yes, it is," Gurn agreed. "But you'd be surprised at just how many cold-blooded people there are in the world."

Katie set down her fork and looked at each of us. "I don't know how much of this I want Skye to know. No matter what she says, Sharise is still her mother."

"I suspect she knows much more than you think, Katie." Chef Walt's voice was firm but kind. "She's the one who insisted her father's killer was Sharise in the first place." He smiled at Katie then patted her hand. "But like all mother hens, you want to protect your chick. Sharise may have given birth to her, but you are her mother in every sense of the word."

* * * *

An hour later, Gurn and I stood by the front door, saying our goodbyes to Katie. Frank had headed out to Tiburon to check with local authorities on the progress. The chef was cleaning his kitchen, a task he preferred to do alone.

"Thanks again for all you did," said Katie. "You risked your life to find David's killer. Thank you. You'll send me your bill, right?"

"You can count on it, Katie. It'll be in the mail Monday or Tuesday, and Merry Christmas. I'm sorry we have to leave before Skye wakes up, but Gurn's parents just flew in and we need to meet them. We thought their flight might be delayed with the rain, but the skies appear to have cleared for the moment."

"Maybe it won't rain for the wedding," Gurn said, looking up at the dark clouds on the horizon.

I turned to the man in my life, putting a hand on his shoulder. "I hate to burst your bubble, but Mom says it's going to rain for the next three days and she's never wrong."

"That's right," Katie said, eyes wide in comprehension. "You two are getting married Christmas Eve. How romantic." She let out a sigh, crossing her arms about her, probably more from the recent events than the damp cold. "It's such a fun thing, a wedding. I wish you both the best. And Merry Christmas to you, too."

"Thank you." Gurn gave her a ready smile. "I'm looking forward to getting it over with, so we can go on our honeymoon." He turned a warm, loving smile in my direction.

"Say, I've got an idea," I said, feeling inspired. "One of my bridesmaids had to back out at the last minute. Her father had surgery and she flew to Boise yesterday to be with him."

"Annette, right?" Gurn looked at me, remembering a past conversation. "She mentioned her father was ill. I hope he's is going to be all right."

I turned to him. "She says he's going to be fine. His spirits have lifted considerably now that she's there."

"Then it was a good thing she went," he said.

"You betcha." I turned back to Katie. "But here's my idea; her pulling out like that leaves me with a bridesmaid's dress and a hole in the lineup. I think the dress would fit Skye; they're about the same size. Do you think she'd like to do it? It doesn't involve much; just marching down the aisle with a lot of other bridesmaids and then we all get to eat afterward."

"Oh, Lee, she'd love it," Katie gushed and snatched at my hand, clasping it to her in a dramatic gesture I didn't think she was capable of. "This might be just the thing for her; a nice diversion from the horrors of what's been going on."

"That's what I thought," I said, "and hoped."

I looked at Gurn for approval. Like the love bucket he is, he usually goes along with anything, and confirmed my invitation with a big grin.

"Sounds like a plan. And why not bring Chef Walt? I think the chef might like to meet Lee's uncle, Tío. He ran the kitchens at *Las Mañanitas* Restaurant in San Jose before he retired."

She hesitated for a moment. "Doesn't Mrs. Alvarez have a set guest list and menu?"

"There's nothing set about this wedding, Katie, believe me." I threw my head back and laughed. "And we'd love to have Skye be part of the ceremony. The dress is still at Angela's. Her shop is on Arastradero Road, about twenty minutes from here. I'm sure Angela can fit the dress on Skye sometime this afternoon or tomorrow. I'll call her for a time and get back to you."

"This is wonderful, just wonderful," Katy gushed then hesitated again. "You're sure about this?"

"Completely; there's no use in having that lovely dress go to waste. Besides, you know Mexican food. There's always more than enough."

* * * *

"I thought the caterer was doing French cuisine," said Gurn as an aside, when we were getting into his car. "I know I can't pronounce half of what we're having."

"If you think Tío isn't going to make a few thousand traditional Mexican canapés for the occasion, you don't know my uncle."

"I thought he was doing the wedding cake."

"It's done. He finished decorating it yesterday. Wait until you see it. I snuck a look at it when he wasn't around. Remember when I told you I asked him to do a rustic Mexican folk art design on white fondant?"

"Not really. I don't even know what fondant is. But as long as it tastes good, that's all that matters to me."

"Sometimes you're such a man, Gurn."

"Thank you…I think. While I'm being a man, let's discuss how Marty got the prototype that you have neatly stored in your cleavage. I didn't want to bring it up in the kitchen, your having stolen it."

"Only long enough to get it back to Read-Out."

"Why did Marty have it? I don't get it."

"An added inducement to do Sharise's bidding. She gave Marty the chip the night she took it from Collier's safe. It's worth a couple of million dollars to the right people."

"So the prototype chip was with Marty the entire time?"

"Yup," I said. "Maybe he was going to try to sell it back to Read-Out when things died down a little or to one of their competitors. We'll never know for sure. But he was aware that a locator chip was attached to the box and not the chip, itself. That's why the box wound up at Ty Deavers' place, to throw everyone off. Smoke and mirrors."

"And when found, it incriminated the band manager." Gurn grinned at me. "Right?"

"Right."

"Very Machiavellian." I could see the gears shifting in his head. "But enough about them. So what is fondant? Maybe I ought to know so I can be appreciative of Tío's workmanship."

"Ahhhhh. That is so thoughtful. Fondant is the smooth icing that covers the cake used as a background for decoration. Our cake has lots of colorful birds and flowers on a white background. It looks like a three-layered painting; simply stunning. I had forgotten what an incredible artist Tío is. But he has all today to make canapés, if he wants. And I know he wants."

"Well, you can be the one to tell your mother about the three new invites. And try to do it when I'm out of the room."

"I was hoping you'd do it." I air-smacked kisses in his direction.

"Fat chance."

Chapter Thirty-eight

Four pm, Christmas Eve. My wedding day, and finally alone. The previous day had been one of rest, spent canoodling with Gurn and the cats. Even the bags under my eyes had started to recede.

I studied my reflection in front of the full-length mirror. I actually looked pretty good, all things considered. True, the wedding dress was a bit over the top and I felt a little like an iced vanilla cupcake. But it was the gown Mom wanted. Lady Guinevere Does California.

If I held the bouquet in my right hand, the black and blue bruising was covered by flowers and lace. If I stood perfectly still or only walked a short distance, I didn't need my crutches. My floor length skirt hid both feet, i.e. the boot encasing my sprained ankle and my other foot, comfy in a white tennis shoe.

A tulle veil clipped to the back of my head not only diffused the light, making any bride look lovelier, but in my case, would cover my face and running makeup as I bawled my way down the aisle. It was all good.

I turned my focus away from my image to the full-length, light oak framed beveled mirror I've loved since always. I remember playing dress-up in front of it as a little girl. It had been carried down from Mom's second-floor bedroom and

272

placed in the butler's pantry, a long narrow room off to one side of the kitchen and dining room.

The pantry was serving as my dressing room and supposed sanctuary. But at times like these, peace and quiet are hard to come by. Mom, Tío, Richard, Vicki, and people I knew or didn't know kept traipsing in and out during the past two hours. If it wasn't family, it was a lost guest or confused last-minute hiree, all catching me struggling with my pantyhose. Not being the sharpest pencil in the pack, I'd come up with the idea of locking the doors only moments before. At least now intruders had to knock.

The cozy room smelled of decades of lemon polish, pungent enough to block out all other scents. Even the aroma of Tío's heavenly mini Chicken Chimichanga appetizers frying in the kitchen had lost the competition. I looked around. I was glad when my parents moved into the house, they decided not to modernize the butler's pantry, a room that came from a time when there were butlers who buttled.

A built-in, ceiling high storage unit ran the length of one side of the room, ending at a tall but slender closet. The closet stored an old-fashioned ironing board and other wrinkle-eliminating paraphernalia from days gone by.

The unit was divided into three sections. At the top, wood cabinets were painted a glossy white and inset with glass. In the center, a deep marble counter was mirrored at the backend. In the old days, the counter held silver salvers, teapots, and other bits and pieces of a more proper era when formal gatherings were all the rage. Now it was crammed with equipment used by Tío in his cooking for shelter residents, of the two-footed and four-footed variety.

Beneath the counter, rows of deep drawers held Irish linens and stuff long out of use, but held onto for sentimental reasons. I scanned the weighty and massive piece from left to right. It remained as it was since the house was originally built, a monument to another time.

I noticed the ironing board was out now, tucked in a corner. An incident involving it came to mind, something happening when I was five-years old. I'm not saying Mom never ironed, but when she took the board out and set it up, I remember turning to her and asking, "Mommy, what's that?"

My mother, being a disciple of the wash and wear or dry clean only school-of-thought, chose her words carefully. "This is something I use to put office files in order when I bring them home." Then she proceeded to spread out files and alphabetize them on the makeshift counter. Talk about unclear on the concept.

I never saw the board out again until my prom night. I'd hauled out the iron and ironing board in an effort to spruce up the bows on my prom dress, only to succeed in singeing them but good. As far as I knew, the board hadn't been out of the closet since that time. But here it sat now, no doubt used by the seamstress to iron my wedding dress which, fortunately, wasn't singed. Talent will tell.

My dress was still loose even after the last fitting. I'd lost more weight at a time when I didn't want to, proving that in my case you can't win for losing, literally. I vowed to have two pieces of wedding cake, maybe three to offset the loss. The thought spurred me to get on with the ceremony.

There was a gentle tapping at the door leading into the kitchen.

"Who is it?" My voice sounded more pleasant than I was feeling. Guppy in a gold fish bowl, that was me.

"It is I, Liana, your mother." Her voice sounded soft, yet echoey, as if she'd put her lips to the crack of the door as she spoke.

"You're sure?" I said with a laugh, heading toward her voice. "You're not one of the new staff you hired today barging in here to serve me some hors d'oeuvres or get a look at my underpants?"

"Stop talking nonsense, Liana, and let me in."

I threw the lock and she pushed her way through the door with more unladylike vigor than I'd seen before. I quickly locked it behind her.

"What news from the Rialto?" I misquoted a line from The Merchant of Venice, Mom's favorite Shakespearian play. I'd like to say I did it deliberately, but come on.

"What news *on* the Rialto," Mom corrected. "Frankly, Liana, I've never had so *many* strangers milling around my house at one time. It's *very* disconcerting."

"That's what happens when you throw a large wedding, Mom, and invite the world."

My tone was unsympathetic but I don't think she noticed. Mom has a one track mind when necessary. She went on as if I hadn't spoken. She was outwardly unemotional in her distress, but I knew things were lurking deep inside.

"And unfortunately, it is *still* raining."

"Buckets?"

"I would *prefer* to use the word 'intensely', but yes. The *good* news is the tent is holding its own against the wind and rain."

"What's the bad news?"

"The outside wall of the family room has sprung a leak. We've had to move the Christmas tree."

"How many people did that take?"

"Six. I believe the *problem* is the gutters, possibly filled with leaves from the recent storms. I've got a call into our handyman who promised to be here within the hour. And the caterer hasn't arrived yet. Some flooding on 101."

"Golly. Sounds like chaos out there."

"We will *not* let this dampen the day."

"No, we'll leave that up to the weather."

Mom let out a sigh and began to pace the small room. "One must *face* these things with intestinal fortitude."

"Sounds like indigestion. Is the groom still here?"

"Of course."

"So at least there will be a wedding. How do I look?"

275

She stopped pacing, concentrating on me for the first time. She looked at me and smiled. I returned her smile. She took her time appraising me, but when she finally spoke, her smile turned teary.

"You're a lovely bride, Liana, *truly*. I like your hair coiled on top of your head. And clustering the gardenias to the side of your grandmother's pearl tiara is a *perfect* touch. You were right. We didn't need any more gardenias than the ones in your hair and your bouquet."

It was my turn to study my mother. She was probably the most beautiful mother of the bride ever, dressed in a crushed velvet lavender gown that gave off a hint of indigo when she moved. The color made her blue eyes sparkle even more than usual. Or maybe the sparkle came from finally unloading her thirty-four year old daughter. There was that.

"Thank you, Mom. You don't look so bad, yourself."

"You could have *phrased* it better, but thank you. Do you have everything, Liana? *Traditionally* speaking?"

I thought for a moment. "Let's see, something old, Grandmother Hamilton's pearl tiara. Check. Something new, I'm going with my wedding dress. Check. Something blue, a blue lace garter." I hiked the hem of my dress up on my left leg, the one that didn't have a cast on it. A blue lace garter was wrapped around my thigh. "Check. And don't say anything about the tennis shoe, please."

"The less said the better. And here's your something borrowed." Mom handed me a small box. I opened it and saw the pearl button earrings Dad gave her right before he died. I was overwhelmed, but tried to thrust the box back in her hand.

"Mom, I can't wear these; you're never without them. You should have them on for the wedding, not me."

"I think it would please your father if you wore them. It will seem as if your father is a part of the ceremony."

"Mom," I said, tearing up. "Dad's always a part of everything I do. Always."

She gripped my arm with a gentle but firm hand. "Then wear them for me."

I nodded, unable to speak. I took them out of the box and with shaky fingers, clipped them on my ears. I didn't mention the diamond drop earrings Gurn had given me as a wedding present. Time enough to wear those as his wife.

"I should get back outside," Mom said breaking the spell. "I'm trying to keep things afloat."

"Every pun intended?" I teased her with a smile and reached out for a hug.

"Every." She embraced me and squeezed harder than I can remember her doing before. "The next time we meet, you'll be a married woman," she whispered then broke free. I gazed into her eyes.

"Let's hope this one takes." My voice was light and teasing.

"It will." Her voice was light and sincere. "And put on a darker shade of lipstick. That gloss makes you looked washed out. The ceremony is scheduled to begin in fifteen minutes. You'll have some peace and quiet until then. I've seen to it."

I barely had time to nod my head before she swept out of the room. I limped to the door, locked it then kicked my train aside for the short walk back to the counter where my travel bag rested. I rummaged inside for the tube of hot pink lipstick called Bright Rose.

I turned back to Mom's full-length mirror, leaned in, and began to apply the lipstick. For the first time I sniffed a scent of perfume over the lemony smell of the room. Simultaneously, the closet door that previously held the ironing board opened slowly. The cloying fragrance became more powerful as the door widened.

Unable to move, I watched as a hand holding a revolver, followed by a woman dressed in the standard white shirt and black trousers of the food servers, stepped out of the closet.

She was a brunette with short curly hair and large horn rimmed glasses. But I would have recognized her anywhere. I would have known her even without the distinctive scent or the bruise on her jaw put there by my fist.

Sharise.

There are a lot of billionaires in Silicon Valley, but in the end,
we are all heading to the same place. If given the choice between
making a lot of money or finding a way to make people live longer,
what do you choose?
Bill Maris

Chapter Thirty-nine

"You didn't drown."

I can't say I was completely shocked. A nagging niggle had been living inside me ever since she took the dive into San Francisco Bay two nights before. Bad penny and all that. But it did surprise me to see her emerge from the ironing board closet.

"I didn't drown, no thanks to you." Her voice sounded strong but playful, with an undercurrent of hostility. "I stayed close to shore and came up maybe two hundred yards away. I have friends close by I can go to, a few who will help me. I store things with them like my disguises and laptops. You never know when you'll need a new look. Like now."

"How did you get in here?"

"One of my friends runs a temp agency."

"You have a lot of friends."

"When the price is right, everybody is your friend. He got the call for extra help, and I signed myself up. I was one of the first to arrive, a real opportunity to look around."

She lost the chit-chatty element of the conversation, becoming hard and accusatory.

"You have ruined everything, everything, you interfering, nosy bitch. I've been waiting inside the closet for the chance to get you alone for nearly two hours. I thought you'd never figure out to lock the door so no one else would show up. I didn't come out when your mother was here. I didn't want to have to shoot her."

My eyebrows darted up right into my hairline. She sniggered before saying more.

"Consider it my wedding gift to you."

Either the snide comment about shooting my mother or the snigger pissed me off. It doesn't do to piss me off; there's no telling what I might do. Sometimes to my own detriment.

"What do you want?" My voice was strong and steady now.

I took a defiant step forward. Sharise took a defiant step forward. I glared at her. She glared at me.

We were at a Mexican standoff. I'm allowed to say that because I'm Mexican-American. On second thought, we weren't quite at a standoff. She had the gun and I didn't. There was that.

"What. Do. You. Want?" I repeated the words, crossing my arms across my chest.

"You're going to call in that boyfriend of yours --"

"Fiancé," I interrupted. "And why would I do that?"

"Because if you don't, I'm going to shoot you."

She brought the gun forward and aimed it right between my eyes. As it was a smallish room, there was no way her shot would have gone wild. Her voice quivered a little when she spoke but the gun's aim remained steady and true.

"Your fiancé has a plane. I read all about him on the internet."

Curse the internet. I said aloud, "So?"

"He's going to fly the three of us to Canada. I can't get out of the Bay Area on my own. Thanks to you, all the airports, bus stations, train stations are being watched. I can't even rent a car."

"So borrow one from your many friends."

"You haven't thought this through, Lee." Her voice dripped with irony. "The Canadian border checks passports and visas. But a private plane is just airport to airport. And your guy is an army bigwig."

"Navy."

"So he's going to take you and me in his little Sester --"

"Cessna."

She took another step forward, almost touching my nose with the gun. "If you correct me one more time I'm going to shoot you, even if I never get out of here. Do you understand?"

I nodded, my eyes crossing. I looked down the barrel of a gun now touching my nose, deciding to use a more tactful approach. Belligerence wasn't working, especially with a woman who had obviously lost touch with reality.

"Let's calm down a little. We can work this out."

She backed up, dropping the gun an inch or two. I let out the trapped air in my lungs and inhaled a snootful of her perfume. It made me cough.

"Yeah, right, okay, whatever you say," I said, while trying to think my way out of this mess. "I'll call or text him. Why don't you hand me my phone on the counter?" I tilted my head in the direction of my cellphone.

Without taking her eyes off me, she backed up until she bumped into the counter. With her free hand she felt around on it for the phone. When she picked it up, I hoped she would toss it to me. But instead, she asked a question.

"What's his name, Gary or something? I can't remember."

"Gurn." Nobody can get his name straight.

"Is he on your speed dial?"

I reached out, nodding my head like an idiot, still hoping she would give me the phone. If I could just signal Frank; he's on my speed dial. Or maybe she'll look down at the phone long enough for me to rush her.

All these thoughts were going through my head as I stood there, inanely nodding. But Sharise didn't toss me the phone. Instead, she gave a quick glance at the last call I made, which was to Gurn, and pressed redial. I didn't even have a chance

281

to move. He must have answered on the first ring, because she gave her short but cryptic speech right away.

"No, this isn't your 'darling'. This is Sharise and I'm holding a gun on your bride-to-be in the butler's pantry. And if you're not in this room in less than one minute and *alone*, I'm going to shoot her. Not a word to anyone or I'll shoot her. If anybody else shows up with you, I'll shoot her. Are we clear that I will shoot your bride at the slightest provocation?" Gurn must have said yes, because she smiled. "Good. I'm starting the countdown now. You have, max, one minute."

He must have said something she wanted to hear, because she disconnected and threw the phone back on the counter.

"He sounds like a reasonable man. Maybe you'll live through this." Sharise stepped aside and with the gun, gestured to the ironing board closet, door still open.

"Get in."

"What?"

"Get in the closet. I'm going to shut you in there until it's time for us to leave."

There must have been an expression on my face, defeat, fear, I don't know what. But it was there and she saw it.

"You really didn't think I would leave the two of you together in this room? I don't like to be outnumbered, even if I am armed. I'm not as stupid as you think. Or as you are." She let out another snigger.

My piss level rose again, so I stood my ground. There was a knocking at the door, firm but just under pounding. Not a sound you could dismiss.

"Lee, Lee, let me in." Gurn's voice was quiet but powerful. I know him when his tone is like that. It means he's scared, but in complete control.

"That's him," I said.

"Don't open the door."

"I am opening the door. You started this. Let's finish it."

Even Silicon Valley investors have put well over a $1 billion in new energy technologies.
Daniel Yergin

Chapter Forty

I unlocked the door, and opened it slightly. Gurn slipped in and stood beside me, closing the door behind him.

Gurn looked at me. "You all right?"

I nodded, but didn't relock the door. Something in me hoped Sharise wouldn't notice. No such luck.

She came to life and snarled, "Lock that door!"

Gurn flipped the lock behind him and turned his attention to the woman holding the gun. "I don't know what's going on," he said easily. "But whatever it is I know we can resolve it without anybody getting hurt."

Gurn has mastered Negotiating Skills 101. His tone and body language made even me believe a happy ending was possible.

"Glad to hear it." Sharise snarled again. She had this snarling thing down pat. Then her lower lip quivered. It didn't make her any less aggressive.

"Here's what's going to happen. The three of us are going to go into the kitchen, out the back door, and to your waiting car, bridegroom. I know you parked it near the gate so you two could sneak away after the reception. It was the talk of the kitchen staff. You're going to drive the three of us to the airport and fly us to Vancouver. I have another friend there who's going to help me. Once I'm safe, I'll let the two of you go."

"Your daughter's here," I blurted out. It was completely out of the blue. Even I was stunned to hear the words come out of my mouth.

Sharise looked all around, her eyes searching.

"What?"

"Skye is outside waiting for the ceremony to begin. Actually, she's in the ceremony. I asked her to fill in as a last-minute bridesmaid. You sure you want her to see any of this?"

Sharise's reaction was big. Her breathing became swift and shallow, the blood draining from her face. Hesitation and confusion colored her entire body. I never saw a woman spin out so fast.

"You invited my daughter to be in your wedding? Why? You hardly know her."

"She's been going through a rough patch, what with her father's death."

I didn't add the part about the woman standing before me being the one to do him in. It seemed unnecessary.

"Lee wanted to give Skye something pleasant to be involved in," chimed in Gurn, seeing we might have an advantage in the dangerous game we were playing. "Don't do this, Sharise. For her sake."

"You don't know anything, do you? Not either of you."

Sharise regained some control and scowled at us, waving the gun in our faces.

"I did my child a favor. She didn't know what her father was like, not really. How he controlled everything around him, no matter how it squeezed the life out of you. She's still young, but as soon as she met a boy, fell in love, or wanted her own life, it would have started. His obsession, his mania to control the ones he supposedly loves. David used anything within his power to make you do his bidding. If he broke you, he didn't care, as long as he controlled you."

Gurn and I stared at her in silence. She went on, rage enveloping her.

284

"Do you know he approached two of my musicians a few months ago? Said he'd give them five hundred thousand dollars if they never played with me again. One of them took the deal, but the other came and told me. David wouldn't be satisfied until he brought me to my knees; gave me no alternative but to go back to him and his tyranny. In time, my daughter will understand what I've done."

"Maybe someday you two can even be friends," Gurn said. "But that's only if you stop what you're doing. Turn yourself in." He took a step forward, both hands opened in an appealing gesture. "Let me help you."

"Come any closer," Sharise said, aiming the gun at him, "And I'll shoot both of you, I swear. Remember, I've nothing to lose."

Palms toward her in supplication, Gurn backed up with a shrug. "I'll have to call the airport, register a flight plan. The weather's a little dicey --"

"Screw the weather," Sharise said, her voice shrill. "Do it!"

"Whatever you say." Gurn's tone was even and agreeable. "I can do it right now or in the car. Which do you prefer?"

Sharise opened her mouth to answer but before she could, there was a knock on the door. A young girl's voice, muted and soft, froze all three of us in place.

"Lee? Lee? It's Skye. I think you have my bouquet. At least your mother says it might have been left in the room by the florist. We can't find it anywhere else. Could you search for it?"

"Just a minute," I called out, never taking my eyes off Sharise.

Skye jiggled the doorknob. All three of us looked at one another in horror. Careful not to make a sound, we scanned the room frantically with our eyes. Sharise found the blood red roses tied together with a forest green ribbon hiding behind a carton on the counter. She snatched at it and threw the flowers to me. Gurn unlocked the door and opened it just

285

enough for me to squeeze the bouquet through. I reached around him and forced the flowers through the crack.

"Here you go, sweetie. Sorry I can't invite you in. I'm not dressed. You'd better get back to the others."

Gurn eased the door closed. We both leaned against it. Sharise quivered, even the gun shook in her hand. Once again, we three were silent, fearing any movement might give us away.

Go away, go away, go away, I thought.

But Skye didn't leave. She called out to me.

"Thanks...and Lee?"

"Yes, sweetie?"

"Can I talk to you for a moment? I want to tell you something."

A flicker of fear crossed Sharise's face, and then it blanched white, so much so I thought she might pass out. Before I could reply to Skye's question, Sharise shook her head vehemently, not to me or Gurn, but to herself. Closing her eyes, she took a step back hiding her face behind a free hand.

That was the opportunity Gurn needed. In one quick, silent action he threw himself forward. Reaching for the hand holding the gun, he pushed it to the ceiling. A flick of the wrist and he twisted the gun from her taking it into his. In almost a balletic movement, he was behind her. He wrapped his arm around her neck gripping her in a vise-like hold. It took less than two seconds. Sharise let out a soft cry, more animal than human, the only sound coming from the room. But Skye heard it.

"What's going on in there?"

She pushed against the door, the door I had forgotten to lock. It moved inward, coming flush against my back. Skye's voice raised in volume.

"Are you okay? What was that noise?"

286

Rigid with fear, I pressed against the door to keep it from opening. Gurn and Sharise, locked in their combat embrace, froze as well. I fought to keep my voice cheery.

"I'm fine. Just squealed when I dropped a hanger. All is cool in here. Are you cool out there? We're cool in here."

I forced the door back in place and threw the lock.

Skye was not mollified. The sound of her voice raised in pitch, becoming almost musical in her concern. "Who's 'we'? Is somebody in there with you?"

At that moment she sounded a lot like Sharise. I'm sure her mother picked up on it as well, because the singer threw me a haunted look.

I let out a laugh that didn't have a trace of musicality about it, more like a referee's whistle announcing a bad play. I did some fast thinking and shrugged.

"Just me, myself and I. Sometimes I like to think of myself as royalty. You should really get back with the others, sweetie. Okay?"

Skye giggled. "Okay. Lee, I just wanted to thank you for inviting me to be a part of your wedding."

The girl sounded young and sweet, a one hundred and eighty degree turn from what was going on inside. I leaned against the door frame, trying not to shake, but my answer was sincere.

"You're so welcome, sweetie. I love having you a part of it. Now go back to the others, all right?" I could feel her hesitation through the door. "Is there something else, Skye?"

"Lee, remember us talking about my grandparents, the Fitzhughs? I just wanted to tell you, I heard from them."

I inhaled a deep breath and looked at Sharise. But my reaction was nothing like hers. She looked as if she'd been physically struck, eyes wide, shaking in terror.

I kept my emotions contained. "Really? What did they have to say?"

"They said they just learned about Daddy's death. They were sorry they hadn't called me in all these years, but they were only doing what Daddy wanted. They said he told them he'd cut Sharise out of his will if they contacted me." She hesitated. "Do you think it's true?"

I glanced at Sharise then Gurn then back at Sharise. She shook her head slightly and turned her eyes away, the only movement she could make with Gurn's hammerlock on her.

Did Sharise shake her head because that *was* the reason her parents gave up contact with their granddaughter? Or was it because now with D. H. Collier dead, they had a shot at his money through the kid? Nothing was revealed to me by the expression on the rock singer's face. Skye asked the question again.

"What do you think, Lee?"

"I don't know, sweetie."

"Do you think I should meet them? They're flying in day after tomorrow for the funeral."

Sharise seemed unable to stand, and would have slid down to the floor, if Gurn hadn't held her up. I answered her child.

"I don't know, but maybe you should meet them. See what they're like. If you like them, if they're nice people, if your gut tells you they're telling you the truth, you can go from there. Take Katie with you and listen to what she thinks. She has your best interests at heart."

"Yeah, I will."

She paused for time. I even thought she might have gone away. But no.

"I hope they are. Nice, I mean. It would be like, cool, to have grandparents." I could hear the hope in her voice.

"Yes, it would, Skye. Family is always cool."

There was a moment's silence. Then Skye spoke again, this time more upbeat.

"Okay, I'll see you in, like, a few, Lee."

"You betcha. I'll see you."

"Bye."

"Bye."

288

I heard her move away from the door. Finally. I wiped at the sweat dripped down my forehead and at the back of my neck. A sense of relief flooded through me.

"Thank God she couldn't barge in here. I didn't want her to see any of this."

There was a moment's silence. Sharise's faraway voice made me look at her anew.

"Oh, God, what am I doing? That was my little girl out there. Let me go, please. I won't give you any more trouble." She leaned the back of her head against Gurn's shoulder. "Please."

Something in her voice caused him to release her. He stepped away, put the safety back on the gun, and shoved it in the waistband of his tuxedo pants.

Sharise sank to the floor, wrapping her arms around her legs. Drawing her body in, she rocked back and forth, as if to comfort herself. When she spoke, it was hard to understand the words, but we let her talk.

"You think I don't love my baby, but I do. I just taught myself not to think about her or let it get in the way of my life. I hope my parents mean it. I hope they learned their lesson. But you never know about people. It's all a crapshoot."

Throwing her head back, Sharise let out a hollow, empty laugh, so sad it brought tears to my eyes. She spoke again, this time in a firm, unemotional tone.

"Get me out of here. Call your cop friend but let's make believe I never showed up to where my little girl is. Please. I don't want to hurt her any more than I already have."

I looked at Gurn and he looked at me. I took my phone off the counter and speed dialed Frank.

I basically apply with my teams the lean startup principles I used in the private sector go into Silicon Valley mode, work at startup speed, and attack, doing things in short amounts of time with extremely limited resources.
Todd Park

Chapter Forty-one

Mom and I stood at the rear of the family room, having entered from the butler's pantry on the sly. The lush sounds of chamber music filled the air. The string quartet had arrived late due to the weather. Fortunately, the wedding had been delayed by the police's hasty departure with a subdued Sharise. Showing up miraculously two minutes before the new scheduled time, the quartet trooped in just as we were wondering how we could do the ceremony without them. Boom box, anyone?

Around one hundred and fifty guests sat on folding chairs crammed together in the connected living, dining, and family rooms. Sliding doors that can fold into themselves provided opened walls for just such an occasion, courtesy of an architect with options on his mind.

The wedding guests sat facing the temporary ceremonial altar backlit by the blush of soft lighting emanating from the bay windows. Dozens and dozens of cream colored LED candles glowed on various levels, flickering between bursts of holly, pine cones, and fresh baby's breath. After the chapel incident, Mom swore never to have a real candle in the house again.

Tugger and Baba had more or less loped down the aisle a few moments before, rings tied to their necks by two gorgeous satin bows; red for Baba, green for Tugger. Guided by the steady hand of Tío, the single lead separated into a double at the bottom and attached to a harness on each cat. It controlled them somewhat as they scurried down the aisle almost as one.

The only iffy moment came when a child reached out and grabbed Tugger's tail. Spooked, Tugger leapt about four feet into the air, landing on the other side of Baba. She panicked and together they picked up speed, racing down what remained of the aisle, dragging Tío behind. My elegant and cool-headed uncle made it look like the quickened pacing had somehow been part of the ceremony. He retrieved the rings from the cats' bows, gave them to the padre, tucked a cat under each arm, and sat down in the front row, bride's side. During a round of applause from spectators, I felt my heartbeat return to something resembling normal.

Then in rhythm with Pachelbel's Canon, all ten bridesmaids, two by two, started down the aisle. How my mother managed to find over a hundred cream-colored LED candles at the last minute I don't know, but their placement on either side of the narrow makeshift aisle, served as warmth, light, and delineation. Space being at a premium, the women walked as closely together as they could without banging into one another.

There was a clear view of the ceremony site for an instant, as the bridesmaids crowded on either side of the altar, one grouping gowned in forest green velvet, the other in ruby red. So Christmassy, so perfect.

In front of the decorated bay windows was the marital archway, white roses woven in and out of its lattice frame. Under the arch stood the padre, Gurn, and my brother. The setting was absolutely beautiful. Why I doubted Mom could pull something like this off in less than forty-eight hours I'll never know. She's a miracle maker.

"I wish Gurn had allowed me to put concealer on his black eye," Mom said, leaning into my ear. Her voice was resigned rather than annoyed, as she had initially been. I studied my beloved waiting for me at the end of the aisle.

"The yellowing does clash with the tuxedo," I said. "But every man has his limits, even Gurn. He really isn't into makeup."

The padre noticed me and moved to the center of the ceremonial archway. A shift of his eyes in my direction and a slight nod was all he gave. Bride in place. Good to go.

Just then the man I loved saw me and shot me one of his glorious smiles. A sense of calm came over me. I knew it would be all right. Everything would be all right.

The string quartet stopped playing and silence filled the grand room. Richard caught sight of me, as well, and stepped away, taking the empty seat in between Tío and Vicki. Vicki was holding Stephanie, quiet and sleeping.

Everything was perfect. Even though it seemed like everything had conspired against us, from burnt out churches, murderous ex-wives, and howling rainstorms, this was happening. I was getting married. Nothing could interfere. Nothing could go wrong.

The quartet began to play the Wedding March. It was time to retrieve what I called my 'cheat sheet' from inside the bodice of my gown.

Whoops!

Missing.

Gurn and I were supposed to write our own vows, more to appease my mother than anything else. One could say I hadn't had a lot of spare time recently, so it didn't get done. In fact, I'd forgotten about it until a few hours before the wedding.

Too clever by half, I decided to cheat. I went on line, and found Elizabeth Barrett Browning's "How Do I Love Thee," a poem of which I knew only the first two lines by heart. But that didn't matter, I told myself, I would simply read it aloud. So I printed out a copy for the ceremony.

I took a deep breath and reached inside my bodice for the absentee paper again. It still wasn't there. I groped and groped. I heard the strains of the Wedding March. Everyone stood, turned, and glared at me. I panicked.

"Mom, I can't find the paper with my vows," I whispered. "How will I remember what I'm supposed to say?" I looked at my mother, sheer terror enveloping me. "It must be here somewhere."

I began a really frantic search, patting down myself from shoulder to waist. There wasn't much room for anything else inside the dress besides me, but you never knew. Watching, the room began to giggle. Well, not the room, but everyone in it.

"Liana, Liana." My mother grasped both of my shaking hands in her cool, serene ones to stop them in their quest. "You don't need any paper."

She let go of my hands and reached behind me. Gathering up my tulle veil, she brought it up and forward, covering my face. Adjusting it, she went on.

"Just say what's in your heart, dear."

"I can't remember what's in my heart," I croaked.

"You will."

She held on tight to my arm and gently pulled me down the aisle. I tried to follow in time with the music.

Left pause. Right pause. Okay, got it.

I'd asked my mother to 'give me away' as the saying goes, because with Dad gone I felt closer to her than anyone else on earth. Except the man I was heading toward. But it probably would have been confusing to ask Gurn to give me away.

We walked closer and closer. I don't even remember breathing.

When we arrived at the end of the aisle, I resisted the urge to pat myself down one more time. My mother took the bouquet from my hands and gave it to my matron of honor. Then, after lifting my veil and kissing me on the cheek, she placed one of my hands in Gurn's and took her seat on the aisle next to Tío.

"Hi," Gurn said so softly only I could hear him.

"Hi," I replied, just as softly. I felt giddy with happiness.

The padre cleared his throat, stepped forward, and began the ceremony. I would like to say I heard every word he said. I haven't a clue. All I could hear was my heart pounding in my ears. All I could feel was the love I bore this man.

I'm sure the words had something to do with 'do you' 'forsaking all others' and 'til death do you part'; the standard, wise old saws unless you're the one standing in front of loved ones and your community listening to them. Then they become the most important words in the world. Too bad I missed them.

"And now Lee and Gurn would like to make a declaration of their love for one another in their own words," the padre suddenly said.

Gurn nodded, but I shook my head. Until that moment, and filled with such joy, I'd forgotten I lost my cheat sheet. No one paid attention to me. Gurn took my left hand in his again, my new gold wedding ring sparkling on my third finger, and looked at me. All I could think was,

Jeesh, when did he memorize his vows? In the midst of fighting for his country? And no cheat sheet?

"Lee, you are an amazing, loving, funny, and beautiful human being. I'm so fortunate you decided to share your life with me. At first I thought, can this be happening to me? Can I be this lucky? Can I have everything in the world? Maybe, maybe not. But I'm going for it. I'm going to try to be worthy of you, try to give you the love you deserve. I vow to love you each day just a little bit more than the day before. And that will be for now and for always, *ad infinitum*, an eternity of you and me. You are my one, true love. Thank you, my beloved, for returning that love."

He stopped speaking and looked at me. I looked at him. It was my turn.

"Oh, Gurn." My voice trembled with emotion. "Backatcha."

A titter arose from the onlookers. A titter arose from Gurn and then he winked at me. I winked back.

"A woman of few words," he said in a clear, loud voice. "Could it get any better?"

The crowd burst out laughing. So did I.

Gurn looked out at the happy throng of those near and dear. "Only kidding, folks. She can say anything she wants, at any length, and at any time." He paused dramatically. "Just try and stop her."

The crowd roared, during which time he turned to me and said in a quieter voice, "I love you; no embellishments."

"I love you; no embellishments," I whispered in return.

"You may now kiss your bride," said the padre, returning us to a more somber state.

Gurn drew me into an embrace.

Your time is limited, so don't waste it living someone else's life.
Steve Jobs

Chapter Forty-two

"I'm sorry I didn't have time to memorize my wedding vows." I didn't look at Gurn when I spoke, but laid my head on his shoulder.

"That's all right, babe. It went just fine. Actually, it went better than fine. It was funny."

"When I locate my cheat sheet, I'll read you what Elizabeth Barrett Browning wrote."

"Don't worry about it. I know how you feel."

"Good, because I'm not sure I'll be able to find it."

Exhausted after five hours of wedding festivities on top of everything else, we were in bed looking up at the ceiling, laid out in our matching pajamas. The cats were draped across our feet, sleeping soundly. Gurn turned to me.

"You know the saying, 'No good deed goes unpunished'?"

"That's when you do a good turn for someone and instead of thanking you, they smack you for it?"

"This time your good turn saved our bacon."

"You mean inviting Skye to the wedding."

"Skye being there is what caused Sharise to give up without someone getting hurt. Congratulations, Lee, on setting another old wives tale to rest."

"I think the reality of what she was doing hit her when she heard her daughter's voice. It changed everything."

"I was glad Frank snuck Sharise out, so as few people as possible knew she was there."

I looked at Gurn. "But then he would. He's a father. He tried to protect Skye, especially as it didn't make any difference to the final outcome. Sharise confessed to everything."

Gurn patted my hand. "Let me ask you a question, is your mother talking to me?"

"Not really."

"The makeup thing?"

I nodded. "She'll get over it. While we're on the subject of mothers, do you think your mom is mad at me because of what Tugger did?"

"The scratches will heal, hun." Gurn kissed me on the forehead. "It's all fine."

"Never sneak up on a cat."

"Lesson learned."

I nodded and yawned in my new husband's face. "Sorry." I stifled the next yawn. "I could sleep for a week."

"I've got other plans for you."

"That's if you can stay awake, yourself, bub. I wonder if Mom was pleased overall with the wedding? I mean the ceremony went beautifully, but the reception didn't go quite the way she'd planned. On the other hand, your dad's toast was just the best."

"I know. Too bad the section of the tent over his head decided to collapse from the rain just then. I think the applause would have gone on a lot longer, otherwise."

"At least it didn't come down on the wedding cake. Or the booze. That would have really put a damper on things."

"When did we get the call from the caterer saying his van was trapped in a flood on 101 and there was no way he was showing up with the food?"

"I can't remember, Gurn. It's all a blur."

"I thought for sure we were screwed."

"But we had Tío's canapés and wedding cake."

"Unfortunately, there weren't any entrees."

I turned and looked at my new husband, searching his face for an answer. "Do you think the guests noticed?"

"You're kidding, right? People were passing out TicTacs, until we cut the cake. Thank God there was enough of it."

"And everyone went back for seconds, because it was delicious."

"Because they were starving."

"I hope the photographer meant it when he agreed not to sue us for his camera getting ruined. But I think the tent people have something to answer for. Canvas really should be sturdy enough for a little wet weather."

"It was a monsoon with gusts up to thirty-five mile an hour, Lee. That's not a little wet weather."

"My gawd." I let out a sigh. "No wonder my veil blew away."

"I'm surprised you didn't blow away."

"But still and all, I would have liked to have had some pictures of the wedding."

"A lot of people took pictures with their phones. We'll have something. You looked beautiful, sweetheart, every man's dream. I'll always have your image in my head. I don't need any reminders." He reached over and nuzzled my neck.

We were silent for a moment then intertwined our left hands together. We stared at the gleaming gold rings adorning our ring fingers and what they symbolized. I interrupted the silence with a whisper.

"I hate to use the word catastrophe..."

"...and yet it seems so apropos," Gurn whispered back.

We shared another moment of silence. I felt a giggle rise from the center of my being. I heard Gurn rumble with a chuckle next to me. Both came to the surface at the same time, and we burst out laughing. We didn't stop for a while.

"Poor Mom," I said, wiping tears from my eyes. "She'll never live this down. Even the toothpicks washed away. I'm sure Lila Hamilton Alvarez is wondering how this could have happened to an event she planned so long. Should I ask her how she felt it went?"

"Don't, Lee. That's sort of like asking, 'and other than that, Mrs. Lincoln, how was the play?'"

I wiped my eyes again. "It's over for our guests, but you and I still have to go on a winter wonderland honeymoon in Tahoe, when neither of us can ski. I can't help but feel a little bad about that."

"I postponed it."

"You did?"

"Early this morning. I didn't think we'd want to spend a week looking out the window at all the other skiers. We'll go sometime in March. I hope that's okay. I forgot to tell you what with one thing and another."

"Hostage taking and all that?"

"Yes, but I am sorry. I should have mentioned it. Are you okay?"

He took my hand and stared at me. He was concerned. I was relieved.

"More than okay. Say, isn't there something else you wanted to tell me? Something from when you first came home?"

"Yes." Kissing my hand, he dropped it, twisting on his side to face me. "Lee, I've been promoted, so to speak. I've been assigned to naval intelligence in the future. No more fieldwork. I can't go into specifics, but let's just say what I could do in my early twenties I can't do anymore in my mid-thirties."

I sat up, and shifted myself on the pillow, dislodging Tugger. He gave out a disgruntled yowl before settling down again at the foot of the bed.

"Did something happen?"

"Yes and no," Gurn said. "Split second decisions have to be made in the field. It's the point when your instincts take over. You've done the thinking and planning ahead of time; the field is for doing. Lately, I've been hesitating, small

299

hesitations, but there nonetheless. Nothing bad; I don't think anyone else noticed or knew. But I knew. It's time for me to let the younger guys take over, the way I did when I was twenty-two. It's been fourteen years. Vice Admiral Saks was in complete agreement."

"Time to be the brains behind the brawn? How do you feel about that?"

"It is what it is. I am content." His lopsided grin made an appearance. "On to a new chapter of my life, our lives. Besides, why should you have all the fun here in the states while I'm crawling on my belly in another part of the world?"

"Yeah," I said dryly. "Why not crawl on your belly in good ol' sunny California? But what about your CPA business? Are you giving that up as well?"

"Are you kidding? I love numbers. The most peaceful time of the day is when I'm reading a column of numbers, especially since I met you."

I settled back down on the bed. "So what should we do for the next week now that we're not going on a honeymoon? Stay home in the rain and rust?"

"As an alternative, I was thinking we could fly to Kauai the day after Christmas. Tío was looking after the cats, anyway. I'm sure he won't mind the change. But that's only if you like the idea. We could sit on the beach in the sun; have a Mai Tai or two while we get better. I have plane and hotel reservations on hold."

"Spend New Year's Eve on a beach looking up at the stars? Sounds wonderful." I snuggled into him. "Thanks for coming up with it."

"I never let the grass grow under my feet."

"The day after Christmas. That's good. It gives me a chance to return the prototype to Rameen Patel, now that he's paid D. H. Collier's estate for it. No matter what, I wanted to protect Skye's interests, even if she doesn't need the money."

We were silent for a moment. I, for one, reflected on the human fallout from all of this. Gurn was the first to speak and along the same lines. I guess we were both reflecting on a teenage girl caught up in her parent's folly.

"She's a good kid, Lee. I think she wants to stay friends with you."

"I hope so. I really like her."

"And I think she needs you in her life right now."

"One older sister coming up." I looked at Gurn with a grin.

"So, Lee, are you going to take the prototype to Rameen or make him come to you? It's quite a prize and you worked hard to get it back."

"Now that it's all over, I'll call him and tell him to drop by after he and his kids open their Christmas presents. After all, I'm giving him the biggest present of all, a chance to save Read-Out."

"Does he celebrate Christmas?"

"I have no idea. But I think he'll come running for it tomorrow, regardless. About Kauai, what's the weather like?"

"Kauai: sunny, blue skies, low eighties. Palo Alto: rainy, grey skies, low fifties."

I listened to the rain beating down on the roof. "No contest. Let's do it."

We kissed long and hard. I looked up into the face of the man I loved and pushed him away.

"You're okay I didn't take your name, aren't you? It's just that I thought I should keep my own name for professional purposes. It doesn't mean we're any less married."

"Beloved, I told you before, who's called what is not where my ego goes. Of course, you'll have to square it with my mother; she can be pretty old fashioned. Dad's like me, though. He doesn't care."

This time Gurn sat up, dislodging Baba. She let out a small squeak and joined Tugger at the end of the bed. Gurn watched the two cats cuddle for a moment then turned back to me.

"I've got a great idea. Now that we're going to be here tomorrow, let's take the elders out for Christmas dinner. There must be some restaurant open that can accommodate us. Tío didn't plan anything, right?"

"The family Christmas was going to be very laid back after the wedding. Tío said something about heating up leftovers. But there aren't any, what with the caterer not showing up. That also means both of us can take the opportunity to make things right with our new mothers-in-law tomorrow instead of later on."

"Then it's perfect. They thought we'd be gone on our honeymoon, so taking the folks out for Christmas dinner will be a nice surprise." Gurn wrapped an arm around me. "Word to the wise: we need to give my mother a lot of wine. It makes her very receptive."

"My mother responds quite well to a strong martini."

"I see two boozed up ladies in our future."

"Okay," I said, brushing my hands together. "That's settled."

He lay down again. I hunkered into the comfort and security of his arms, leaning against his shoulder again.

"Gurn, right now, I feel like we have everything."

"So do I."

"Are we jinxing ourselves by trying to keep it going?"

"I don't think so, Lee. That's what life is all about, the struggle to have it all. And right now, we have it all." He looked at me, green grey eyes brimming over with love.

"Merry Christmas, darling." He leaned in.

"Merry Christmas, darling." I leaned in.

And once again, when his lips met mine, the room temperature soared.

Ho, ho, ho.

And they lived happily ever after....until the next murderous adventure.

~

About Heather Haven

After studying drama at the University of Miami in Miami, Florida, Heather went to Manhattan to pursue a career. There she wrote short stories, novels, comedy acts, television treatments, ad copy, commercials, and two one-act plays, produced at several places, including Playwrights Horizon. Once she even ghostwrote a book on how to run an employment agency. She was unemployed at the time.

One of her first paying jobs was writing a love story for a book published by Bantam called *Moments of Love*. She had a deadline of one week, but promptly came down with the flu. Heather wrote "The Sands of Time" with a raging temperature, and delivered some pretty hot stuff because of it. Her stint at New York City's No Soap Radio - where she wrote comedic ad copy – helped develop her long-time love affair with comedy.

Heather lives in the foothills of San Jose, California, with her husband and two cats.

~

If you enjoyed this book, please consider going to http://www.amazon.com/Heather-Haven/e/B004QL22UK/ref=sr_ntt_srch_lnk_1?qid=14666976 38&sr=8-1 and leaving a review. Then email me at heather@heatherhavenstories.com to let me know, and I'll send you the next Alvarez Family Murder Mystery, Book Six, for FREE! Thanks so much.

Also by Heather Haven

The Persephone Cole Vintage Mysteries

- *The Dagger Before Me* – Book One*
- *Iced Diamonds** – Book Two*
- *The Chocolate Kiss-Off – Book Three*

A 1940s holiday vintage mystery series featuring a five-foot eleven, full-figured gal named Persephone 'Percy' Cole, a trail-blazing female detective with the same hard-boiled, take-no-prisoners attitude as Sam Spade, Lew Archer, and Phillip Marlow, but with a wicked sense of humor.

- *Death of a Clown*

Winner of the Silver IPPY, for Best Mystery/Thriller 2014

- *Corliss and Other Award-Winning Stories*

A collection of her favorite suspense and mystery stories.

*Formerly Persephone Cole and the Halloween Curse
**Formerly Persephone Cole and the Christmas Killings Conundrum

The Wives of Bath Press

The Wife of Bath was a woman of a certain age, with opinions, who's on a journey. Heather Haven and Baird Nuckolls are modern day Wives of Bath.

www.thewivesofbath.com

Made in the USA
San Bernardino, CA
04 March 2017